air burial

air burial

jean shields

CARROLL & GRAF PUBLISHERS
NEW YORK

AIR BURIAL

Carroll & Graf Publishers
An Imprint of Avalon Publishing Group Inc.
161 William St., 16th Floor
New York, NY 10038

Library of Congress Cataloging-in-Publication Data is available.

ISBN: 0-7867-1100-0

Book design by Paul Paddock
Printed in the United States of America
Distributed by Publishers Group West

Do you recognize me, air, full of places I once absorbed?
—Rainer Maria Rilke

air burial

part I

chapter 1

That night of the wake, my father in a mahogany casket in his study, the house smelling of whiskey, of freshly showered skin and dry cleaning, sliced lemons and horseradish, of votive candles and furtive cigarettes, even a hint of marijuana, which I wanted to follow after days comparing embalming costs, chipping down the price of the monument, selecting flowers and lining up eulogizers, after so much death and detail, I deserved a drink.

I deserved more than that, actually, and I got it, but first of all I got drunk.

Leaning against a wall, I savored a scotch, feeling its smoked velvet unfurl across my tongue. His thirty-four years of judicial decisions, favoring tenants or disabled drug users, meant people loved my father in an abstract way, the way you could love a flag or the picture of a saint. So a motley assortment of admirers filled the house. These were fighters from way back, in dashikis or peasant blouses from Guatemala, who'd advised him on this or that case, and of course lawyers lawyers everywhere.

Their voices all meshed to a din. No one cried.

My brother Royal mingled, easy beside the old family friends, remembering the names of their less-than-lovely daughters, impressed by the new grandchildren, the strings of letters acquired after infinite schooling. Mona, my mother, sat in a wingback chair in the center of the room. Her hair swept into a bun was like a tempest tamed with bobby pins. She never rose to receive people, had deep confabulations with an anointed few, and just lifted her chin to the rest. She smiled now and then, how she always smiled. Its severity had nothing to do with this particular death, or her widow's grief, but with life itself.

The Davies family was receiving at home. A tray of drinks skimmed by, all amber liquid and jiggling ice. I helped myself.

I had started with a warm-up shot before the guests arrived, the house quiet, except in the kitchen where the caterers filled mushroom caps. A reliable scotch, or two, was it, to loosen the tongue and allow all those stiff words to dance more naturally.

But by the fifteenth time I'd said, "Thanks so much for coming," I felt those s'es giving me trouble, and that c-h sound in *much*. Words lost their edges, the syllables suddenly dense with moss. I needed some sharp consonants to slice through to the hard meaning of things.

I couldn't look at my father when they brought him home. Mona had insisted on having him rouged up, and the thought of him in makeup—the orangey pancake of a high-school drama production, the villain's arched eyebrows—made me want to laugh when it crossed my mind, and the more I drank, the more it crossed my mind. All the black bunting and white lilies depressed me, looking so much like death, but not real death, rather someone's idea of it, death by Disney.

The doors separating the study from the living room were open, so I could see the gleaming casket across the room from where I stood. Just another fucking party, people yielding to the inevitable lusts—food, drink, companionship—then I'd catch a glimpse of that box, and it felt as if the floor were slowly turning, like it might just be the rotation of the earth, tangible at last.

Now seemed a good moment to have a look at him.

But a woman's laugh rocked my first steps. I teetered forward, then slammed on the brakes, which seemed to be somewhere in my stomach. My uncle, Virgil, caught me. My mother's brother. "Steady, girl," he said, and his hand felt welcome on my waist.

Virgil could always make me laugh, so I knew he was dangerous. In my girlhood I sought him in the musicians I imagined as husbands. Suits looked well on him, loose on his lean frame, always that sense of space about him. Dark brown hair, darker brown eyes, pale skin, pink cheeks—he looked like me.

"I want to see him," I said.

"Whither thou goest." Taking my arm, he smiled at people, excuse me excuse me, making it seem so easy, this getting around rooms. Then he closed the doors behind us, sealing out the overwhelming talk, here where for one night at least, the house became a portal to the unknown.

They had parted my father's hair too far to the right. His chest did not rise in breath and I felt, noticing this, that I should call and demand a refund, surely they had mishandled things somehow. Then I froze. I didn't breathe and I couldn't look.

"Do you think he knows we're here?" I said finally.

Virgil's hand rested on the casket, eyebrows pushing together in thought. Then he seemed to catch himself, and he smiled, his forehead smoothing out.

"I'm hardly the metaphysical type," he said.

I closed my eyes, and stood still, ready for the transmission, a message, anything other than the memory of pipe smoke curling away from him. I felt arms around me, then smelled a warm scent, something between skin and tea.

I was being kissed. This was unexpected.

I opened my eyes. "Uncle, you should know better."

"I do," he said. "But it doesn't help."

I looked back at my father. Some makeup had rubbed off on the collar of his suit jacket. How sad to spend eternity in a suit.

I took the handkerchief from Virgil's breast pocket, and rubbed the lipstick off my father's mouth, the foundation from his cheeks. Then, with a yellow highlight pen from his desk, I outlined my hand on the thin linen and slipped it beneath his palms.

Our second kiss, deep inside and hard against, was in the foyer, by the rented coatrack, squished against a mink. I liked the tropical heat of his lips.

What I really like, though, is the space on the other side of a rule, and that's where his kiss put me. I stroked his neck, learning the wrinkles.

"The crippling effects of gravity," he said.

The doorbell dingdonged, and we jumped apart. I alternated steps on the black-white of the tiled floor, marking my way toward the luminous red door.

"Caroline, we're so sorry," Mr. Jenkins said, entering with his wife, she in a felt hat studded with tiny pearls. He'd laid the dockets on my father's desk, helped him into his robe, brewed coffee, and stonewalled callers. He held my hands in his, and his were spotted brown and black like a horse's flank, dense with hair and thick with age. I leaned against him. He felt so good and solid, I very nearly cried.

Virgil, who stood to the right of us, they ignored.

"I loved your father like a son," Mr. Jenkins said. He held my face now, the mammoth thumbs on my cheeks. His nose flared into a bell, and his lips were cracked. "He changed things, don't ever forget that." My tears dropped back down into me at this. The great man, that for-mulation, tapped into the font of rote response. *Thank you, thank you so much, that's very kind of you.* In these words I disappeared altogether.

We stood, not speaking, his wife glancing toward the living room, the voiceless language of marriage noisy between them. Virgil, his hand on my elbow, led me toward the kitchen.

"Let's get some air," he said.

Mr. and Mrs. Jenkins smiled a small complicit smile and walked into the living room.

On the deck off the kitchen, Virgil pulled a pack of Dunhills from his jacket.

"No, thanks," I said. "I've quit."

He lit one and handed it to me. "You're in no condition to deny that you want this."

I took it and inhaled, enjoying the raspy warmth on my throat.

"Hell of a party," I said, observing the golden light of it framed in the windows.

He leaned against the rail, and held his own cigarette down and away while he exhaled blue.

I shook my empty glass, and he returned to the bar. Someone said, "Forgotten but not forgiven," and I turned away from the door. Dusk had softened the lines of the flower beds, fallow in early spring, that in the sunlight had looked like brown gashes. The moon rose, an edge of light hovering just above the trees.

My mother stepped gingerly onto the deck, in heels for the first time in years, leaving the door open behind her. She looked intently at the gaps between the lumber.

"I want to thank you for doing such a lovely job with everything." Her voice was tight. The brakes in my stomach screeched. "I don't know what happened to me."

Neither did I. By the time I got home to Chicago, the funeral director had nearly sold her a burnished copper coffin with a spring mattress and maroon satin lining trimmed with gold, guaranteed to last twenty years. This to a Unitarian minister, who had helped countless congregants navigate the treacherous waters of death. Though she was sobbing, I said, "Wait a second, aren't you going to cremate him?" She looked at me with daggers and gratitude, and from then on, I planned everything, which I didn't mind. It's what I do for a living, and I'm good at it, especially negotiation. I can walk away.

"No problem," I said. We stood in silence, both of us leaning on the porch rail and I felt an age-old urge to cup the cigarette in my palm. "How are you holding up?" I ventured.

"Oh, you know." She gestured toward the yard, her voice trailing off, and I didn't know at all. "How about you, honey?" she asked.

I thought a moment. Whatever I felt, I didn't feel it yet.

"I'm really tired," I said. That much was certain. We were quiet again. "Mona, are you scared?" I wanted to touch her hand, saying this, for there to be some tenderness so that she would know she could answer. But I didn't. I dragged on the cigarette.

"Your father provided for me. We own the house outright, so that's an asset. And there are stocks, you know, all that stuff. I'll be fine. Carl Sanderson called about the will today, so I'm fine."

"Why would you let him handle it?" I didn't mean to say this. I meant, wasn't she scared, after thirty-eight years beside the same man, night in, night out, to sleep alone? Wasn't she wondering about her own span of time, didn't she fear its boundaries?

"Just who would you suggest?" Her voice had an edge to it now.

"Any of them would be better," I gestured toward the window, where silhouettes vibrated in conversation. "Virgil could do it."

"You don't know my brother very well. Carl, at least, I trust." She paused and looked at my cigarette. I let it burn.

Virgil, carrying two drinks, closed the door with his hip. "We just voted and everyone agrees you should discuss this some other time."

"Carl asked us to dinner tomorrow," Mona continued. "I thought it would be nice if we could all go. He's been a great friend to this family."

"Virgil," I said. "You should handle the will. Talk to her."

He shrugged his shoulders. "Don't ask me."

"That's the story of his life he just told you," Mona said. "Don't worry"—she turned to him—"I wouldn't dream of imposing."

"I just think we should keep it in the family," I said, taking the second drink.

She turned back to me. "You've got it all figured out, don't you, darling? Where to put the candles, what to serve." She was rolling now. "And free legal advice to boot."

"Mona," Virgil said. "Don't say things you'll regret."

"You're just the person for parenting tips," she said. Her eyes glittered with tears.

"I do not need this." I gulped down the drink, and I pitched the glass into the flower bed.

"Don't you walk away from me," she called. But I did.

Inside, the party roared. The air felt close, thick with syrupy perfume and reduced sauce. I pushed the door open. Virgil moved toward his sister. He said something in hushed tones, to which she replied, "She doesn't know the first thing about love, and she certainly didn't love him." Then she stepped into the yard, and stooping, retrieved the glass.

My room had the same wallpaper as when I was a girl, flowers with Latin names in slanted script beneath them, filigrees of dots breaking up its unrelenting vertical. Faded posters of rock stars, photos of high-school friends (big smiles, everybody's happy), dolls with their painted-on congeniality staring into the middle distance—these things made the room mine, a mausoleum of my childhood.

I folded my clothes as if they were origami. I loved to pack.

A metal sound scraped the night, a garbage can being dragged down a driveway. Donald might be at our office. I found an old pack of cigarettes in my desk and lit one. It tasted leathery.

"Donald Hearst."

"Donald, hi."

It took him a moment to recognize my voice.

"Caroline, my God, I've been thinking of you all day. Did the caterers work out? They owed me a favor. I hope they were good to you."

"Everyone's stuffing themselves, so it must be fine."

I waited for him to ask me how I was doing.

"I'm drunk." I said. "And I'm tired, and my mother and I fought even though I promised myself that I wouldn't and I really need to come back to New York tonight. Can you meet me?"

He didn't say anything.

"God damn it, Donald. You have to."

"I can't tonight. I just can't."

"Margaret," I said. His wife.

He didn't say anything.

"She's got some smarmy dinner planned and you're too guilt fried to tell her you can't go, crisis at work, 'Gee honey, I'm sorry.'" I took a long drag on the ancient cigarette. "You're so disappointing."

I clicked off the phone and looked at it for a while. It didn't ring.

My bookshelves bowed beneath heavy texts from college, comp. lit. comp. religion, art. Here was a long way from there. But it would have to do—my stomach sour from the scotch, anticipating tomorrow, the bags that would balloon beneath my eyes. I'd look like hell, and I hated that.

I'd get off, though, an ironclad alibi to shield me—grief. It might make all kinds of things possible.

"Knock-knock," Virgil said, standing in my doorway with two drinks.

"Who's there."

"'Tis the east, and Juliet is the sun." He stepped in and raised a glass toward me. "A toast," he said.

"To what?" I stubbed out the cigarette on the hard wood desk and took the drink.

"To our trip, of course."

We touched glasses and downed the slushy scotch.

"Where're we going?"

"The Grand Canyon. A mule ride would do you good."

I started to laugh, but only a long breath came out, like a breeze.

"What if I don't want to go?"

"Doesn't matter," he said. "You need it. And you need me, too."

The Grand Canyon. That seemed right.

"I'm all packed. Can we go right now?"

chapter 2

Motorboats grounded in driveways, ladders tilted against bare trees, tires planted in yards. The headlights turned up these oddities, like creatures from the deep ocean, as I stared out at the dark world.

He hummed, eyes adoring the road, body easy behind the wheel. I trusted him completely. The leather seats of his Volvo had electric coils in them, turned on even though the spring night was warm.

"Jesus, Virgil, you're way too pampered."

"I haven't been to the Southwest in"—he paused, counting—"four years. I climbed in New Mexico that time," he said. "It's a hell of a place, Caroline. Like the moon or something, it's so different. I hope you love it."

"Keep talking, okay?" He looked over at me with a concerned glance. "Don't start, Virgil. If you get too tender with me, I swear I'll knock you."

"I forgot what a tough guy you are." He laughed, and I felt relieved. I wanted him to take care of me—why else would I have come?—but it would have to be a stealth operation, a silly dance we'd make up as we went along.

"The girl says keep talking. Right. The rock is red as blood at sunset, not candy apple, not brick, not cordovan. Not sexy. Sangre de Cristo. You're the religion expert, what does that mean?"

"Blood of Christ."

"Exactly. Even the gold-crazed Spaniards got it. Climbing there is the holiest thing I've ever done."

"More than the Himalayas," I asked, studying the dials on his dashboard.

"I was too young then. It was me against the mountain. I ought to go back, but I'm not strong enough anymore."

"Poor old man." I imagined pinching his cheek but found myself suddenly shy.

A semi flew by on the left.

"What was that about with Mona?" he asked.

"Didn't you hear? I never loved him." I shot him a glance. His face looked pained.

"You know she didn't mean it. She's extra crispy right now."

"Don't defend her, Virgil. You know? It's always like this."

"Trust an old man. No matter what else there is, she loves you."

"Yeah? Well, hear this: Love is not a bottom line. It has responsibilities. Like, it's supposed to feel good once in a while."

We floated silently on in the halo of our headlights. Our scents mingled, my Chanel, his something else that I would get to the bottom of. I nodded off, then jerked awake again and watched as the two median lines revealed our immediate future.

I couldn't stop thinking of the smeared makeup on my father's jacket. Something elemental was lacking, like there might not have been a body in that suit. Something felt hidden, veiled in modesty so that even in death, this ultimate departure, I could not satisfy an ancient curiosity. Tomorrow the casket, the body, the suit would all be hauled away after the service at the Unitarian church like so much detritus, then slid into an incinerator and burned.

His smoke would rise toward heaven, that was one good thing.

"How do you want to die," I asked him.

"I don't."

"But if you had to." I cracked the window a little, and the car cooled quickly.

"Warm in bed, beside a woman I love—Jayne Mansfield, maybe— the happiest man alive."

"I think she was decapitated."

"Well, there you go."

"I always pegged you for a dashing death—in a crevasse in the Andes, or swept down the Amazon. Definitely something South American."

"Too many bugs there." He clicked on the cruise control and took his foot off the accelerator.

"You know, I couldn't have cared less about that wake," I said. "I mean, about arranging it. It was all for her. I wouldn't have done anything like that."

"What would you have done?"

I thought for a long time. Graves were out, too much like charmless studio apartments, no light, no ventilation, too isolated. Burning was a little better, it was more efficient, and it offered the possibility of a pyre. But nothing at the local mortuary touched the horror or the mystery, and that bothered me. Shouldn't the form match the feeling?

"I'd have given him an air burial," I said at last. He looked blankly at me. "You leave the body out—animals eat it, it decomposes. Then you grind up the bones, mix them into dough. Your body feeds other bodies. That's the way to do it."

He was silent for a long while. "It would take forever."

"It should," I said.

The moon, high and nearly full, bleached the landscape blue. Dark and empty fields flanked the road. There were no sprouts, nothing to disturb the rows of dirt. I was tired, high on talk, eager for more—let's talk all night, let's never find morning. I didn't want to go to bed and wake up to what I'd done.

A Howard Johnson's sign shimmered turquoise up ahead, reminding me with its promise of beds that Virgil and I had kissed rather passionately.

Virgil took the exit.

Fluorescent lights bore down on the lobby, hardening every edge, highlighting scuff marks, crescents carved into the Formica tiles. The plants had plastic stems, and wadded straw wrappers mixed in the fake sphagnum moss. Virgil pressed a buzzer and for a long while we heard nothing but the che-che-che of a sprinkler in the night.

"I've got a headache," I said. He stroked my neck, just below my hair. His touch was warm, slow, incidental, the way you might scratch a dog's belly while reading the paper. It felt marvelous, but it detonated a panic in me.

"We're not having sex," I said, as the night attendant emerged from some inner chamber. He looked at me, then tapped some keys on a computer and it whirred into life. Through the door he'd left open, a soprano's voice vibrated.

"Passing through?" the clerk asked, looking up, then back at the computer screen. He had dark hair, on the long side, big eyes. Handsome. Horny and lonesome. Going nowhere. Why else would he be here?

Virgil asked him about breakfast, chatted about the highway, our route, yak yak yak. I wanted a cigarette, and ignoring this made me jumpy.

"One room or two?" he asked.

"Two," I said.

The clerk gave us our keys, and on a blurry map, drew a line from the office through the courtyard where the pool was, to our rooms.

The body of a drowned wasp circled the pool's edge, pushed along by invisible currents. Lights in the deep end illuminated a film of leaves and plastic sandwich bags. A few lounge chairs lay on their sides, their straps shaking in the breeze as if plucked.

Virgil kissed my forehead, yawned. We unlocked our doors. "Sweet dreams, sweetheart," he said and the bolt on his door clicked.

The wallpaper in my room didn't meet at the seams. Rust blossomed around the screws holding up the light over the bed. The television had fake wood paneling. The only way to get fresh air was to leave the door open, so I did that, and stood on the walkway outside the room, regarding the dark houses across the street, the American cars with foreign names in the parking lot, and listening to the sounds from the highway as if they were words.

Under the best of circumstances I'm a nervous sleeper, waking hourly, responsive to noises or thoughts that coalesce into dreams, dreams that seem to mean something, that sometimes wake me and I have again my thoughts.

In the five nights I'd been home, I'd stayed awake thinking through death's logistics. This death involved two caskets—the mahogany, rented for the wake and the service, and a pine box in which he would be burned. I called six morticians and had them bid on the job, evaluated different grades of mahogany, playing cost against effect, and then I'd glimpse myself, totting up the costs, so unladylike *at a time like this.* This was not what I was supposed to feel, at a time like this. It made me wonder if I felt anything at all. I knew I did, if only I could . . . what? And here I was.

So now, climbing into the tightly tucked, scratchy sheets of this cinder-block motel, now I finally felt my exhaustion, exacerbated by the drink, battling the manic energy of the cigarettes. Light from the street lamps seeped in beneath the heavy curtain, orange, garish, a man-made sun.

I had to pee, but didn't. I just lay in the bed. I tried relaxation techniques but I'd snap back as soon as my mind drifted. Do not stop visualizing the white, warm radiance. It looked cold in my mind, and a long way off.

I had never been so afraid.

I told myself it was fear of silence, that I wasn't used to doing without the noise of work. I wanted it to be something like that, a thing that seems bad scary, but turns out to be good. But I suspected that. It was wishful thinking, denial. Fear is fear, a natural phenomenon—like an ice storm, cold and still, locking everything into place, yet oddly beautiful. All I could do was keep on lying in it.

My life in New York shimmered in front of me, aurora borealis in neon. First it was innocuous things, broken pavement by where I sometimes bought cocaine; a spindly tree outside my apartment, rising from the sidewalk, ringed with metal bars.

Then it was my working days, splayed on the dissection tray.

A.M.: Liz enters my office with faxes and contracts. Four years younger, long legs, shoes in the dominatrix mode—thick soles, high heels, always black, complicated straps. She doesn't like me much, because for sure she didn't do poli sci cum laude at Yale for such an underpaid, bullshit job, and I once told her that's where everyone starts, early on when she whined about it. No one wants the hard news. I saw her think, then think the better of, *yeah, well you started on your back*, which is unfortunately common knowledge, about me and Donald, because he was such a chump the first two years, following me around like a baboon smelling estrus, then we were seen kissing somewhere, the elevator, the stairs. I wasn't too cautious, what did I care, just passing through on my way to better, then wham-o, it's a full-time job with equity, and I've been there six years and it feels like ten. How does time do that?

Of course, there's the drawing. That's the good part, designing a centerpiece, choosing the colors of napkins, as if it mattered in the slightest, people will use them to rub sauce off their lips, yet it matters. And I like it, I like line and saturation, all the art school stuff. And this way I can pretend that I'm not so far off the mark, I'm still working with line and saturation and chromaticity, except that I call it color because chromaticity scares the clients and makes Liz snicker.

I flipped through channels on the television. Dolls and knives were selling in alternating lots. Only one doll sold at a time, but each kit of knives widened to include increasingly unruly blades.

Then the phantasms started: Mona in bed, withering now that Father wasn't beside her, pale and paler until she became her own sarcophagus; Royal, old and arthritic, massaging his joints, unable at last to kick a soccer ball. When the camera turned my way, I got up to pee. I wasn't about to watch this happen to me.

But even in the bathroom, pressing my calves against the porcelain of the toilet for reassurance (cold, hard, definite), the warmth literally draining out of me, even there with my eyes averted, I saw that death had touched me and would do so now again and again.

I wanted a cigarette. No doubt about it, something with menthol, better than brushing my teeth, smokier, all dragon mist and gathering fog.

A line of light shone along the edge of Virgil's window, but I wasn't going to go begging to him. There must be a cigarette machine in the lobby. I dumped my purse out on the bed, gathered up the loose change and some singles, and walked out, closing the door.

The air had a balmy touch, a first warm night, softening the edges of things, an invitation to uncover. Little pictures of each cigarette brand stuck out in plastic above the levers. I put my change in, but it wouldn't take my rumpled bills. I walked back to my room to get some newer ones, and realized at my door that I didn't have my key.

Virgil's light was out now.

I went back to the lobby and pressed the buzzer.

"Sorry to get you up," I said to the clerk.

"No problem, I never sleep at night."

"Do you have a passkey or something? I'm locked out of my room."

He stood back and regarded me, stroking his chin. He was tall and thin, wearing loose jeans, a baggy green shirt with a tiny collar, buttoned all the way up.

"There are no accidents, you know," he said.

"Tell me about it. Key? To my room?"

"Let me check. I'm Druid. Come on in." He opened the little half-door cut into the counter. I rolled my eyes, what the hell.

On the sofa, we shared a warm can of beer, smoked his Camels and listened to Wagner, one of his passions, he told me. Smoke made the room bleary.

"You're here every night," I asked.

"Except Sunday and Monday. That's my weekend." He slid off his shoes and his toes were bony, very white but tufted with long, dark hair.

"Doesn't it get kind of depressing?"

He shrugged his shoulders, then put his arm around me.

"Not when I get to meet sexy ladies like you."

"You meet a lot of sexy ladies at this job?"

He shrugged again and drained the beer.

I reached over to the coffee table and shook another Camel from the pack. He slid his hand onto my back and caressed me. He had a nice touch, and I stayed forward, granting my spine, my ribs, knowing I'd grant more, always, always unable to resist my loneliness.

"You're real pretty," he said.

I leaned across his lap and his hand went under my shirt, a few cursory revolutions, to show me it wasn't just my breasts he wanted, then straight for them. I felt him grow in his jeans. I unzipped him. He raised up and together we slid off his jeans and underwear.

His hip was sublime, undulating like a sand dune, a landscape in microcosm. I kissed it, then circled it again and again with my tongue. It was a place to worship, a place of beauty and mystery. He guided my face toward his penis, bobbing freely now, and I raised up, unbuttoned my blouse, and quickly dropped my pants. He reached down to his knapsack and rummaged a moment, coming up with a condom, and opened the package with his teeth.

Then we were together, him on top, then me, his eyes closed, mine open. He felt good in me, almost comfortable. But I couldn't stop looking. His eyes rolled beneath his fluttering lids, and his mouth made an exaggerated O. He was a hatchling, flimsy new beak gaping wide. And I, I had nothing to feed him. Oh dear, he said. Oh dear, oh. That good?

Was he asking me? I thought so, but I was deep in thought and uncertain. If we were communicating, I didn't want to miss it. I strained to hear and heard his breath, felt sweat break across his back, a warm dew. That feels good, doesn't it. Say it. Good.

Yes, I said. Yes, good.

In a while it was done. His lips relaxed, he slept. His penis in its silly sock became small as a child's hand beneath me. Squatting over him, my hips started to ache. I climbed off, gathered up my things, dressed, and went back outside. Still no key. The night was creepy, with its wind shifting branches and planes crossing overhead, sounds of things distant.

Outside Virgil's door, my hand in the softest fist, I stood, poised to knock. What was I doing here, lost in the middle of the night, onward toward dawn? I had ditched my family, my job, the knowns—although everything you think you know is just bandage wrapped around the unknown.

And so I understood, standing there, a thin door away from something, or nothing, that this was where I had to be.

I knocked. A car sped by on the highway, a shriek, a meteor ripping through this small universe. His light went on. The door opened the length of its chain.

"What's the matter?" He squinted at me.

"Do you have a cigarette?"

"You know I do." He opened the door.

"I'm locked out of my room," I said, stepping inside.

He tapped a cigarette from its pack and handed it to me. I fumbled with his lighter, then when I caught the flame, I inhaled too deeply and coughed.

Sleep had left pouches beneath Virgil's eyes, and his hair stuck out at sharp, twiglike angles. His clothes were neatly draped over one of the white wicker chairs, his shoes placed right by left on the floor. This was his bivouac—everything in its place, set for the next day's action, quickly to hand at first light. He could sleep burrowed into snow or suspended on stone. He knew the necessity of rest.

He didn't smoke, but sat on the edge of the bed, watching me, waking up. His stillness made me all the more aware of my agitation.

"Get any sleep?" he asked.

I shrugged, and sat down beside him. I wished the lights were out, I wished the TV were on, I wished he were smoking too, and that our two glowing tips were the only light in the room. I wished to be invisible, here but not here, with him but alone. I wanted a thing and I wanted its opposite, to willingly transgress and to not be interested in such things, protected, somehow, from my dreadful propensities.

"I might go back to New York tomorrow," I said.

"Really?" he asked. "Is that what you want?"

He reached out and stopped my arm from delivering the cigarette to my mouth. The question echoed in the silence between us. My chest hurt from smoke.

If I went back, it would mean that my father's ashes were enough, a stingy allotment of grief, an insult to what was possible. It would mean the day after tomorrow I'd walk into the office, listen to voice mail, then pick up the handset of the phone and start talking, as if nothing, none of this, had happened. It would mean seeing Virgil at some New Year's or Fourth of July, and he would kiss me on my cheek and I would kiss him back on his.

My mind stopped where his hand touched my skin.

I gestured helplessly with the cigarette, drawing a ghostly circle in the air. He stroked the hair away from my face, brushed it off my neck. The breath of him so near, the warmth emanating, that old sinking feeling.

We kissed. All was still.

The cigarette fell, and Virgil reached for it, then stubbed it out in an ashtray. "No," I said, and I said it more than once, around the room in stomps and staggers, tears shooting up from my molten core.

"Hey now," Virgil said, trying to slow my stumbling with an embrace. Funny how quickly you can read a touch—this was sympathy and safe home, not the no-man's-land we'd been in a moment before. But still. I would have none of it.

In the courtyard, I pulled down a lounge chair to wait out the last small darkness. I felt raw between my legs and smelled that briny scent. It meant nothing, not even a momentary flicker of joy. No father, no lover, no work worth doing, no home worth inhabiting. Forward or back, at this moment, either direction seemed the same.

I gazed out on what was becoming morning, the sky lightening to bruised purple, phantom shapes solidifying into their day jobs. A raccoon climbed to the edge of a Dumpster, the metal booming like stage thunder. I hissed, long and slow. The raccoon snapped his head my way, twisting his coy nervous hands, but he didn't jump.

chapter 3

Virgil eases into his running shoes, on top of the orthotic arches, custom molded to the rippling contours of each foot. Pulls taut the laces, double ties the floppy wings of the bow so that they won't release mid-run. Stretch the calves, the quads, the hams—at least twenty seconds each, no bouncing, a karate teacher had told him once, years ago now, but it stuck. Twenty seconds was the minimum. Otherwise you don't become any more flexible.

Birds, small and brown, twitter and reel above him in the lavender morning sky. Virgil has slept well, as he always does, despite the impetuosity of the night, or because of it, despite the recent diagnosis or in rebellion against it.

This is day, and day promises all good things.

Then the first footfall, like the beginning of rain—gentle to start, tentative, finding the ground, adjusting to its hardness. A jolt in the joints of each ankle, a sensation he looks forward to, marking as it does a beginning—pain initiating bliss.

His knees rise, the muscle curves beguilingly around the patella, and he is a white horse running, a thing without aches. Speed just right, fast enough to look good to passersby—though here, on the access road beside the freeway, there are no admirers. But not so fast that he develops a stitch, like a woman's irresistible fingernail twisting his gut.

Distant trees, utility poles, brindle gray asphalt underfoot, cracked sidewalks, car mechanics not yet open, their garages locked down tight. The road starts on an incline and he digs in, sprints the hill. His legs burn, and his lungs.

Caroline in the wee hours wrapped in a smoky corona. His beloved Caroline, noble whether weak or strong, but he cannot shake the desolation of her, the fatigue behind her eyes. Arthur stiff inside that absurd coffin. Virgil had felt ignored, slighted. Those kisses, his shameful delight. Ridiculous. Love at a time like this. He paces himself to an 18-wheeler.

I am the very model of a modern Major-General sings itself, the line begetting the line. Right leg, then left, call and response as physiology. Air in, its soft moisture cool going down, tainted with diesel, with pollen—the first blast of spring. The paved-over world, this bit of earth unlike any other, this the one time he will see it. *And he's hardly ever sick at sea.*

From *Penzance* to *Pinafore*, Virgil runs on.

A tingle singes his left knee, a premonition of pain, a foreshadowing of inadequacy—you can't do it, old man. Just another mile, a measly eight and a half minutes, I'll slow down. Just let me run, breathe this air in and send it out. Isn't it for the whole world, this breathing? Doesn't it matter, this moment of concentration?

He has learned more about pain than he cares to know in the last three weeks, since seeing the oncologist. The specialty itself telegraphed the relevant information, the man merely colored in the specifics: Virgil's pancreas, an aggressive cancer, treatment options limited. Chemo and radiation might extend things out by weeks, hardly worth the vomit and hair loss. Weeks. These words that slice up time.

What, never? No, never. What, never? *Hardly ever.* The *Pinafore* sings on, time is music. *Hardly ever sick at sea.*

He speeds up on the straightaway, outrunning the choke at his throat, the tight fist of his heart.

The pain subsides and he is free again, in Nepal, at the base of Nuptse, a few down from Everest, reading its gray expanse. Always a good student, he knows which routes the famous ascents took. Can he see what they missed? Can he be famous, too? The answer is no, and he has learned to live with it, after a bad drop that time into a glacial crevasse, its blue ice blackening with the sun's descent. He had been certain he would die there. And he had been wrong. Wrote a mental will, thought good-byes to Jane and David. He heard his partner yell his name, and didn't dare answer for fear of bringing the ice down in shards around him. Instead he concentrated, and there, there was the rope, not his imagination, real rope. When he returned from Nepal, he and Jane had their one reconciliation. He had been so sure that if he only survived, he wouldn't need anyone but her. He still can't believe it wasn't true.

A pickup truck passes him. Wafting from its open window, a snatch of drive-time radio yuks, and cigarette smoke, a blue smell. Eking out more strides, he envisions Jane that summer she came to care for them, his fifteenth, her seventeenth, her hair the color of narcissus petals. Dirt beneath her toenails, golden down on her legs. He took it all in the instant he saw her, her unexpectedly dark eyebrows, how she had the faintest freckles beneath the straps of her sundress.

How he followed her that summer, pretending disinterest, smacking ten-year-old Mona with a big brother's prerogative, but following all the same, into the woods, where Jane taught him to see wild carrots and chamomile. Virgil's father said she used medicinal plants because her family couldn't afford a doctor. "Wouldn't you like to marry such a fine boy?" he taunted, indicating Virgil on the porch. Jane threw a red ball to Mona and laughed. But Virgil blushed violently, yes, he would marry her, then and there. He would be her champion.

The last strides of the run, the last good ones, even, consistent. *The very model.*

All these memories. He will run through them and come out on the other side.

She never seemed poor. The fabric of her clothes didn't shine from too much ironing. "Virgil, how about I teach you to call a thrush?" Jane's musical voice.

No, not that one. Not today. He is almost back to the motel, his gait a near limp. Not to mention the heat inside—his pancreas, he guesses, though if pressed, he couldn't locate it on the map of his body. Somewhere in there. When he stops, he bends over against a wall by the parking lot, breathing hard. A family packs its car—large sedan for large people. Then he vomits. Red, saline—more blood than not.

Caroline reclines on a lounge chair, arms clutched around herself. Her long lashes tuck against the uplift of her cheekbone, a bone he has loved since he first saw it, when she was fifteen.

"Caroline?" She doesn't stir. The day warms now that the sun is out and about, light plays in the pool.

Thanksgiving or Christmas, it would have been, a turkey holiday, the rich smell of it stifling the house, the air humid with butter. She was a bad girl then, out on the porch behind the kitchen, smoking a cigarette. Her inhalation made this bone flower in her cheek, like a time-lapse wonder of nature—the woman inside the girl. She wore a leather motorcycle jacket with so many straps and zippers and buckles that he couldn't help but think of a straitjacket, and it seemed apt, how she must feel in that house of turkey stench.

He has always liked her more than his son, David, boy genius with the pressed khaki pants, double 800s on his SATs, and wasn't the boy proud of that. Virgil ought to have been proud, too. You reap what you sow. And now look at him—David is walking proof of that adage. Then Virgil has the thought that scares him, the thought that must not be thought: Even though what he is reaping isn't that great, it also isn't that bad. This is dangerous knowledge, because it undermines fear, and fear, above all else, is necessary. Fear keeps your integrity in tact. But if you know that a bitter harvest is still a harvest, what then?

"Caroline, you all right?" He coughs to punctuate the question, and tastes the bile he retched earlier. He must brush his teeth. She mustn't smell this diagnosis.

Caroline, though, she has something else. Smart, certainly, but no need to grind you down with it. Savvy. Her clarifying anger, her wet-soil eyes, earth promising growth.

"Darlin'," he says, jostling her lightly, making light of the endearment. "What are you doing out here?" She opens her muddy eyes and reaches her arms up and around him and he feels as if he might collapse.

He'll get her back into her room, he'll feed her breakfast, cure the hangover. They will drive, and each mile will be a mile further from where they began.

chapter 4

Heigh-Ho, Heigh-Ho, it's off to bliss we go.

Thus sing my veins walking along Napoleon, fifty dollars closer to heaven, my beloved Horse stashed in my skivvies. Heigh-Ho, Heigh-Ho, over there's an apartment I know, where I squat with another gent in similar dire straights, but I can't go there, no sir, no way, because the junkie's way is to avoid sharing when you've got, and to facilitate sharing when you want. Right now I got, and I want it all.

I feel in my pocket. Lighter, check, spoon, check, rubber hose, check check check. But where's my needle, and my sweet syringe? Shit.

So I have to go home, because home is where the works are. I don't have two nickels to rub together to buy a new rig, and besides, that old one and I go back, back back to the first time, making it a sanctified kind of a deal. It's the only one I've ever used, will ever use, being of a loyal, persnickety bent. It's insurance against question marks—whose arm, toe, or groin did this needle last visit, plunged by hands that last saw soap and water God knows when. These are not my questions. Hygiene has made me the man I am.

Heigh-Ho, Heigh-Ho, it's through the door I go.

"Yo, David, where you been?" says Baby Duck, my ruminate, as I call him, prone as he is to stillness and brooding, then venting in long-winded philosophical loop-de-loops. Should have been an ancient Greek. He makes to stand from the double-decker twin mattresses he's sitting on, our couch by day, and at night, our beds. Quite efficient. Hand out, he expects me to slap mine sideways to his, in loose approximation of soul-brother bonding. Pathetic for a couple of white guys like ourselves, but it speaks to the absence in our hearts of a true bond. "Thought maybe you came into a little wealth," he says.

I slap his hand. He always hits too hard.

"Ha, yeah, good one," I say, sneaking through the gym bag in which

I keep my worldly goods. " 'A man of means by no means,' as the song goes, Baby Duck, and when has a song ever lied?" Heigh-Ho, the dairy-o, here we go. Svelte plastic, friend of my friend, enemy of my enemy, power and the glory, my life works. I'm a-jangle with anticipation of the good meal to come, the sweet cessation of tension, which is a rare and precious thing in this life of thought.

They say our pupils widen when we see something we desire. I squat by the gym bag, clutching the device, unsure of my next move, and slowly lift out the syringe. Baby Duck has his eyes fast upon me, the look of avarice dilating there.

"Songs lie all the time. Especially love songs. I wish they'd tell you how it really is, you know, about how she'll tell you she doesn't think it's going to work, and how your rage is getting in the way. What a joke, especially that soulmate stuff, you know, because right away, you have to posit a soul, and well, as a sensualist in the formal sense, I take issue with that. Trust what you see, hear, smell, taste, touch. And that is it." He makes a wiping-his-hands gesture, another dazzling display of Aristotelian prowess. What a stud.

"Did you see the paper today?" he asks. "Those fuckheads." He doesn't take his eye from me, and indicates, with the minutest lizard flick, the *Times-Picayune* lolling open on the mattresses. "There's an article on the death of gentility. Personally, I don't believe it."

His voice lowers to the growly registers. Baby Duck is not what you'd call a happy junkie. Smack dims the aggression and aggravation of his thoughts, which totally explains his addiction. If it were me, I'd need relief, too. But I am motivated by the broader possibilities that getting high makes visible. I like vision, and heroin gives you time enough to see.

"David, my boy, my pet, David." He leans toward me from the bed. "You did come into wealth, didn't you, you schmuck, and you weren't even going to tell me, were you, you self-aggrandizing arrogant little putz."

I try to stand up but it feels safer to crouch. I'm a tall person, and slender, so when I am my full height, a feeling of vulnerability over-comes me, as if with all my landmass, I need a wall like the Great one in China—brick-by-brick protection.

"It's only modest wealth," I say lamely, then noisily pull the syringe out of my bag. Why not, my cover's blown. "I don't have enough."

Baby Duck hops off the bed and slaps my hand again, hard like before. The rig clack-clacks across the warped wood floor, skittering into a corner.

"You selfish runt." He slaps me, on my shoulder, close about the neck. I stumble, then quickly turtle up. "I am your brother. Have we not discussed this?" He hits me now at the bottom of my biceps, a par-ticularly painful spot due to an abscess that's sprouted inside my elbow, then takes my arm and bends it behind my back. I breathe hard. Pain blasts me like last-day trumpets. When I look at him I almost laugh, his fury is so cartoonish, nostrils flared, red pate getting redder, the tremble of his strength rumbling from his body to mind. He feels around my groin, and finds the baggie. Reaching in, he squeezes my nuts just because he can, and wrenches out the smack.

"No, come on, no," I say, crying now, which I hate. "I just bought that. Come on, Duck."

The Duck doesn't even hear me, though. He's holding up the bag and batting at it, mentally weighing and sifting and heating and plunging. He drops my arm. Then he goes to the corner where my works sit in a tangle of dust bunnies.

"Mind?" he asks, reaching for it.

I do mind, actually. I rush him, all slaps and fists, and he drops the baggie. It falls by the lantern that we light for a little while each night, and I dive for it. He steps on my outstretched arm, and I duck and roll, a survival drill from long-ago elementary school so very handy now. The floor smells of fennel, which I can't account for. The baggie is nearly in reach, but Baby Duck has my rig.

"I remember, you told me about this," he says, holding up the syringe. A soft, mellow voice, the guy could be an easy-listening DJ.

He pulls out the plunger and tosses it down the airshaft. Then he snaps the new needle and lets it fall to the floor, puts the chamber in his mouth, and chews. It snaps in his mouth.

"My works, you asshole," I say, wailing. I collapse on the floor and rock, knees to chest.

"Grow up." The next blow I see in its arcing flight, destined for my cheek. Duck, duck, goose, and the Baby's fist nearly buckles my temple, but I dodge, grab the baggie, roll again, and get my ass out the door.

On the street, I wheeze for a moment, and stuff the good stuff down my pants, precious unsharable Horse.

"David Harris, you're history," Baby Duck yells from the window. *Good one*, I think, loudly—my thoughts sometimes yell, though I rarely do—*let the world know where you're squatting*. Then I start to run. People on the sidewalk stop and watch me, then look up to the window. One man whips out his cell phone, and in no time, I know, the sirens will sing down the street and the world will be a different place.

"You're a former person, chap," the Duck rants on. "A dim and distant memory."

Oh no I'm not.

I just run.

chapter 5

The Volvo was a navy blue sedan with bell here, whistle there—leather interior, a key that flicked out from a plastic fob like a dangerous blade. The fob had other buttons that locked or unlocked doors, armed or disarmed alarms, pushbutton security. There were separate temperature adjustments for driver and passenger so that even in the same tiny space, we needn't feel the discomfort of someone else's preferences. Virgil had not personalized it in any way. No bumper-sticker joke or screed, no Hail Mary full of grace swinging from the mirror. Bland as bologna, a mere vehicle.

It had windows, though, which I made use of while Virgil drove. The vast Midwestern sky, billows of glorious white gray clouds, wet and remote, large in a small way, the sky as paradox. Virgil listened intently to classical music—a Haydn string quartet, he told me—on his CD player, which rotated through myriad discs stashed in the trunk.

"This is a later work, one of the darker ones," he said of the music. "I've become enamored of it."

Enamored of string quartets. This was a man I didn't know.

"What else?"

"What else what?"

"What else about you is going to shock me?"

"I sing a little."

"Slay me."

"Papa Haydn's dead and gone, but his memory lingers on," he sang. "That's the *Surprise* Symphony."

It was just past eleven in the morning, and I knew the day's schedule by heart. The mortuary would have transported my father's body to the Unitarian Universalist Church, where my mother would officiate, in her Kente cloth vestments, maybe, or something more somber—the velvet tunic I had embroidered with dragonflies when I was twelve. I wondered if she had slept, and how I could be here, not there. She would be at the church by now, sitting in her office, meditating and listening to the swell of the event—voices as people filled the pews, the solemn organ music we had selected, Barber's *Adagio for Strings*, except not for strings, a favorite of my father's. The church was of an intimate scale, dark and thoughtful, a fieldstone base, oak floors mitered into interlocking ovals and deep blue stained glass regulating the notion of light. A horizontal fountain burbled like a stream in the reception hall, the Peace Fountain. The service would be small—family, close associates. The wake was to have been the public event. Afterward, in the reception hall, there would be coffee and cookies, quiet conversation—condolences, that's the word, isn't it, for such talk.

"Isn't there anything else," I asked. Virgil flipped around and landed on Caribbean music, steel drums and guitars that shimmered, palpable warmth. I turned it off. "Do you mind?" If he did, just now, I didn't care.

I took out my cell phone, dialed Mona's office number, and waited for the connection. The white line along the side of the road framed blur: bushes, houses, silos, a swath of maple forest, then a tractor slowly scratching out furrows, dancing dust. It smelled of manure, a dairy must be nearby. What could I say to her that would make me in this car on this road on this day the gleamingest, all-rightest of alternatives? The ring trilled. I turned off the phone and stuffed it into my purse.

"How come Jane and David didn't attend?" I asked.

"David's in New Orleans, I think, and Jane," his voice trailed off.

chapter 6

Virgil inhales fumes beside the gas pump. Caroline stands some distance away, smoking his last Dunhill, her back to him, facing the road.
She has been so quiet, she seems so exhausted. Worry will make it
turn out all right. Worry is prayer. But then, this might be a mistake.
The thought must be entertained, an unwelcome guest still a guest.

"I need to use the rest room," she says, tossing the cigarette care-
lessly toward a storm drain. And away she goes.

There are four islands with four pumps each—sixteen cars pulled
up, most with multiple passengers. At one, a man in white T-shirt and
shorts attends his car, while two young girls bounce in profile in the
backseat. Say on average there are two people per car. That's thirty-
two people. If each person would give him one day of their lives—and
what's a day, after all? he has blithely wasted scads of them—that
would add a little over a month to the unspecified allotment of weeks
he has in the bank. The pump rattles and stops. He squeezes the
handle and the gas flows again. How about a week? That's more of a
sacrifice. A week is, for instance, seven dinners in Brittany. A week has
meaning. But for the sake of argument, say a week. Thirty-two weeks,
about 60 percent of a year. He would accept that. A month, that's too
much to ask, no one would grant it, and a year, well, only lunatics and
martyrs would offer up a year, and you wouldn't want their addled
time, anyway. Besides, in thirty-two years he'd be ninety, doddering
and infirm. He could forgo that.

Everything's negotiable, why not time?

He continues pumping, the fluid surges through the hose. Gas
smell and its oily rainbow when it drips from nozzle to ground, and
all that it implies—barrels of crude dredged up from beneath arctic
wastes or Saudi sands, transported in tankers and trucks to this spot,
so that Virgil can take his niece where she's never been, so that on a

whim they can depart, just like that. American freedom at its most literal.

And now the car is full, ready. He inserts his credit card into the pump, no need to say hello to the young man reading his hot-rod magazine in the cashier's booth. A faceless transaction. No security like a full tank. One more place his unconscious belief used to cluster, now forever blown apart. No security, full tank or running on empty. The new security of no security.

Perhaps if he offers compensation—what would a week of life cost? He has modest wealth—a thousand? $32,000. Such a deal.

Just drop it, he thinks. He parks the car.

Caroline stands outside the door of the travelers' center, with its smell of fried food and janitorial supplies. She talks on her cell phone, leaning away from fellow travelers, hunched down like a girl sneaking candy. He puts an arm around her waist, kisses her cheek in a manner befitting an uncle. Determinedly affectionate. She wiggles free, her hand out. *Just a minute, just a sec*, she says, then *thanks, that's it, okay, good-bye*. No clues. He does not want there to be another place she goes. He wants to be her world.

"What's up?" he asks. *Who were you talking to*, though he doesn't ask.

"They have hamburgers," Caroline says. "Real ones." She smiles for the first time today. He would buy her anything to be so rewarded. She can keep her secrets.

"And just what makes a hamburger real?"

"Come find out." She slides her arm through his and the warmth of her, her mere aliveness jolts him. A week? Would she give him one? Would he, if the tables were turned? The very idea makes him cringe. A miser, as he's always suspected.

Inside they push trays along a metal cafeteria shelf, protected from the steam tables by thick glass. Vats of mashed potatoes, green peas dimpling in the heat, meat loaf and roasted chicken—these choices bathe in pools of fallen condensation.

"See what I mean?" she says, when they near the grill. A slim young man in an apron and a white paper hat flattens and flips burgers of uneven diameter. "Handmade!" Small rounds of raw ground meat await his touch. She orders one for herself, and fries. "The grease cure," she says. "I'm so hung over." Virgil takes the chef's salad, hard-boiled egg halves obscenely bright and smiley in the plastic bowl.

She smothers the burger in ketchup, very little mustard, and nothing else, and practically skips to the table. She's happy, she's happy, he says to himself, proud, justified. See, he says to his resident jury. See?

Bad weather. Driving the late-day road, he hopes for bad weather, for trials and tribulations and the ties that such things bind. She sleeps, the window her pillow. The silence between them—*their* silence, he thinks—fills with German soprano, Strauss's *Four Last Songs*. Sinuous voice, that final chord of the fourth song, the musical equivalent of orgasm and the moment beyond, twilight, hope, rest. Oblivion. Do not say death.

"You all right? You've been driving all day," she says, stretching her arms toward the windshield. "I could take over." Her first words since lunch, where she performed 'loquacious' for him, the living dictionary.

The sky grays and begins to weep. Such powerful wishes. But the wrong ones.

"I'm fine. No worries." Rain smears across the glass. He turns on the windshield wipers. Clarity appears with the wipers' slaps, then drowns again, reappearing, drowning. "You regret this?"

She looks over at him, which is all he wanted, for her to need to see him.

"I hope not."

"Anyway you want to do this," he begins. "I mean . . . It's up to you."

"What a dreadful thought."

"Hey, no pressure," he says, and she laughs a little. "Look," he says, pointing out a mileage sign. "Forty-five miles to St. Louis."

The mileposts ding in his mind, a subtraction problem in motion.

Mile 33, 32, 31, 30. All the world is math, expressed in the points of maple leaves, in the aerodynamics of bird wings, in vectors of distance and time. Even emotion—there might be a geometry underlying sadness, supple enough to describe the viscosity of a tear.

Mile 23. *Caroline, I'm sad.*

He considers this statement from all sides, as his lawyerly training dictates. Would the defense be so kind as to define 'sad'? No use, not worth wasting the air. Its heft will be too burdensome. She has just lost her father. She must be sad, too. So she will empathize but fail to understand, fail to know his sadness as he can know hers. That's the joke age plays—thinking you know how others feel because of what you felt in the past. His own father died eleven years ago, and when he did, Virgil's life lightened in unexpected ways. No more conversations where the old man tried to trick Virgil into thinking his thoughts. "Are you sure you're not being reckless?" his father had said once of a trip to Europe. Could he tell her that, to look for the benefit?

"Let's stop in St. Louis," he says, though she seems far away, out the window again, lost in the gloaming.

"Any way you want to do it," she says, a wry tone in her voice. "It's up to you."

chapter 7

The rain stopped by the time we reached the city's outskirts, and the air was crisp with ozone.

"See where we should stay," Virgil said, still driving, pointing with his head to an AAA guidebook.

"Something posh, with a pool," I said. The hamburger had diminished the physical symptoms, but there was more to a hangover than dehydration, headache, and sour stomach. There was the guilt. For that, a swim might help.

Neither of us had a suit, so after we booked rooms, we went to the mall. It smelled of vague perfume and lemony cleaning compounds, the way, in someone's mind, air should smell. No residue of wind or grit, of exhaust or blown leaves.

"What is it about malls?" I asked Virgil.

"Other than their being spawn of the devil?"

I rolled my eyes. "Dear God, an idealist."

"Malls are fascist states."

We had reached the center court by now. A teenage couple spooned on one bench, then two boys came up behind them and the girl jumped up and chased them. Children squalled in strollers while their mothers window-shopped.

In a department store, we went our separate ways, me to ladies, him to menswear. I selected a navy blue tank suit, plain as could be. Regarding myself in the mirror, it looked as if a chalky, powdery deposit had accumulated on me. Not fresh, not vital, barely alive. I needed a good scrubbing. I needed sunshine, some fresh air, and absolutely no more cigarettes or hooch. I needed to stop not sleeping, to straighten up and fly right and to not want unwantable things. I needed to be altogether different than who I knew myself to be. The blue suit, just right. I could measure my progress against it.

In the men's area, Virgil sat in a chair by the swimsuits with his head nearly between his knees, breathing hard. I rushed up to him.

"What's the matter?" I asked.

He sat up quickly. "I hate shopping is all." He winced. "Choose for me."

I rifled through the suits and held out a pair of Day-Glo orange baggies.

"Very me," he said. "Good call." And though it appeared painful, he smiled.

We selected forest green trunks with white stripes down the sides. "This is killing me," he said, holding his side, and I believed him.

Moorish furbelows, blue and white and yellow tile, the closed in smell of chlorine, the dance of light on the vaulted ceiling. The pool was part Turkish bath, part junior-high natatorium. I crawled and butter-flied down its length and back. Virgil slid himself gingerly into the water, then held onto the gutter.

"Stop slushing around," he said. "I'm getting wet." He smiled then, and let go of the side, kicking off the wall. Under the surface, sleek, he swam the length of the pool and I watched him, loving the odd elongations of limb, the lines of his body refracted and wobbly, arms outstretched then his body surging forward as he swooped them in close to his sides. When he reached the other end of the pool, he came up sputtering.

"You are so beautiful," I said, and I dove under, determined to swim the length as he had done.

chapter 8

In the night, or the early morning, in darkness untouched by sleep, he thinks, death is failure. We all fail eventually. There are his clients— who of the tax lawyers he knows should take over? Names say themselves, a mental list he will transcribe in the morning, phone calls and to-dos that he must do. To hear Caroline breathing, the sound of her body shifting against the sheets. She is next door, a world away.

Go home, get treatment, any medicinal cocktail at all, a few weeks more is a few weeks more. He had thought himself so brave to say no, but discretion may really be the better part of valor.

He turns on his light and takes up his book where he left off, mid-hunt in a mystery, a detective, a serial killer.

Bugger these ghoulish stories. He gets out of bed, and stands naked by the window looking out on the dead of night. Twelve floors down, a car turns right. Its headlight beams swivel in arcs across the pavement. He would like to call Jane now and get it over with, the hearing of her voice for the last time. But he'll let her sleep. Virgil the magnanimous.

What to say? 'Oh by the way, I'm dying.' Offhand and macabre. What's mine will be yours, just like when we married. For yourself and in trust for David—until such time as he is free and clear of heroin, a meaningful condition. Wrap the emotional in the legal. As in a divorce.

A police car starts up a street over, rooftop cherry spinning wild red across the walls of nighttime buildings, no siren, no need. Virgil puts on his briefs, his pajama bottoms. Takes his key, leaves the room. Long corridor, wall sconces and striped wallpaper, floral carpet, Biedermeier chairs and Queen Anne tables at twenty-foot intervals. At the elevator bank, a potted palm, a large mirror, a house phone on a glass table. Then he walks around the other hallway. A man delivering morning papers looks up at him, "good evening, sir." Virgil nods. The patterns, the furniture, comfortable yet neutral, unnoticed things that get walked past. Virgil feels duty bound to notice. His final gesture, to see the unseen among us. Cherish the mundane—perhaps those will be his final words, he thinks hopefully. He would like to go out on a wise note. In front of Caroline's room, stomach-first, leaning against the door, he inhales her sleep. Soap and sun-filled, the scent of his hope. May your dreams be sunny as a field in Provence. He would knock as she did last night, not afraid to disturb his rest, needing contact more than politeness.

In, he pulls air down into his lungs. Thirty-two weeks would be so nice. He will knock, Caroline I'm sad. Caroline, cherish the mundane.

But no. He pushes back and unlocks his own room. Not from politesse. Silence will be his gift. Back in bed, lights out, he feels his chest rise and fall with his breath. He'll leave out the bit about his copulating cells, the battle already lost, how he waits for attrition.

chapter 9

Light spills out from an RV's doors and windows, creating a semicircle of jovial possibility on this otherwise-dreary New Orleans night, shifty with the electrical crackle of an imminent storm. Tenderhearted souls pour coffee from a large tureen, and I smell soup. From out of the darkness, I join my ilk milling about with steaming cups, chatting, shifting nervously, a cocktail party if ever I saw one, but with serious intent. From the can't-beat-'em, join-'em school of social engineering, the needle exchange is under way. Accept that people inject themselves with chemistry, accept that the associated health risks are costly on the back end. Discard the moral valences, the condone/condemn dichotomy, and do the math—a needle costs less than a hospital bed. Thus does compassion seep into our world. But there are moral valences. Every junkie knows that. We just forget them in the moment, in the unadulterated now.

My talisman in smithereens, what choice do I have?

To go clean. That's a choice, I remind myself, standing at the farthest border of the light. One I'd like to make. The warm cups look inviting, a friendliness pervades. I feel the Horse in my pants. After this bag, I think. No more. After this bag, I will walk away from New Orleans. I will live on a commune and drink spring water, chop wood, and know healing. Maybe finish school.

I could give this bag away. That's a choice.

I step up to the doorway. The sooner I shoot up, the sooner I move on.

"Hello," says a woman with golden hair. "Here you go." And just like that, she hands me the plastic-wrapped syringe. I cradle it like a newborn baby. "Would you like something?" she asks, indicating soup, coffee, even Oreo cookies, and smiles as she waits for an answer. I recognize her from Botticelli, she's the allegory of spring. Love strikes me dumb.

"Some soup," she answers for me. The right answer. She dishes it into a Styrofoam mug, yellow broth in which chunks of orange, flecks of green swim among languid noodles.

"Thank you," I manage to say, and I blush and leave.

I have no place to go, now that I'm persona non grata chez Baby Duck. My veins don't actually care, even when rain begins to fall. It rains on the other team, as a high-school cross-country coach used to say. Lightning cracks the sky with thunder hard upon it, and again. Branches suddenly silhouetted, mad arms flung skyward in dance. The load-in for a grocery store, dark, covered, a ledge, some Dumpsters. Part of its roof has fallen. It has been a bathroom if smells don't lie. I zip in and hoist myself onto the ledge.

One thing I will want to take with me into straight life, I decide as I stage my operation on the lid of a Dumpster, is this focus. How rare it is, really, to care for one thing to the exclusion of other comforts. That marriage vow, forsaking all others, makes sense to me. I flick my lighter and hold it beneath the bowl of the spoon. I will probably never feel this way again, know this level of sacrifice. New needs will impinge and compromises will follow. The powder liquefies, a caramel fragrance rises as the bubbles burst. I feed the needle with fluid, lift my sweatshirt, press hard below my navel raising the vein, and in she goes.

I lean back against the security door pulled down tight and locked to the loading dock. Its ridges poke into my back and I don't care, they're eiderdown to me. Or I'm eiderdown to them, which is it? Lightning strikes again, filling my cave with momentary white. It makes me laugh and I laugh so hard I cry. Most excellent good Horse.

"On Donner, on Blitzen," I say, Santa in liftoff. The storm fugues my words.

I don't know what time it is that the sirens start. But I wake suddenly, stiff, wanting the next shot. But the sound of justice is rising, a thing to be honored.

Baby Duck's wallops slow me. One more small shot for lucidity, for luck. I swab the needle with a moist towelette, cook and plunge, again into my groin, but the vein spikes and the pain makes me jerk. Blood seeps into the waistband of my pants. The sirens bend around the corner and multicolored lights swirl against the interior of my cave. Running footsteps echo. I toss the works onto the ground. But everfastidious, I repackage the Horse, with intent to chuck it into the Dumpster. Maybe I can hide, and maybe I can seek it out later. I'd hate for it to go to waste.

Blood trickles down my belly. The police car has stopped, but its sirens blare on. The little bit of Horse from the aborted shot has me enthralled by the blue-red lights, circling, all-seeing like the eye of God. I open the Dumpster lid. A stench of garbage blooms in the still night air, and the screech of old metal draws sudden sharp white light to me.

"Hold it right there," a male voice says. I toss in the Horse and drop the lid.

It bangs with solemnity, and no one has to tell me, I'm plumb fucked.

chapter 10

Virgil and I got into a rhythm, crisscrossing I-55 between Missouri, Kentucky, and Arkansas, heading toward Memphis. Virgil wanted to see Memphis. We'd drive a little, then stop at birthplaces, Underground Railroad way stations, embankments where armies had forged long-dry creeks. If it had a plaque, we stopped. I was already writing a mental memo for the next trip: Things I'd Do Differently. Action item one: lay in a supply of food that I actually like. We kept trying to picnic at sites of historic interest, and having to make do with corn dogs.

This was Virgil's idea, that I should actually see the country, not just flash over it at 80 miles per hour, a speed that seemed to suit thought, deceiving with its appearance of purpose and precision. I objected at first—we were going to the Grand Canyon, weren't we? But I came to like the slowness, the little back roads, the forlorn motor-court hotels left high and dry by the big bad Interstate, the time I had to notice the movement of dust.

The car, which had been rather pristine when we began, shiny with wax, its leather seats supple and austere, was now acquiring signs of life. Cracker crumbs wove themselves into the carpeting. Pen marks marred the upholstery from where my hand had slipped doing crossword puzzles. Maps remained half open, their accordion leaves shimmying with the motor's vibration. I stopped wondering what I was going to do. I just sat, still in the midst of movement. I drove or I looked out the window, I hummed with the radio. Maybe this was the simplicity I'd always wanted but didn't believe myself capable of. We weren't exactly tearing up the turf at this pace, but I secretly wanted to continue forever, just drive around, arguing about politics, or about which direction was north. For long stretches I forgot about my phone, of things to do, good and honest works. It was fun.

* * *

"I'm hungry," I said the afternoon of our fourth day, outside Paducah.

"You have but to ask, fair lady, for it to become my command," Virgil said.

I rolled my eyes at this elaborate courtliness, but inside I softened. There was such an ease in him. But it wasn't anything he did. It was all he didn't do that made you notice other peoples' dodges and weaves: the spastic tapping feet, rattled change, ruffled hair, the glancing past you, midsentence, toward doors. He emanated something else. His eyes smiled for him, as his lips stayed closed in a polite, wistful arch, but he smiled often. And when he did it was like an embrace.

"You really are a handsome man," I said. "I wouldn't mind knowing everything about you."

We pulled off at another rest stop, red brick, one story, lush grass and sycamore trees, dogs walked and watered, legs stretched.

I ate an open-face turkey sandwich beneath a slick of gravy, mashed potatoes that were purely conceptual as they had no actual taste. It sat inside me, refusing digestion. The server's white dress held her body too close. When I asked her how long she'd been at the job, she nodded at the woman a table over, as if giving me directions. I wondered if she had any lipstick in her bag, any private cache of hope for when she looked in the mirror. That sounds glib, I know, but I wondered. She appeared to live on a tiny ledge, and she must have known life was larger than that—if nothing else, she'd see it on television, and while TV lies, it also reflects.

My cell phone rang. I pulled it out of my purse, quick to answer, then saw Virgil looking at me.

"I won't be long," I said to him. He didn't believe me, I could tell. "I promise. Hello?"

"Caroline, how are you?" It was Donald. "Listen," he lowered his voice to a tone of dangerous intimacy. I had given in to it any number of times, it had proven me weak and flimsy, so in need of love that my resolve vanished like a magician's dove. "I am so sorry about the other night. God." He was quiet a moment. I filled the space with longing. "Hell, I disappoint myself."

I murmured in response.

"I hope you won't mind my asking," he continued. "But when are you coming back? Whatever mojo you've got, honey, we need it. Everything's going to hell here." He laughed in a way that I recognized as professional, not so much about humor as it was a way to draw the listener—me—into his gravitational field.

I tightened my lips, trying not to get taken. Virgil gazed across the room. A willowy young woman sat in a booth there, rhythmically eating french fries, as if doing factory work.

"I'm not coming back." Virgil smiled at me when I said this, and I was content that I had his attention now.

"It's no problem. You absolutely need some time. But—and I really apologize for pushing on this—do you think it will be more than a week? It's just I can't imagine sparing you longer than that."

Virgil opened up the business section from the newspaper. I looked at the tips of his fingers holding the pages, the even crescents of his nails.

"I'm taking a trip, to Arizona," I added.

"You know I only want what's best for you." Now he employed his recitation-of-facts voice. "You ended it. I still love you, so of course I want your best interests. Did you get the bouquet I sent, by the way? Now let me think. We have contracts with Demwalt, Mason, and Fernandez, right? Which one do you want to keep? I'll give Liz the others."

Liz? She was my assistant. Why would he give anything to her?

"Time out, Donald." I looked quickly at Virgil. He smiled again, folded the newspaper and touched my hand. "I'm not coming back. As in at all, ever, I quit."

I could hear him thinking.

"Caroline." He stopped. as if searching for the words. "You are under extraordinary strain right now, and your well-being absolutely comes first." He waited. I didn't say anything. "But, well, you're a principal in this firm, and we have a contract. It's binding, and it says you have to give me at least thirty days' notice. Technically, I could sue."

Angry tears gathered hot behind my eyes. "Jesus Christ, Donald."

He paused, an effect he always used well.

"Look," he said finally. "Demwalt really needs your touch. You know how those Texans are." He laughed that laugh again. "How about this: Be a consultant. We'll talk, you can look over a fax or two. Nothing heavy. I'll keep you on the payroll."

I could run away and play it safe. Donald could make yes seem the only sane answer.

"I'll think about it. That's the best I can do. Don't bother me for a week." I clicked off the phone.

"Don't do it, Caroline," Virgil said. "Whatever it is."

In the car later that afternoon, driving, I replayed Donald's call in my mind. I felt jumpy in my gut, spoiling for a fight. I pressed down the accelerator, and took us up to 95.

"Stupid bastard," I said.

We were on a small two-lane road, and something moved across it—a cat, a coyote. Or nothing, a shadow, a plane passing by overhead. I lightened off the gas. The car slowed. Virgil looked at me.

"Don't," I said. "I don't want to hear it." I felt him looking at me still, considering.

"Sure you do," he said. "A friend of mine has a farm near here. Why don't we put that stupid phone of yours to use and see if he can put us up? I haven't seen him in ages." He fumbled with my purse, spilling the five lipsticks and three eyeshadow trios into the footwell, then looked at the phone helplessly.

I explained how to do it, reaching over from the wheel. He batted my hand away, "I get it, I get it."

Reaching into the backseat, rummaging through the detritus—more makeup, books, sweaters—he turned to the front with an address book, and dialed.

"Kevin, you'll never guess where I am."

They set it up, and from a long series of "uh-huhs," I knew Virgil was getting directions. When he clicked off the phone he was beaming.

"Kevin's a wild man. You'll love him."

I hated him already.

Virgil talked on and on, about how Kevin had leased some land, and stood up to the power company when they came to claim it, took them to court, chained himself to a tree, his rifle pointed at the driveway.

"He won, you know. He won. I thought he was nuts, but he did it. They backed down."

I could hear the awe in his voice, how the sentences didn't end, they merely swirled into an eddy of private thought, where the truth as he constructed it existed, and the comparisons ran rampant.

chapter 11

"Virgil, my man!" Kevin took Virgil in his arms, lifted him off the ground. "Damn."

Fine wisps of sandy hair gently curled around his head. Round wire-rim glasses with lavender lenses drooped over the bridge of his nose and red blood vessels coiled around his nostrils. He was well past six feet. A T-shirt clung to his round gut, and he had on shorts and sandals, though the day had cooled.

Situated halfway up a hill in a valley of hills, the farm was actually a rickety prefabricated one-story house. A cyclone fence delineated a large yard, barely containing a barking German shepherd who swayed on hind feet, tethered to a pole by a doghouse. I hated the dog for its noise, and Kevin even more for tying the poor thing up. The fence seemed gratuitous, as there didn't seem to be any sign of humanity, except a distant electrical substation. Trees clattered in the chilly breeze.

"Virgil and I go w-a-a-y back," he said, letting us carry in our own bags. He was drinking a Heineken, and smoke from a joint wafted up from his hand. "Yessiree, we had us some good times together, did we not?" He held out his palm for a slap, and my heart sank when Virgil smiled—not just a subtle eye-smile, but a full mouth, thirty-two-tooth salute—and slapped him back. "Let me light one of these for you, my man," Kevin said, inhaling deeply on the joint, and we were inside.

Looking around I had to wonder if the fight had been worth it. The floor was covered in strips of shag carpet that had not been tacked down, each a slightly different shade of brown. A massive desk dominated the tiny living room, with two computers and paper strewn about as in a hamster cage. There was also a large-screen television and a brown velour lounge chair preset in recline mode, its footrest doubling as a table. It held an ashtray, two Heinekens, and a bong.

"Ever the decorator," Virgil said, and the two of them laughed.

Kevin licked the edge of the rolling paper and expertly tightened a joint.

"Who's on first?" he said, and again, he and Virgil laughed so much that I knew this went way back, and that it would be a long night indeed. I grabbed the joint.

"Light my fire," I said, and Kevin laughed all the more and pointed at me and said, "Hey, all right." He held out his palm for a high five, and I wagged my finger, with its large lapis ring, Pope-like, for him to kiss.

His lenses had cleared now that we were inside, and Kevin's eyes were almost black, like little ball bearings. He dropped to one knee, tenderly took my hand, and turned it palm up. Then he blew hard against it, trumpeting loudly.

To my astonishment, I blushed.

"Chiclet, walk," Kevin called, and the dog started up again, a bounding frenzy as we neared. She had a young dog's thinness, and her body curved like a letter C when she wagged her tail. "Yeah, girl, yeah," Kevin said, circling the leash over her head, inciting her to dance on two legs. Rivulets shone in the hills, silver in the pale moonlight.

"Your uncle and I, we worked for the forest service," Kevin said, strolling with me up the hill, away from the house. Virgil was calling clients, said he'd join us. "He was a wild young Turk, yes he was. Could've climbed a pane of glass."

We moved through a thin stand of trees toward a clearing.

"I never knew he worked for the forest service," I said.

"It was what they called 'alternative service,' you know, for us pansy-ass boys who wouldn't carry a gun all the way to Vietnam. We made the most of it, though."

"You mean like conscientious objectors?"

When we got to the next rise, Kevin let Chiclet off the leash and she loped off, her nose reading the ground. A few trees circled the hill, new buds softening the branches. Wind moved through the valley, bracing and fresh. Kevin had brought an old Mexican blanket and, with a crisp snap, shook it out and spread it on the ground. He sat, then extended a hand and helped me down.

"The very same. I grew up Quaker, but Virgil was the real pacifist. I was always getting into fights." He lit a joint and inhaled. "We'd go into bars and the old guys, who'd killed Japs or Krauts or whoever, they'd say, 'Why the hell don't you defend your country?' and me, I'd just start swinging." He inhaled again and looked up at the sky. "But Virgil, he was into it. He had to convert each and every one of those VF-fuckin' Ws, like a Hare Krishna." He was silent awhile. "This one guy, he stubbed out a cigarette on Virgil's hand"—Kevin pantomimed this with slow, grinding gestures—"said, 'That's what I think of your conscience,' and Virgil didn't do shit. Man, he was into it."

He puffed, inhaled, puffed, then passed the joint my way and said, "Finish her," through clenched lips. I contemplated the story, wondered if there might be a scar on Virgil's palm. He would have been my age, or younger. I dragged on the joint.

It was peaceful, slowly tuning in to the raspy wind, the wet smell of saturated earth. I lay back, closed my eyes, felt this place—clover underground, working within its seeds. Ants tunneling, birds newly back from southern climes. Blades of grass, chlorophyll that would eat tomorrow's sunlight, then exhale out oxygen. The elegance of the system—I thought of my father with a tender stab.

"Ow-ooo!" Kevin howled. "Damn what a nice night. Great that you two came. I needed a little face time. What do you do, way over yonder in the big city?"

"I'm an event planner."

"What the hell is that?"

"I plan events." Why did I feel embarrassed?

"Okay, but how do you know they're events?" He said each word slowly. "I mean, isn't that, like, for history to decide? Like JFK's assassination. Now, that was an event."

He looked meaningfully at me, glasses down his nose, and his face looked rubbery, as if I might stretch it in different directions, then release and watch it snap back into place.

"You're not too up on the real world, right?" He shrugged. "Here's how it works: People pay money to plan parties. Could be a product launch, an announcement, anything they want. I figure out who should come, what the experience should look like, feel like, taste like, smell like, sound like, how long it should last, everything."

"So you're saying it's the money that makes it an event."

It was rough spin, but it wasn't wrong. I nodded.

"But that's my point, Caroline. Exactly my point." He pulled out another joint and lit up, then passed it my way. I took a few tokes. The grass was singing to me now.

"Um, what's your point?" I asked when it was clear he wasn't going to say anything more.

"Money doesn't make something an event. An event depends on fate, on circumstance. You can't promise them a successful launch, can you, just because they spend money on it."

"Depends how much they spend." I laughed, but he didn't. "Here's the thing, Kevin." I took another draw on the joint and held it awhile, working out the thought. "Money is a fetish."

He raised his eyebrows at the randy word.

"Like in anthropology—a thing that guarantees power," I said. "These guys are only happy if they spend a lot, because the more they spend, the more power they get. And I'm the priestess. I know this year's colors and the hottest band. I have the knowledge, and they pay for it."

"Man, oh man," he said. "A priestess, right here in River City." He fell back as if faint, laughing.

A yell drifted to us, and presently Virgil ran past us, then turned, ran back and tackled me. Then he hopped back to his feet.

"What are you kids doing," he asked, leaning over, breathing hard.

"Caroline's explaining religion," Kevin said.

"Well, I just made a client ten thousand dollars," he boomed out the amount.

"Damn if she isn't right," Kevin said, pointing to me. "It is a fetish."

Virgil looked quizzically at us a moment, and we both laughed. Then he pounded his chest, Tarzan-style. "I need height," he said, and he spun in circles with his arms out. "That one"—he pointed at a tree—"she is mine."

He ran to its trunk and caught its lowest branch. Then he swung back and forth, but not fast enough to create momentum, and fell to the ground with a soft thud. Chiclet bounded after him as he walked back to where we sat.

"Give me a toke," he said.

"Bet you can't smoke it all," Kevin said, handing Virgil a fresh joint.

"How much?"

"Ten thou."

"You're on, buddy." Virgil struck a match and held it to the joint, then inhaled deeply and choked. "That counts," he said, coughing out smoke. His next few draws were more delicate. When he'd smoked it down, he stood swaying, flimsy in the breeze.

"Isn't it weird the way trees just stand straight up," he called, walking back to his chosen conquest.

"So, how do you like it," Kevin asked me. We watched Virgil catch the tree's lowest branch and swing, gaining momentum.

"What," I asked.

"Planning events."

"Once more with feeling," Virgil called, and swung his legs up, hugging the branch with all his limbs. Then he found his purchase and began to climb.

"It's . . . ," I paused, watching Virgil ascend into the tree's highest arms. The wind moved him around, and stars twinged distantly behind him.

I'd overseen a party the night before coming home for my father's funeral. The theme was disco. We'd hired dancers, including a John Travolta look-alike in a white *Saturday Night Fever* suit. We'd installed a translucent dance floor undergirded with clown-colored lights, hauled up in the freight elevator to a law firm on the eighty-second floor of the World Trade Center. I had arranged an open bar and dance lessons, so for two hours, the paralegals and partners spilled drinks and cha-cha-cha'd behind a girl in a clingy dress whose every move was pure light. Their steps became heavier as the night wore on, sodden with drink, as if a line of telephone poles had suddenly taken the notion to shake it. I went to the ladies room and sat in a stall and cried. Why did this fun, my remarkable feat of legerdemain, look so paltry and pathetic?

Up high in the air, Virgil capered along a branch, beautiful and free, a spirit, a jinn. I felt so lucky, watching him, so profoundly relieved that he had wrenched me from that other world with its ceaseless phone, its hours spent talking to plastic.

Never again. I would never be oppressed by my own handiwork again. In the morning, I'd call Donald and tell him no.

I stood up.

The sky shimmered with more stars than I'd seen in years. Big ones, little ones, hazy swaths of them, yellow blue and pink, a large one falling and then gone from sight. Falling still, just not visible. I lifted my arms to embrace them all, tiny holes in an impenetrable velvet hung to shield our eyes from glory.

"I love you," I called, walking toward Virgil's tree. Grass crunched with my steps. "I love you, I love you."

Virgil threw a walloping kiss, his hand way back behind his shoulder. A moment of stillness, fresh and cool, then he wobbled. His back went too far out. His shoulders followed. An arm was still up high, but a leg was low and getting lower, its foot dangling, tapping, feeling for a branch. The tree shook. I heard repeated thunks, a hollow, drumlike sound, and the air rushed from my lungs. A branch broke with a sharp crack and came softly to the ground. A moment after, Virgil landed, on top of it, draped gracefully across its thickest wood.

Chiclet pounced on him, barking, licking, eager to play this new game.

chapter 12

"Name?"

"David . . . Johansen." I pull out my fake ID and show him.

The clerk types this into the computer then looks at the screen. There are five other desks here at Central Lockup, each occupied by a gentleman like myself, slouched in the chair, speaking in the shortest, curtest possible tones, monosyllables need only apply. One man, he's maybe two years younger than me, cries.

"First time, huh?" he says. As if I'm getting a tattoo, as if this were a choice.

It is a choice. I need to remember the causality that I initiated. Big ocean waves may have landed me on this shore, but I did in fact enter the ocean.

Given my druthers, though, I'd be elsewhere. Anywhere elsewhere. So there's a disconnect. It does not feel like choice.

"Address."

I roll my eyes and give up Baby Duck's squat. The walls have not been painted in a while. They're faded around 8 ½" x 11" pieces of paper, some with pictures, front and profile, most just with words, underscored, bolded, declamations, important things to remember in the meting out of justice. The room smells like stale sweat, like fear.

I scratch my elbows. My knee bounces like a sewing machine's needle. The bitter jones, metal shavings in your veins.

"We'll put you in with the virgins," the clerk says. He watches while my stats print out, pulls the paper and staples it into a file. Why do I feel like I'm at the doctor, not about to enter jail for the first time in my life?

*   *   *

After a shower, I give up my worldly possessions and take on the mendicant's saffron jumpsuit, Orleans Parish emblazoned in block letters. It could house a small Bedouin family and, slim as I am, I get lost among the folds of still cloth. When they unlock the cell, I try to imagine the desert, a sandstorm blowing, anything to obscure the eyes looking out of thick faces, looking at me. These are hungry eyes, yellow at the whites, narrowed, trained on me. These eyes have seen men die.

Fool's way, best way. I dive in and begin to swim.

"Hello, gents, I'm David Johansen and I'll be your host tonight, and I want you to know the request line is wide open."

Though no one moves, the air tightens. Three men occupy two bunks, while on the other side of the cell, another bunk bed remains unoccupied. On the lower, a large black man in a do-rag picks at his fingers, a hangnail maybe. He's thick, with steroid-fed forearms contracting and releasing mid-manicure. On the upper, a slim white man with blond hair, a goatee, a look of Jesus in his blue eyes, lets a dark-haired man tattoo him with a ballpoint pen.

"Who's that? Verna, from Seattle? Welcome to the show, what's your request?" I pause. "I have a dream? Far out. We all have dreams, Verna, and I want you to follow yours. Now here's what MLK had to say on the subject." I make a clicking sound with my tongue, pantomime the hanging up of a receiver.

The three of them stare at me now, and the air tightens even more.

"No, no, we are not satisfied," I say, and it pretty much sums up my feelings. " . . . and we will not be satisfied until justice rolls down like waters and righteousness like a mighty stream."

"Mind shutting the fuck up?" the black man says.

I walk a little closer to his bunk. "I am not unmindful," I continue, looking at him now. " . . . that some of you have come here out of great trials and tribulations." I say this with a soft question in the tone. He looks down at the floor. "Some of you have come fresh from narrow cells. Some of you have come from areas where your quest for freedom left you battered by the storms of persecution and staggered by the winds of police brutality." I pause on that one, maybe he nods. "You have been the veterans of creative suffering. Continue to work with the faith that unearned suffering is redemptive."

The two on top of the bunk laugh unkindly. "Douglas," the dark-haired one says. "We got us a singer."

chapter 13

Pain is so clean. Elegant, precise. Right side, searing, burning. Virgil shakes. There's a cool dab in the center of the heat commanding his focus, an icy edge bordering the expanse of hurt. Caroline holds him on the left side, Kevin on the right. She breathes rapidly, and her exhalations—ha, ha, ha, ha—pound his shoulder. Sweat beads along her hairline. He would kiss her there, taste her salt.

However. Pain is not to be enjoyed. Pain is pain for a reason. It's protection. A swift kick. As they carry him, they are unevenly matched, he so tall, she so short. He would laugh if it didn't feel as if a thousand tiny fires had been lit along his side, each step igniting another switch of wood, a martyr's pyre.

"There you go, buddy," Kevin says, carrying him across the threshold in both arms like an exhausted bride, plopping him into the lounge chair. Kevin glistens from the effort, and the room fills with his perspiration. Virgil inhales. The scent reminds him of climbing, the days without bathing, how you come to smell yourself at last.

"Look, I don't care what kind of contract you need." Caroline on the phone, taking no prisoners. "He needs an ambulance now." Used to having her way. She'll get help. He can rest and when he wakes up . . .

"Hey man, don't fade out." Kevin snaps his fingers in front of Virgil's face. Virgil wants to swat these hands, these pesky bugs. But raising his arm a tiny inch freezes him in red-hot pain—how can it freeze and scorch?—but it does. It does.

"Gently, gently," Kevin says, taking one of Virgil's hands lightly in his own, stroking the top of it. Virgil begins to cry.

Virgil watches Caroline swing the phone cord. Her knee bounces up and down. He endeavors to hold a hand out to her, but she faces the window. The absurdity of the moment is not lost to him.

"There now, hey." It's Caroline's melodious voice. Her warm hand strokes his forehead. "They're on their way. Nothing a little money can't fix," and she lobs this at Kevin as he pulls back the tab on a can of Heineken.

"Right-e-o, campers," he says in a Mickey Mouse falsetto, then takes a deep swig.

The air felt good. It was good to fall through it, the way it whistled, its cool absence.

Kevin turns on the television. "They'll be slow," he says. He lights the bong and the water gurgles while he inhales. CNN comes on, stock symbols and a woman's blond head twitching, her eyebrows gesture.

"How can you smoke that at a time like this," Caroline says, really angry. Kevin breathes in more perfumed steam. "What a waste." She gets up. "Truly a fucking waste." She goes outside with a slamming of the door, and Virgil winces.

No running after her, no walk beneath the stars.

Chiclet begins to bark. "Hey, puppy, it's only me," Virgil hears her say. He imagines her arms around the beast.

chapter 14

A heavy woman sat beside us in the emergency room, moaning, her hair perfectly coiffed, her grown son reading contentedly beside her. Children in unzipped jackets wove a game of tag around the lounge, zigzagging through the hard-backed chairs. Someone had vomited earlier, and though it had been mopped up, its acrid smell lingered. Virgil, pale and withdrawn, clutched his side and stared stoically at the floor. In the ambulance, he had recited the Lord's Prayer, tripping on "Give us this day our daily bread."

I squeezed his hand. No way was I letting go.

"You can tell me how stupid I was," he said, slipping his hand out of mine. "Falling like that."

Kevin had driven behind the ambulance in the Volvo, and now he wandered the room. Lighting on a chair for a moment, he flipped through a copy of *People*. "Everyone's Pregnant!" its headline gushed. A woman looked at it over his shoulder, holding his arm to read the captions. He tossed the magazine into her lap—"Here, take it"—and walked the room again, rattling the change in his pockets like beads from a rosary.

"You were beautiful up there," I said to Virgil.

"Oh Christ!" He looked at me angrily. "Don't do it, Caroline. Don't say things you think I want to hear. I was a fool and I fell to earth."

"You were beautiful up there." He was. "You were free."

"Now it's all scotched." Virgil put his face in his hands and his shoulders heaved in silent sobs. It stabbed me. Not the sobbing so much as the dryness of it, as if he were a desert trying to squeeze out a tropical storm.

He shrugged off the arm I wrapped around him, and I felt my renegade hopes from that night of my father's wake—escape! rescue!—drain out of me beneath the blue white medicinal light.

I ran away out west. I got as far as Missouri. I saw myself heading back

to work, tail 'tween legs, saw the blackened gum of the subway plat-
form, an urban rune I ought to fathom by now, New York in its ugli-
ness and glory, spring coming on, then the swelter of summer with its
rank garbage and bare skin and once-in-a-while salt-sea breeze. Me
on the phone through it all, my imagination leaching away, by turns
more decadent or less, getting lazy, repeating myself, piling up loot
and not caring what it got spent on. Finnish licorice? Divine. Sene-
galese nectarines, four bucks a pop? A dozen, please. I'd stuff my face
with the finest money could buy and not taste a bite.

Kevin sat down beside me and started humming the old Dylan
song, "A Hard Rain's Gonna Fall."

"So true, isn't it?" he asked me.

"What?"

"It is a hard rain, gonna fall."

I just looked at him, and he wandered off again. Names were
called—Lupe Valdez, Preston Billings. They hobbled off behind the
nurses, into that healing realm of blood-pressure cuffs and otoscopes
and examination tables made up fresh with paper. Everything stainless
steel and sterilized and ready.

"You'll see the doctor, it'll be all right," I said. "Come on."

"It will not be all right. I won't see a doctor." Virgil stood up, and
immediately buckled back down into the chair.

"Okay, now you're a fool," I said, my hand out to steady him.

He looked back at the floor, his face chartreuse, and let my hand
rest on his. What was he telling me?

Kevin returned to us, sitting now beside Virgil and massaging his
shoulders with furious pulsations. "How you feeling, man?"

"Like I don't belong," Virgil said.

"I hear that," Kevin said. "This is just the worst, isn't it? All these
people, all sick, God you can smell death coming off them. If I were
you, I'd skedaddle."

"You are so right," Virgil said. I glared at Kevin, which had no
effect, going unnoticed as it did.

"Way to help, Kevin," I said. He looked at me with injured eyes—'What did I do?'—and I walked to the nurses' station, cursing him under my breath, *fucking clueless baby.*

The two of them sat with their heads together, Virgil talking in emphatic tones, Kevin nodding.

"Look," I said to the nurse. "I know everyone says this, but we've been waiting a long time, and my uncle wants to leave. I'm scared he's really hurt." I looked at her with as much plaintive longing as I could muster. "Can you help us?"

"If you'll just take your seat, the doctor will see you as soon as he can," the nurse said.

The kids playing tag jumped a man's outstretched legs, and one of them tripped and began to cry. Where were their parents?

"Doesn't this get to you?" I asked her. It was getting to me.

"There's a coffeeshop on the second floor. You might want to go up there." She looked at her list. "In all honesty, I think it will be a while before they see your uncle."

"What did she say," Virgil asked.

"Hang tight. You're practically next."

"Let's just go. I feel okay."

"Virgil, you can barely move."

"He looks all right to me," Kevin said.

"Well, you're the one who thought it was prudent to live without medical care in the first place, so I'm really not too interested in your opinion right now, unless you want to help me convince my uncle to take care of himself."

"Yow, baby. Better soften that tongue. Never get a man like that."

"Yeah? And you should learn to help out when a friend's in need." And I started to cry, which only made me madder.

Both Virgil and Kevin looked at me, along with everyone else in the ER—this was as much fun as they'd had all night. I drew in some deep breaths to steady myself.

"Shit, I didn't even think of everything you been through," Kevin said, and he said it so tenderly that I started to cry all over again. He tried to embrace me, but I rebuffed him. "I am so sorry. About everything. This guy," he indicated Virgil. "Your dad, all of it. I never got along with my father, and sad to say it, when he died, it didn't mean that much. Then, like, six months later, I was in a bar, just a cheesy place, big ol' rack of antlers over the bottles," he squiggled his fingers, drawing stag horns in the air. "There's a guy who looked just like the son of a bitch, and I picked a fight with him. An old guy, but never mind. I slugged him hard, got my ass kicked six ways from Sunday, and sat on the curb crying my eyes out. I'm a prick."

And with that, Kevin began another perambulation, hands rattling change.

"Hey, ease up on him," Virgil said. "He's easily hurt."

"Ask me if I care."

The two children chased in front of Virgil, one reaching to hit the other.

"I can't stand this," Virgil said, voice wobbly. "I really can't."

I felt like hitting those kids myself.

Virgil's breath caught, shallow in his throat. Everything about him looked battened down, bracing for blows. It was nearly three in the morning. A voice said, "James Alton?" and an elderly man politely raised his hand.

"You need to see someone, Virgil. You know you do."

He looked dead at me. "Please."

We studied each other, and he reached over and wiped a tear from my cheek, then took it to his lips.

"This is wrong," I said, as I helped him up and into his coat.

chapter 15

"So, um, where do I sleep?" I ask, and Douglas and Tyrone, the big black guy, ignore my question. There are two sets of bunk beds in the cell, but it isn't clear who's where. All the beds have stuff on them, though as far as I can tell it's just we three who make up this cozy coterie.

"This one?" I sit on the bottom bunk opposite Tyrone. "Too lumpy."

I climb to the top, and Douglas cuts me a hard look. "Uh, uh, uh," he says. "The man don't like little singers on his goods."

"So that's a no, I take it."

Douglas sidles down from his bunk and comes over to me, very close, his front practically touching mine. He is extremely thin, with wisps of blond hair like dandelion down blowing around his face.

"Has anyone ever told you you look just like Jesus?" I ask.

Douglas doesn't look too pleased with the information. His face flowers in hues of rose, and sweat makes it moist. Tyrone, who I can see from my vantage point, laughs. To my immense surprise, Douglas pops a piece of gum into his mouth—his maw with darkened teeth— the smoking-cessation variety, and he's so close that I can hear the candy shell break as he begins to chew.

"Trying to quit?" I ask, inching away from him, and slumping back down into the lower bunk. Lumps and all, it's home. "Me too. Not smoking, though. Never have been a smoker. I'm a Horse man. So if I get a bit twitchy, or start to sweat like I have dengue fever, don't worry. It's just the Horse. It won't last forever, so I wouldn't want you to get too concerned."

"You a mouthy motherfucker," Tyrone says.

"It's my gift," I say. "To you," I bow toward Tyrone, " and you," this time to Douglas.

"Asshole," Douglas says, and he retreats for the moment to his bunk. But I know him, I knew him before I met him. He's scalding water bubbling and jumping in the pot, a bad thing coming my way and no barrage of words will stop that, so I lean back against the wall—my wall—and survey things, in this moment of reprieve.

The lock up has cinder-block walls painted vague mint green. Tyrone has pictures of Louis Farrakhan and Elijah Muhammad taped above his bunk, and over Douglas, Christ preaches to a group of children. A small window lets in a square of southern light, the filtered kind that's part river mist, part atmospheric haze, and part oblivion. Very white. I like southern light. That and the weather are why I stay on in New Orleans. The sky is safe here, it never feels too big.

This is where I'll wait for arraignment. Mr. David Johansen, né Harris, you stand accused of possession of a controlled substance, how do you plead? Not guilty in the least, sir, by reason of I'd already thrown the stuff in the Dumpster, so I didn't technically possess it, now did I? A court-appointed lawyer is supposed to turn up later in the day, and I plan to tell him almost everything.

"How do these lawyers work," I ask, hoping one of them will answer.

"He a real lawyer or a public defender?" Tyrone says.

Douglas laughs, and says in mocking falsetto, "Will it hurt?" and then in his regular guttural tones, "Virgin!"

"Public defender."

"Forget about it. Those guys process twenty or thirty of you at a time, so you better know your shit. Ask me, you got to use your influence. You clearly a rich boy. Your daddy must know a guy who knows a guy."

"So you think this lawyer will show up today, then?" I ask.

"Where you got to be?"

I have never been so aware of the length of a second. The clock in my head ticks and each tick elongates Gregorian-chant style, stretching, the moment bent in a thousand shapes before it's released and the next moment begins, doing the same damn thing, world without end. Now I see the dread of that.

It's not unlike Horse time, this way time stretches. But even though I know that when on Horse, I'm not truly free, the difference is, I think I am.

Someone calls, "Hello." No one answers. Scrapes and clangs of cell doors opening and closing, voices, bombs of laughter going off above or below, and I'm not sure if that's two seconds or ten minutes.

"Yo, Tyrone, Wheel of Fortune, bro." A man stands at the cell.

"I'm there." Tyrone gets up and joins his friend. "Television?" He asks me.

I don't say anything, lost in the refracting moment. Douglas strokes his new tattoo, a cobra on mag wheels etched into his forearm. Open, close, open, close he makes a fist, then releases it, flexing the viper.

I know his blows, smell his gum as he whispers "Virgin" in my ear. He's every fear I've ever feared.

He slides from his bunk and stands over me. He is the only thing in the whole world, all I can see. A moment of true focus. I whimper.

"What's the matter, little Virgin? You afraid? You told me yourself, I look just like Jesus." He puts a hand in my hair and tousles it, then tightens his grip till he's pulling hard.

"That hurts," I say, amazed at my voice given the rushing in my guts.

"Good," he says, and he pulls harder, turning me onto my stomach.

"David Johansen," a guard comes to the cell.

"That's me." Douglas quickly lets go.

"What are you doing," the guard says to him. Douglas shrugs. "Come on, Johansen."

He leads me down the cell block, and being the new kid in town, I get whistled at. I don't know how to work with that, so I stare at the guard's belt, rigged with hardware, gun, cuffs, club. He's wired to the other guards and their voices crackle around him.

"Sir," I say, my stomach about to heave, "I need to use the toilet."

"Jesus Christ, Johansen, you think this is kindergarten?"

But it's too late. I retch, and hold the vomit in my mouth. More whistles.

We go through a set of thick metal doors, which require his keys and keys on the other side to open, and then I'm in an area of conference rooms. Inside one, a dark-haired man in a rumpled gray suit paces back and forth, talking into a cell phone.

"Twenty minutes," the guard says, closing the door. Video cameras watch from two corners of the room as I release the vomit into a trash can. The lawyer looks at me with disgust. He waves distractedly and says, "I know, I know," into the phone, and listens a minute more, writes some notes on a pad of paper and says, "I gotta go, he's here and he just puked."

"So David, I'm Sam Bauer, your defender. I understand you got caught with—let's see here"—he leafs through a file—"looks like a little under twenty milligrams of heroin, is that right?"

"Do you have a Kleenex?" My mouth is gummy at its edges with vomit. I taste it, feel its acid in my stomach. I'm sweating, withdrawal and its "flulike symptoms" now cranking up, adding to the misery.

He rifles through his pockets and doesn't have one.

"Can you get me some water?" I see a water bottle in his briefcase.

"No, once they close the door they don't like to open it. So the charge is heroin possession, right?"

"Well, technically, no." And I start to say more, but he cuts me off.

"Right, so a possession charge"—and he looks through his notes again—"depending on circumstances, can carry a mandatory four-year term. Or you might just get probation. How do you want to plead?"

"Well, like I said, I didn't actually have anything on me. So I think I should plead not guilty. I could really use a sip of that water."

He ignores that. "You plead not guilty, you go to trial, and I'll tell you something. They're not too nice about heroin down here. Makes New Orleans look unsafe. Scares away the convention business. You end up doing more time. I say cop the plea, get the minimum, and you walk after six months or so." He starts to fill out a form, and he writes in *guilty* where I think it should say *not*.

Six months, of Douglas chewing gum?

"Um, excuse me, but that's not what I want to do. I didn't have the heroin on me. I'm not guilty as charged."

Sam looks at me a little longer, then goes back into the file and reads. All the while, that clock in my head is ticking, except now each tick is gone before I hear it, no more meandering, it's *tempus fugit* time. Twenty minutes, twenty minutes, the guard's voice keeps saying. Twenty minutes, six months, four years. Shit. My knee begins to jerk up and down. My stomach surges, I feel Douglas's hand in my hair. I retch one more time into the trash can.

"Jesus Christ," the lawyer says. This time he finds a Kleenex, and at last hands me the bottle of water. I sip gratefully. "Junkies," he says, sotto voce, but I hear it.

"Okay, so your report says you showed signs of having ingested the substance, and that a needle kit was found on the ground just below your feet."

"You're the lawyer, but isn't that circumstantial? Isn't there a reasonable doubt?"

"Look, basically what I do is file your paperwork and show up on your court day. You wanna plead not guilty, it's your call."

"Not guilty. I'm not guilty of what they're accusing me of."

"My professional opinion is, you're screwing yourself. You got anyone you can call? You need a lawyer."

"I thought that was you."

"You need a real lawyer. Did they give you your call?" He leafs through the notes again. "You declined. How stupid was that? Why?"

When you're someone like me, if people love you, the way, say, my mother loves me, they'll always help. Do you need money? (When does a junkie not need money?) Are you eating, why don't you come home—we can beat this thing, David. And probably we could, if I would ever go, if I could bring myself to let her send me the bus fare or the plane ticket or the twenty dollars I owe in library fines, whatever. And I'd like to, actually. I'd like to go home, to be hugged, forgiven. I'd like to get clean. But I always need help. So I never ask for it. That is the fundamental deal. I can't be my mother's worst fear realized, and if it means accepting less than adequate representation, I don't deserve any different. I deserve to be a mop sopping up a dirty floor.

And Dad, well, forget about Dad.

"Really, why?"

Then I realize I haven't said a thing, just sat here staring into the land of nod and by now almost all of my precious time has ticked away.

"Not guilty, Sam Bauer. Remember. I am not guilty."

All shuts down at 10:30 with simultaneous lights-out, and were it not for the clanging of metal doors and a wronk sound of the one lock locking us all in, I would almost think summer camp. I lie in the semi-darkness—a light is on every ten feet or so outside the cells, greenish light. A guard moves around down the block. Tyrone snores already. He tells me he's been accused of breaking and entering, they found him with $30,000 worth of jewelry. Douglas won't answer my inquiries as to his malfeasance, but I'm sure it's not pretty. I listen to hear his respiration and since I don't hear it, I don't think he's asleep. Which means I won't sleep either.

As if I could. My stomach still heaves and my elbows itch. Fever bastes me in sweat and my joints ache. I'm constipated beyond belief, with the sense of pressure that gives. And I wonder what I'm doing here, how I got to this particular place. When did I become so friendless, so in the shadow of God?

"David." It's Douglas, whispering. "Come here."

I pretend to sleep.

He climbs down from his bunk. Tyrone snores on, or simulates it well.

"David, didn't you hear me?" He sits on my bunk now, and again moves his hand into my hair, but gently. I expect the tightening pain, and watching for it makes the tenderness gruesome.

He strokes on. "Feel how hot you are. You're burning up." He strokes my forehead, my neck. He takes my head into his lap.

"Please," I stammer. "Leave me alone. Please." I cry.

"No tears now. You know Jesus loves you." He strokes my cheek and it feels nearly good.

He leans down and kisses my cheek and God help me, I soften. It seems this is how badly I need a caress.

chapter 16

The thought of being stuck amid the paper and bong water at Kevin's did not strike me as a healing prospect. So, after leaving the hospital, I checked Virgil and myself into a hotel, just one room, in case he needed me in what was left of the night. But he slept straight through, and in the morning, we surveyed the damage. He had a bruise the shape and practically the size of Australia wrapped around the left side of his rib cage.

"I'm fine," he said. CNN poured into the room, and he sat shirtless on the bed gazing at the screen. "Let's just go."

"One tiny bit of healing and you think you're good to go," I said.

"It's not that bad," he said. "We should just get moving."

"You should ice it for a day."

"This just isn't what I wanted."

I rolled my eyes. "Well, it's what you got. We're staying put. So do you want breakfast or don't you?"

He wanted pancakes.

As I drove, I couldn't resist peeking at my phone. While turned off, it had logged three calls, all from Donald. No doubt, calling about Demwalt.

The town was like a place in a commercial or a dream, conceptual, reduced to its rudiments—one-story buildings lining two sides of Main Street, a median running the length of the street with raised brick planters, hyacinth tips pushing up. A grand old bank built like a temple commanded one corner, while Delehant's for Ladies presided across the street, with orange blinds pulled down, casting its headless mannequins in sherbet glare. A café-donut shop, a stationer, a jeweler,

American flags flapping outside each. Large ponderous cars occupied the parking spaces, yet no one was on the street, and there was no restaurant. I drove on. Maybe there'd be something farther out.

I could just imagine the hysteria at the office. Archer Demwalt demanded special handling. He was given to big business affirmations requiring quotation marks, the "maverick"—he used that word when we met—son of an old Dallas family, which meant he'd made his money in computers with the money he already had from oil. Extremely good manners in the Texan mode. I'd known him six months before he stopped calling me "ma'am," and only then because I said, "Arch, I'm not your goddamned grandmother."

I pulled into a gas station, filled the tank and when I went in to pay, I bought a pack of Camels, and didn't ask about a restaurant. Back in the car, I lit up.

Over the years I'd done several events for him, and he "liked my style," as if my taste had anything to do with it. He liked his own style, blustery evocations of the West of the mind, Frederic Remington hyperbole and sentimentality. And he liked that he could call me twelve times a day "just to check in." Now he was getting married. It had been a "whirlwind romance," he'd told me, he'd met the lady of his dreams—the daughter of a Dallas police bigwig—and was going to "make her his wife." I believed the element of force in the word *make*.

I listened to the messages. "Caroline, what are cymbidiums?" Donald's voice squeaked with desperation. "Caroline, he wants fondant icing on the cake, what do you think?" "He's asking about twenty-pound card stock versus thirty-six. What should I tell him?" By the last message there was audible sweat breaking on his forehead. Donald had never been a detail man—that was my forte.

Let him sweat. It was not my problem. This was precisely what I had run away from.

I drove a little farther. Still no restaurant. The air was crystal in its clarity, no humidity thickening the atmosphere, just unmediated light. Enjoying this did not stop me from lighting another cigarette.

Cymbidiums were lovely, especially the pale pink varieties. Arch's fiancée hadn't voiced much in the way of preferences when we'd spoken, other than to ask if her dapple gray Arab stud could somehow be in the wedding. The horse's gray and the orchid's pink would look stunning together and, after all, it was Texas. Why not mount the bride on her favorite stallion? I imagined her sidesaddle, veil rippling in sunny, buoyant waves. The veil would need to be a sheer fabric, woven through with the merest hint of gold. Arch would like that. Donald needed my file on florists.

As long as we were grounded here, Virgil resting up, it couldn't hurt to call. I punched in the number, fumbling with the phone and downshifting at the same time. The car stalled. I started it up again and noticed a cop on a motorcycle behind me, his finger pointing to the curb. I pulled over and rolled down the window.

"Morning, ma'am," he said.

"Hello. Is my taillight out or something?"

"No, ma'am. You just drifted through that stop sign. Coulda caused a accident."

This seemed highly unlikely, given the paucity of inhabitants, but I bit my tongue. I hadn't seen the sign.

"You know, I just got my uncle out of the hospital last night and I guess I'm a little distracted. I'm sorry. I would never want to be a menace." I smiled sheepishly. He was probably forty, trim, eyes little slits of mercury.

"He wanted a pancake breakfast this morning, so I'm trying to find a place. Would you know of one?"

"Can I see your license, please?"

"Absolutely." I felt in my purse for my wallet, and realized then that it was in the hotel room. "I can't believe it. I left it in my other pants, the ones I was wearing at the hospital."

The cop began filling out his citation. "Driving without a license," he muttered. "Ignoring posted traffic signage." This did not bode well.

The situation required tears. The brightness of the day, its shafts of warmth hinting at summer pleasures, these pierced me, especially coupled with the image of my father in that gaudy box. He would never call again, talking about seeing an article I might like, or about a case he had, sharing its fascinations.

"Hey, miss, don't cry, please. My kid was just tested over there for leukemia—I know how scary it can be."

"Leukemia?" This broke my spell. "God, I'm sorry." I felt ashamed.

"Parkview has good pancakes. I'll take you there."

I followed him to a chrome-sided diner on the far outskirts of the town. Beside it, a fenced-in yard of stacked bald tires, acres of them, waited for discovery, as if someone would eventually arrive and drop to their knees in praise, finally, Lord, my prayers answered. In the meantime, a pair of Dobermans growled around the perimeter.

"This is perfect, thanks," I said, ready to order and go.

"Break bread with me," the cop said. We sat. The coffee was very dark and bitter and going down by the gallon at the counter and the tables near us.

"What'll it be, Duane?" the waitress said. He ordered for us, including my order to go, pancakes all around.

He drank his coffee and scanned the room. Voices whispered faintly from the radio attached to his epaulet.

"What made you become a cop?"

"Runs in the family. Dad, my two brothers, a couple of cousins—all cops."

The sun lay across the table, a square of heat. I rested my hands in it. The booth had its own little jukebox, mounted on the wall. "You like music, Duane?"

"Sure. Who doesn't?"

"Pick out a song. My treat." I tossed him a quarter. He caught it mid-flight and smiled, and his smile was like a long-forgotten thing. His smile had memories of when it used to happen all the time, for no good reason.

He went to Barbra Streisand, "People Who Need People," suitably maudlin for my mood, for the warmth on my hands. His lips were colored like peonies.

"I'm sorry about your child. What happened?"

He shrugged. "My wife didn't get pregnant too easy. We tried a long time and were just about to, you know, do it some other way. Then out of nowhere, she's pregnant, and we're both so happy, like God just smiled on us. He's the cutest kid." He opened his billfold to a picture of a blond boy, about two, in blue overalls, clutching a stuffed lion.

"He looks really happy," I said, touching the plastic holder.

Our pancakes came and I had no appetite. Duane ate a few bites in silence. His face was turned toward the window and to my amazement there were tears sliding down his cheeks.

"I'm just, well, so sorry," I said, panic rising. Should I reach across the table and take his hand? "I shouldn't have asked." My father's wake came back to me, its absence of grief, my anger at the mourners who would not mourn. Smile! Be brave! Buck up! Surely I was more courageous.

"No, that's exactly it," he said with surprising volume. "You should. No one does. They all feel sorry for us, you know, but it's like we did something wrong. All we did is love him." He had been leaning over his plate, elbows on the table. He looked up now. "You got kids?"

I shook my head.

"You'll find out what love is when you do."

The radio at his shoulder chattered again, and something in its vibrato caught his attention. He listened a moment.

"I gotta go. Thanks for—" he didn't finish, but tore up the ticket and let it snow down onto the table. I remained in the booth a long time, resting my hands in the sun, looking out the window, then at the shards of the torn-up ticket, smelling its faint carbon-paper smell. It was good to be alone, unknown in this unknown place. I didn't have a thing to say to anyone.

After a little while, I pulled out my phone and called my office.

"Donald," I said to his voice mail. "No deal. Consider me gone."

chapter 17

Virgil lies on his good side and holds a bag of ice to his bruise. He rotates his arm, assessing the degree to which it makes him flinch. It hurts, but tolerably, a bad bruise that will fade with time.

CNN bombards him with facts and figures of serious intent, dished out by lovely women. All these women, all talking to him, telling him important things about the world that will impact the bottom line and affect his clients come April 15th. He struggles to attend, but the cooling ice, the white sunshine angling onto a table, the occasional piping of a bird—these have greater allure.

He pulls the phone to him on the bed and dials his herbalist in Chicago, tells her of the fall. She already knows about the cancer. "Not to worry, I Fedex you arnica root and a few others, you brew." He drafts a letter to his clients, his resignation letter, the only one he has ever written in his entire career, a fact that swells him with foolish pride. One commitment honored. After a few scratchings and rearrangements, he calls his assistant.

"Darla, I'm going to dictate a letter that needs to go out to my clients no later than tomorrow. No interruptions while I'm reading it. Got it?"

He reads, and arriving at the information about his illness—alluded to, not named—she gasps and through the rest of the call, she sniffles. She has been with him three years, the longest any assistant has lasted. Virgil ignores her emotion and instructs her to arrange a call with another attorney, so that he can negotiate the transfer of his clients' interests, and then says good-bye.

Caroline hasn't returned and he tries to imagine her, out in the bright day, driving. In his mind she's humming, music emanating from her like a scent.

Now the real work. He should write to David, or call, and starts the letter.

"Dear Son,

This is your father speaking, your father on a bed in a hotel room, your father with a bruise, perhaps a broken rib and your father with metastasizing cells running amok from the organs out. That's no way to tell you what I have to say, but . . ."

After ten minutes, Virgil notices that he isn't writing anymore, and that the letter is all wrong and that he has no idea what to say to his one son, what his parting line should be.

Not should. Shoulds are for choirboys. What does he *want* to say, in his one last conversation? The sun jumps from table to floor, its angle widening. *I love you.* He can't remember when he last said it, overwhelmed as the tender feeling is by the apologetic urge, and the sorries are chasm deep, echoing endlessly, and so he has been a silent father.

Maybe dying will loosen his tongue.

Virgil takes the ice off his bruise and feels along his rib cage until he finds it, the hard knob in the gap between ribs four and five, like a fireball from a candy machine. Red-hot candy delight. He touches it, this tumor, this new part of him.

A knock on the door and a voice, "Housekeeping," prompt Virgil to cover himself.

The maid opens the door and apologizes.

"No, it's all right. I'm a little bit ill, so if you could just give me fresh towels, that would be great."

She bustles about in the bathroom, stands his toothbrush up in a glass, straightens his soaps and shaving kit.

"No vacuum?" she asks.

"No thanks." Virgil smiles at her. He loves her, too. When she leaves, a burning surge of tears wells in his throat, and he puts his face deep inside a pillow and allows it all to come.

*   *   *

In the night, after Caroline has returned and fed him pancakes and watched television with him, then gone out to find the local paper and brought it back and performed its articles on high-school baseball and town-council meetings and made him laugh because she renders it absurd with a quaver in her tone, after she has distracted him so beautifully from the hard candy on his side and the epic bruise and the tears that were mercifully finished before she came and the ghosts of women he has had or desired who appear to him now in parts and wholes, through all of that, she was with him. But now it is late and she's next door, and he wonders if she's reading or asleep or watching TV, if she's sad or blank or happy or calm, if her hair stretches out on the pillows around her, what her breath smells like, how her heart sounds through her chest.

Virgil reaches for the phone, thinking to call her, invite her back over, slumber party. Instead, he dials Jane. He knows her number by heart—that's where it's stored. She lives in Utah now. It's earlier there. The phone rings, his heart lurches. She answers.

"Jane? It's Virgil."

I need to tell you, he wants to say. He says nothing.

"Where are you?" she asks, and her voice thrills him, deep with river melody. "Didn't you get my messages? I've been trying to reach you all day. Do you know where your son is?"

part II

chapter 1

"Look," Caroline says. "Houses." Virgil can't look, speeding intently down the interstate, Jane's voice in his head. *David hasn't called*, she said. That's not like him. Usually once, twice a week, now three weeks without a word. She had tried the police—maybe he'd been picked up. Nothing.

The southbound highway spans a swamp. Cypress trees rise out of it, spindly, gray with muck. They glide above the water, the air viscous, a species of liquid. Caroline keeps looking out the window, then looking backward. The houses must have disappeared. "Can you imagine," she says.

All he can imagine is what's ahead, the boy emaciated, shivering despite heat, pale, shiny with sweat. Sick. *I've got the flu, Dad, that's all.* Virgil knew better, but had once given him some codeine, left over from a climbing fall. David was so surprised, so grateful. Oh David, what would make you do this to yourself? This is a question he would like answered. Didn't he have the right, as a father, to know? He has to laugh at that, the righteous, indignant daddy. What rights does a father have? You're just an instrument, a vehicle for life, and once it's here, walking, talking, re-creating itself, well— progeny slip away from their progenitors just as fast as they can. You are the past. That's one thing every child tells his parents. I'm making off with the future and there's nothing you can do about it. Except this stupid child.

Signs herald New Orleans—Metairie, Slidell. Vast graveyards, with their angels and crypts and decay, bracket the road. The flatness, the patois on the radio, the plantain trees mixed among the pines indicate that this is someplace else altogether.

Through will alone Virgil accelerates.

Something beyond will, actually—obligation. Dread mixed with a drop of redemptive possibility.

*   *   *

They get a corner room at the hotel, three large windows overlooking a kink in the eel-colored Mississippi. He has stayed here before, and it pleases him to see Caroline in this grand old place. He stands and pushes the curtains back to watch a ferry's stately crossing to Algiers. Caroline does what she has done each night, assess the quality of accommodations based on the bathroom amenities. This hotel she likes. French-milled soap.

"I've never been to New Orleans," she says, as they step out onto the Rue Royale, a thin street, dirty like the floor of an old movie theater, too much stuff thrown down, too many feet walking heedlessly over it, grinding it into a permanent stain. It has rained and the street makes a sparking noise when cars roll over it. He is exhausted and these streets hold other memories that he would rather not meet, a younger man walking, younger and happier. To age is to confront ghosts, his old selves rearing up at unlikely junctures.

"Come on," she says, when she stops and realizes he's not beside her. "Let's explore."

Despite the weather, lumpy women in sweatsuits, raincoats draped over shoulders, umbrellas half open, wander the streets. Titillation buzzes through the air. This is Gomorrah. Hope springs eternal—the wish to see something lurid. Virgil's prick tingles with the same expectation.

"I have to find David." The words sound like a death sentence. He looks down, then back at her, squarely. "It won't be good." Clenching everything inside, he still chokes. "He's probably strung out somewhere."

"What?" Her voice registers genuine astonishment, but he expects to see amusement. He is prepared to hate her just now. The wet air chills him. He dares her to laugh. "You can't be serious," she says. "I can't believe it. David? With the fossils?"

"He's been on and off of heroin for years. Jane thinks he may have OD'd." He stops and looks down a cross street. "You don't have to do this, you know. I mean, it's my problem, not yours." He waits.

To his immense surprise, she cups her hand softly to his cheek.

A woman in a striped house dress plays clarinet across the street. She leans back into the notes and they gush out, syncopated, optimistic, full of jive.

Jane has given him David's last address, as if he didn't know it already. When they call, the line's disconnected, so they take a cab over, the driver asking, "Sure that's right?" when he hears where they're going.

Curlicues of paint flake off the building, stretching into the air, ready for flight. The ground below is littered with multicolored flecks. It could look festive, but amid the shards of glass, the fast food wrappers and paper cups, the spots look like hives. There is a rusted fence strung around the building. Four men with brown bags laugh outside a liquor store next door, until they see the cab. They watch its progress sharply.

"That's the place," the driver says. "Don't look like anything now." He stops and twists to face them, the cab still in drive. "Where you wanna go now, mister?"

Away. To bed. With—he tries to imagine a body that could transport him. "I need to—" he says, but stops. He can't say what.

Caroline watches him. She has been quiet this ride, a comforting vibration beside him, unintimidated by the squalor. He admires her ability to just look. For him, keeping his eyes open is penance, but a forgery, as it is still possible not to see.

"Let's go back to the hotel," she says, touching his forearm. "We need to figure this out."

"Ask me, that's the thing," the driver says, still facing them. "I don't know why you want to come here. I don't come myself. 'Less I have to." The meter ticks up twenty more cents.

"Virgil," she says.

He can't answer. He can't breathe.

"I need to. . . ." He steps out and slams the door, then smacks the side panel of the car as if cropping a horse. The driver accelerates and the cab moves on.

Virgil makes himself walk slowly toward the clutch of men. He pretends that his heart isn't racing, that the sweat raining off his forehead is from the heat. He holds his palms out and up.

"I was wondering if you could help me."

No one says anything. They don't look at him.

"I have a son who lives here"—he points at the building—"or he used to. David Harris. Know him?"

The men don't speak and their hostility radiates like flame. One man is tall and slim with a gaunt face, dabs of red in the creamy whites of his eyes. He almost makes eye contact.

"Any of you have sons?" Virgil goes on.

"Why don't you get the fuck out of here before you get your ass kicked?" a fattish man says, younger than the others, eyes hidden behind dark glasses, baggy overalls cut off at the knee revealing ham-like calves. He wears a knit cap that says Saints.

"I've been wondering that myself," Virgil says, and despite himself, despite the anger circulating among these five men—he considers himself one of them now—he keeps talking. "I would like to, you know? You don't know how much. This boy is in trouble, though, and, well, I haven't been much of a father."

"We don't know where your boy is," the fat man says, and he spits when he says *boy*. "But he ain't here."

Virgil nods. "Sorry to have disturbed you."

He walks away, counting to five with each step to even out his pace. The men start to mutter behind him, *dumbass white man*. Footsteps follow his and he braces for a blow, but it doesn't come. The cab went this way, so he does too.

The thin man crosses the street and walks parallel to Virgil. At the next block, the man turns the corner and stops. They stand, regarding one another. Virgil crosses.

"What happened to your son?" the man asks.

"I don't know exactly. He dropped out of school two years ago. He was like a different person, all the fight gone out of him. Then he just drifted. Called one day, from here. It hurts his mother so."

"They just swept that old place clean long about a week ago. Bunch of squatters, junkies. One very angry loud boy. Sound like yours?"

"David's not loud."

"I had a boy like that. Sweetest, smartest. Good second baseman," the man says. "Tries a little coke one day, you know, with his buddies, big jock is always high above the law, right? Had a heart attack and died. Nineteen years old, baseball scholarship to LSU, everything ahead of him. Could have played in the majors." A robin lands at their feet and cocks its head.

"Should have tanned his hide at the first sign," he goes on. "But then, look at me." He toasts Virgil with a bottle wrapped in a brown bag up, then drinks it, and the smell of rye flashes between them.

"Find your boy," the man says. "You got to."

Virgil's side throbs suddenly, nearly buckling him. "I know I do," Virgil says. "I don't know what to do. I've been such a. . . ."

"He's either in lockup or Bywater." The man hurries down the block.

chapter 2

Turning in the taxi to face backward, I watched Virgil walk up to the four men. "I'll give you thirty dollars to turn around," I said to the driver.

The taxi kept moving.

"Come on," I said. "We can't just leave him there."

"The hell we can't."

He maneuvered the car onto a busy street, into the center lane. I couldn't get out.

"I have to help him."

The driver snorted. "What are you going to do?"

"He's hurt. He'll get hurt there. At least let me out."

"New Orleans a rough town. I'm taking you back to the Quarter."

"If he gets hurt, it's on you, Edgar," I squinted at his license. " . . . Wilson."

"Baby, he got out of the cab. That's a choice, see."

I sat for a while, very tight, trying to squeeze out a thought.

"I'll just get another cab back." My voice broke. "Please take me."

"What's your name?" the driver asked. I told him. "Well, Caroline. That man does not want you right now. He got a son there?" He eyed me in the rearview mirror and I nodded. "Then he got some business to attend to because that's no place for a white boy." I started to sob.

"Look," he said, and I looked into the mirror again. "I'll call dispatch, tell them to send someone over, you know, just cruise a little." He handed a tissue back to me. "But you put some food in yourself, you get ready for when he comes back. That's when you can help."

There was a convention in town and the hotel lobby was filled with women and men, waiting for others, undoubtedly off to gorge on New Orleans's vaunted cuisine. They made me sick, their joviality, their denim dresses with appliquéd flowers.

I was in a foul mood. I went up to the room.

Circling through TV channels showed bombs falling, guns blasting, a child cringing in a corner, a pair of cops entering a bar. I stopped there. The climactic moment: Lout spills beer on the lady cop. She storms to the washroom to clean up. Unselfconsciously, she removes her blouse, rinses it in the sink, holds it beneath the air dryer while we viewers enjoy her ample bosom uneasily contained in a white bra. Looking up, Eureka! Righteous indignation. A camera in the bathroom ceiling, the smoking gun, the case solved, justice and hard-on served with equal aplomb.

I turned off the set and threw the clicker onto the other bed. More viewing would require reaching that far. I didn't think I had it in me.

No message light flashed on the room phone, no envelope icon appeared on the screen of my cell phone. No Virgil. That fucking bruise of his throbbed in my imagination, a beacon, his pain calling me even if he himself were too stubborn. How could I not have known about David? If this were work, I would have known. There, people always gave up the dope to me. What else did I not know?

The mini-bar promised surcease of suffering after a fashion. A petite Jack and Coke, perhaps? Vodka and orange juice, or straight over ice, clear on clear, icy biting clarity? Champagne, bubbles of joy to belie this angry panic? Jack and Coke. When in doubt, something sweet and rich in caffeine.

I went to the bathroom for a glass. My cell phone rang.

In my rush to answer I dropped the glass on the bathroom floor, breaking it, and hopped out over the shards.

"Caroline, hey." It was Donald.

"I do not want to talk to you. Figure it out yourself. I have other concerns."

"Wait, wait. Slow down." His voice soothed me, close as a pillow, the strange intimacy of phones. "I just needed to hear your voice. God, I miss you. What are you doing right now?"

I looked around the room. "Breaking glasses. Throwing things. Making a fool of myself, talking to someone who hurt me."

"Someone who loved you. Who still loves you."

"Someone who wouldn't know love if it came up and knifed him in the gut." We were both silent a moment. It seemed I would never forgive him. "What do you really want? Otherwise, good night."

He remained silent. The mushy part was over.

"Caroline, look. Demwalt's calling me a hundred times a day. 'This is going to be the show-stoppingest damn wedding Dallas has ever seen, and now I spent a bazillion dollars with you all, and goddamn you all better do right by me.' Jesus H. Christ. How could you stand this guy?"

I laughed despite myself. Donald had caught Demwalt's hectoring cowpoke twang dead-on.

"He's right. He has spent bazillions with us. With *you*," I corrected myself. "You do owe him."

"I don't know how to do this. That's the truth of it. I need you for this one. After that, spit in my face, walk away, I'll wish you well and write you one hell of a walloping check. But help me."

"I . . ." Before I could say more, the cell phone dropped the call.

chapter 3

Virgil sits on the curb. Down the street a man washes a sedan. Runoff fills the gutter with music, water rushing toward the storm grate. The sun glows on this impromptu stream. A woman moves toward him, light hair glancing her shoulders. She smiles as she passes.

Maybe she smiled, and he turns to watch her. She might turn back— he can harbor the hope. Hope, like a criminal, needs harboring. Like a criminal, it should be brought to justice. But then what would he have? Her hips flare, her bottom a glorious widening. The sky fades, barely blue at all, the air moist as breath. She doesn't turn back. Get on with it.

In a yard, and spilling onto the sidewalk, a boy with dark wavy hair rides a tricycle. A golden retriever trots beside him and wags its tail, lifts its nose to Virgil. A girl, clearly the boy's sister, the same dark waves cascading down her back, draws a hopscotch path on the sidewalk. She fixes him with a dark eye and holds up the lavender chalk.

"Our father's coming tonight," she says. Virgil takes the chalk and draws a tulip.

"Have fun," he says. "With your father." To pick her up and twirl her in the air, what joy.

Then he comes to Magazine Street. Taking out his map, he looks for Bywater, but doesn't see it. The map's cumbersome folds embarrass him, he folds it quickly and scans the street. In one direction the street trails into disarray—broken glass glinting in the gutter, another liquor store, rusted sedans moving in stately cetacean fashion.

Down the other way, Magazine Street hangs between old and new. Shops of folk art and pottery line the street, rented cheap by artists who bring their cats to work, who smoke and chat on the door steps, and smile at him when he nods. David won't be here, despite the lingering funk. Too much happy potential. He should go the other way. David really might be there. It is not too late to turn. But he continues.

A woman's laugh and the smell of coffee grounds waft out to the sidewalk from a café, irresistible. Just one cup, then back to work. It will help him focus, collect his thoughts.

Cigarette smoke curls against the room's vaulted ceiling, sliced by the blades of a slow-moving fan. The ochre walls are both warm and primal. He feels comfortable. His coffee comes in a pint glass that's too hot to hold, so he leaves it on the counter to pick up sports, business, the front page from the *Times-Picayune*. The tables bump against each other in dense herds. Groups of students pore over highlighted textbooks. A few chess matches are under way between unkempt men.

Virgil stands by a pillar, sipping his drink and skimming the paper. A phone by the rest rooms—he could call Caroline, apologize for this disappearance, or the police. Maybe they've picked up David. He should do that, but scans the room for what he really wants—a seat near a woman. In the back of his mind, he knows he might find one.

There aren't many, though. Seats or women. One reading *The Portable Kierkegaard*, but the tables blockading her, together with her chickenish profile, make him disinclined to fight his way through. A lovely Hispanic girl, round in the cheeks, in the bosom, in the calves, full lips glossed almost black, her hair slick and shiny, is alone, but she must be waiting for someone, the way she checks her watch and rations her tea.

A table opens up along the wall, nearer to him. No woman, but it's a good table, and someone might come along, so he weaves in and claims it just ahead of a trio of boys. A couple sits next to him, side by side on the bench, the man leaning toward the woman, gesturing with a cigarette, holding forth in a thick French accent.

Virgil engrosses himself in the paper, checking on the philosophical woman each time he sips. Hasn't he read Kierkegaard? Is he the that-which-doesn't-kill-you guy? No. Wouldn't do to misquote. Let her be the expert, anyhow. Men always think they know it all—he'd been told that often enough.

"Isn't that right, monsieur," the man at the next table asks him. "Monsieur?"

"Sorry," Virgil looks up from his paper. His philosopher queen has left.

"Isn't it true that only a puritanical society like yours would push sex so much?" he says, evidently repeating his question.

"Beverly," he pats the woman's arm, "is chiding me about the ads she saw in France, how—what did you call it—how *graphique* they were. She does not see why it's different."

Beverly rolls her eyes, out of the man's line of sight, making an accomplice of Virgil. She looks small, buried in a slate gray sweatshirt. Bright blond hair frames her face. Very red lips, no lipstick.

"How is it different?" he asks, ready to champion her cause.

"In France, the veneration of the woman is a cultural institution," the man says.

Virgil leans back against the bench they all share, the man in the middle twisted forward, facing him. Beverly leans back too, and, looking straight at Virgil, nods toward the door.

"Gerard, you are the most thought-provoking man I know," she says. "But I have to go." She kisses him, both cheeks in the French style. He holds her a little longer, kissing her on the mouth.

"This woman is always going," Gerard says, his eyes following her out. Virgil looks down at his paper for what seems a decent interval, then rises, nods toward Gerard, and squeezes through the tables toward the door, wondering if he has misinterpreted a twitch.

He doesn't see her when he steps outside. The sky flares crimson in the west, deepening blue overhead, Venus just showing. *I wish I may, I wish I might*, he thinks.

"You made it," Beverly says, coming out of a liquor store with a bottle in a bag. "I didn't know if you saw."

"I thought I was seeing things," Virgil says.

"We all see things. Hardly anyone notices, though."

"What do you see," he says, and they start walking.

"I'm going over to the market. What's your name, anyway? I guess you know mine." Virgil tells her.

Walking toward the market—Virgil doesn't recognize any street names or landmarks, lost for sure—she tells him about art school, about wanting to paint oils but doing illustration instead because it will be easier to get a job. "I've already done a children's book, about a dragon who wants to be friends with kids but keeps burning them. A friend of mine wrote the story, but it's the illustrations that really make it."

Virgil only half-listens, trying to decide if he is amused or bored, wondering why cute girls—she is certainly a girl—think they can enthrall men by talking ceaselessly about themselves. The analog of the man's expertise. He thinks of turning back, maybe finding someone else. But he hasn't marked the turns they've taken. He is committed.

"Tell me about Gerard," he says.

"I met him in Paris," she says, and says *Paris* with a hundred-ton weight on the *pair* part. Pair-isss, the s hissing.

They had a fling when she went there with her family. She never expected to see him again, but he'd shown up at her door one night when another boyfriend was over, which didn't go over well. She'd like to get rid of Gerard, but didn't know what to do. She didn't love him, but she liked his accent and what he could do in bed. All her girl-friends thought he was glamorous, said they wished some Frenchman would just show up on their doorsteps.

"I'm sure he's sleeping with them," she says, glibly. This catches Virgil's attention.

"Would it bother you if he did?"

"No. I mean, he is. One of them told me. It didn't bother me."

"You're not jealous?"

"It's just sex."

Maybe there's hope, Virgil thinks. "Most women I know would mind," he says.

"He's not an important boyfriend. Some guys, I would mind."

"Like that one before Gerard?" She nods, silenced. He's found a spot of pain in an otherwise-insensitive skin. "So he was the one you cared about, but he left when he realized you'd cheated on him."

"How did you know?" she asks with genuine amazement.

He shrugs his shoulders. To answer that would take ages. "Tell you what though, I bet he fooled around on you, too."

"Oh, no. Eric would never do that. He's very idealistic."

"Those guys are the worst. They've got all sorts of rationalizations. Hard to argue with, I bet." She nods. "He probably slept with the same friend who tried out your Frenchman."

Beverly withdraws at this. They near the market. Cars throng the street, jostling for parking. The sky has clouded and a few drops fall. A large woman with a string bag full of vegetables shakes out a plastic rain scarf and spreads it over her hair.

"Hey, I'm sorry," Virgil says. "It's none of my business." He squeezes her arm.

"I brought it up." She squeezes back and smiles a dazzler. "You're probably right, is all. Funny how one person's cheating doesn't mean a thing, but even the thought of another person doing it hurts like hell."

Virgil could love her for that.

He helps her shop, beneath the pitiless expanse of fluorescent light. Compact, miniature men—they might be Mexican, or from farther south—maneuver pallets of bananas, cantaloupe, kiwi through the shoppers. They speak to each other in a language that's not English and not Spanish, and laugh. One man, his teeth are so white when he smiles. He should smile all the time, Virgil thinks. He wonders what they make of this place, all this food, these fat people who pile it into their carts without looking at it, who regard one another as obstacles. Once he walked through a Guatemalan market past a room where branches from banana trees hung, ceiling to floor, in cool green light.

Beverly is all efficiency, a blue plastic basket draped over her forearm by two spindly wire handles. She painstakingly chooses expensive let-tuces with plastic tongs, and fat red tomatoes, spring-colored blades of asparagus. Yogurt, dark chocolate, water from Italy, gleaming coffee beans that smell hopelessly of tomorrow morning. He steals a glance at his watch and wonders what Caroline is doing, where David might be, and quickly snaps back to Beverly, blond Beverly.

"I'm a vegetarian," she explains in the checkout line, rhythmically placing her choices on the conveyor belt. "I haven't had meat in eight years."

"How do you feel?" he asks, because he knows his cue.

"I feel so good." She looks at him meaningfully. "I mean, what you put in your body is one of the few things you control. I can't believe people eat that," and she points her chin at the woman ahead in line, whose frozen pot pies and two-liter soda bottle the cashier is whooshing across the scanner. The soda bottle won't scan, though, and the clerk keeps wiping the bar code and retrying, this one action apparently the only way she knows to solve the problem. Color rises to her cheeks. Virgil calculates her wages, he looks over at the mirror that runs the length of the checkout area, imagines the managers back there, crunching numbers and peering through the glass to spot malfeasance.

Drop it, he tells himself. *This is how it is.*

Finally the clerk gets the bottle to scan. The woman with the pot pies fumbles with coupons.

"Cashiers of the world, unite," he says.

"Huh?" Beverly says, and charges the food on her Visa.

He carries the bag for her.

"I don't know any men who would do that," she says, and it's halfway to insult, the way it comes out, yet she's so sincere. What fools young men are, how much more they'd get if they just carried the goddamned groceries.

She reminds him of Jane. That's why he's hung in so long, not bowed off into any of the many bars they've passed. God love New Orleans, you're never far from a drink. It's her hair, the blinding sunlight of it. Only this one detail, yet it's enough.

They stand a moment outside the market, Virgil not relinquishing the bag, as night mist envelops them.

"I bought rum," she says, tapping the bottle in its brown paper. "You like rum?"

Virgil doesn't like it. Too sweet. But he nods. And they walk. He will do anything to see this through.

If he were to touch his side, bruise or growth, pick your poison, it would sear his finger. *You are not a well man, no indeed, no sir, no way.*

He will do anything to get lost.

"I'd love to see your paintings," he says to say something.

"Yeah?" She looks over at him and he smiles and nods earnestly. "Okay then. You know what I love about New Orleans?" she asks.

"No, what?"

"Exactly nothing."

In 1961, he'd come here, just legal. Got drunker than he'd ever been, previously or since, seven days' worth. He'd wanted to cleaver his head when he came out of it, it couldn't have hurt worse than the hangover. He'd met a woman then, maybe a bunch of women, he always met women, it was his one talent. But there was one, and she was the first he'd slept with besides Jane. It felt so good and free, he'd stayed in her a long time and she liked him there, she was happy if he went hard at it or rested awhile, she was with him either way. He couldn't remember her name, just the feeling of her, the sense of really being with her. Not in, next to, behind or on top of—with. After that he was often lonely.

"I think New Orleans is extraordinary," he says.

"It's tacky and hot and fattening and I'm sick to death of it."

"I'm sorry you feel that way. It's a special place to me." He is not with Beverly, either.

But maybe, but possibly. Hope leads him on.

chapter 4

After talking to Donald, I wanted to put on something pretty. But the only dress I had was the one I'd worn at the wake, a dark brown knit, too dour, too heavy and hot. I wanted something light.

A few blocks away, down a quiet alley, a bay window extended into the street, and behind its glass, satin dresses the color of champagne fluttered off the mannequins, responding to an unfelt breeze.

The shop was called Uta's, and Uta herself was tall and older in a way that was eternal. Her sand-colored hair stayed off her face as if by obedience training. She had a high forehead that peaked just slightly at the brow ridge, giving her face an unexpected sharpness. Deep red lipstick, a black jumpsuit, and a cigarillo drooping in an ebony holder, together with a dense German accent and its accompanying melancholia, rounded out the dissipated glamour that shrouded her.

She looked up from a magazine and tapped some ash into its spine. "I have the perfect dress for you," she said when I was halfway through the door.

She disappeared behind a curtained doorway.

The store smelled of the thin cigars, a thick smell that recalled my father's pipe on Sunday morning. It felt more like I'd entered someone's home, and that the owner had a quirky sense of juxtaposition: heavy Victorian couches and somber sideboards, against austere white walls, all of it softened by the flowing fabrics and muted colors of the clothes.

The dress was stunning. Tea length, sheer white cotton, incredibly soft.

"Your coloring is so rare, so perfect for white," she said, hovering outside the dressing room like a ghost. I stepped out to see myself in the three-sided mirror.

She smoothed the fabric down my back. "This dress has been waiting for you." Her touch surprised me.

"You're smart to have nice lighting back here," I said. "How long have you lived in New Orleans?"

"Since the time when I had a smooth face, like yours," she said with a sly, sidelong glance. She stood behind me and pulled the fabric across my shoulders, tilting her head in serious scrutiny.

"You're German?"

"*Ja.*" She said it with an exaggerated accent, then began laughing.

"Did you come during the war?"

"What a pesky questioner you are. What does it matter when I came or where I'm from? I'm just here."

We stood facing the mirror, looking at each other.

"I'll never keep this dress clean. I'm traveling," I said.

"Ah, a traveler." She warmed up to the word. "The best thing to be. That is what we all are, but we only know it when we're on a trip. Where are you traveling from?"

"I started in Chicago."

"I had a lover from there once. Are you alone?"

I went back into the dressing room. The dress had a tiny scalloping of lace along the neckline, almost imperceptible.

"I'm with my uncle. I'm going to wear the dress," I called through the door. "What happened to your lover?" I came back out with my jeans and blouse over my arm.

"Who cares? He hurt me." She got a bag for my clothes, and I flipped through other dresses on the racks. "Have a whiskey," she said.

She pronounced "whiskey" with a V, and before I answered, she went behind the curtain and brought out a bottle with no label.

"He was such a boy. Married. But still the rooster. Couldn't stand for a hen not to notice him. He came down about once a month and always brought some gauche piece of jewelry—a heart pendant dripping rubies, that sort of thing. Expensive, but depressing. Women should not wear rocks."

She poured out the whiskey and we sat down on a red velvet sofa. "It depressed me to live out a cliché. That's why I left Germany—and yes, it was around war time. I hated it there, perfectly handsome boys suddenly so serious. My mother wanted me to marry this one, then that one, to wear plain dresses and darn socks.

"Then one night at the movies there was a newsreel about America, about New Orleans. Propaganda, horrible racist stuff, blacks shuffling and dancing, and then Mardi Gras, with a voice telling us how vulgar, you can't take the jungle out of niggers and so forth. But for me it was God up there, the movement so beautiful, the costumes, even in the black-and-white film—the way they sparkled. I wanted that. Something in life should shine. So here I am. I worked my way across on a freighter, said I was Swedish. I was very pretty back then. I could smile. It wasn't so hard."

She took a long drag on her cigar.

The whiskey went down smoky and hot. "It's good," I said, and I reached for the bottle.

"A man I know makes it. An old fellow. Such a sad man, but such good whiskey."

"So when did you meet the man from Chicago?"

"A few years after I first came. I landed in New York and went straight to the train station. Just enough cash to get here. Worked as a seamstress for a dress shop, this one, in fact. Then one day he walked in with another woman, a redhead. Playing the big spender and she squealing with delight. Had no sense of her body. Whatever was tight, she wanted. While she was in the dressing room he noticed me, and before they left we'd made a date. A place you love only excites you for so long. After a while you need an adventure with a person. And tacky gifts aside, he was an adventure. I learned some things from him."

I felt lazy from the drink. The sun sank through the lace on the window. She looked into her empty cigarillo pack. "I need another," she said, and went into the back room. "This would look good on you, too," she said when she returned. She held a peach scarf over my head and dropped it lightly. "Why don't we have some fun tonight?"

We drank a few more whiskeys and tried on more of the shop's clothing. She made the clothes, went on buying sprees back home in Germany, where she purchased old dresses and took them apart, fashioned scarves and belts from the notions that adorned her youth. She said it amused her to go back now, to see how busy everyone was forgetting the past, forgetting the world as it was most vivid in her mind.

"That man from Chicago," I said. "What did he teach you?"

"That a married man is married."

I laughed. "Why is that funny?" she asked me.

"I think I knew that same man."

She took me to dinner at a small restaurant with walls three feet thick, an old, old building, Jean Lafitte drank here, she said. She ordered German wine and pork chops for both of us, "I will feed you, you are too thin," she said. Her speech began to slur.

"What are you doing here, anyway?" she asked.

"I ran away from my father's funeral. With my uncle. He's out looking for his son who's supposed to be here someplace."

"That sounds rather complicated. You loved your father?"

"More than I knew." Even that answer seemed dubious. I still didn't know what I felt, beyond the jolt of his absence. And I expected to know more by now, that the act of departure would have freed up my emotions. But it was still a mental experience, images that visited me unexpectedly. Me spinning around in his rotating desk chair, playing in the vestibule where the judicial robe hung. I'd go under it and inhale. It smelled of him.

"Death points out the things you didn't know before." She chain-smoked through the dinner, and between that and the whiskey, we created an atmosphere all our own. "And your uncle? You love him?

I groaned. "You know how it is." I gestured, a circle in the air. "It's like we fall in love with what we want."

At the thought of him, questions sprang nervously to mind. Where was he, had he found David, did he feel all right? Such a contrast to how it used to be. As a man in my childhood, Virgil was the possibilities. He provided the alternative. My father, my brother, they were what's expected—upstanding, sports-playing, God-fearing. Virgil I imbued with nobility wrenched from a life honestly lived— and he played the part, with tales of Himalayan mountain peaks, intense physical struggle, lessons learned at the end of a rope. Now that I knew him, saw his painful spots, sensed his unhealed wounds, felt his tempers and heard his callings-out in the night, I grappled with a new idea: that we begin to love only after longing fails.

I helped myself to another cigarette, and Uta was quick with the lighter.

Waiters cleared away our plates. We downed espresso and lingered over port. Uta liked to dance. "I know a place," she said.

We walked over to Joss House in an old iron work building on Esplanade, passed an empty lot. A dog barked in the overgrown grass. I jumped. She patted my arm, and left her hand there.

When we got inside, Uta went directly to the bar. The barman greeted her like a long-lost granter of good wishes. A mirror behind the bottles, illuminated with flickering votive candles, showed me her face, the large jaw opening, the red lips parting for words and flicks of the tongue as she listened. The walls were painted saffron blotched with gold, the ancient wainscoting dark red. A serpentine paper dragon undulated in extravagant curves from the ceiling, its body coiling around the lights. In the center of the space, a reggae band played a languid groove. A few people danced, nearly stationary, they might be simply victims of a breeze. Swirls of marijuana smoke drifted between them.

"He's my old friend," she said when she returned. "You are the prettiest girl here." She handed me my drink. "We both agreed."

"Your old friend." I looked at her, girl to girl, quizzical. "What kind of friend?"

"Oh, *ja*. You know such men—conquest, denial, and months later, you're his mother confessor." She laughed. "It's nice to be older. You see it coming."

We stood a moment in silence, looking about the room. In the corners, trios and pairs sprawled on pillows. She pointed to the balcony and started out.

The night air touched me like a breath. A few stars pushed their light through the dense air. Uta leaned over the railing and sang softly in German.

"What is that?" I asked.

"A lullaby. My mother used to sing it to me. Now I sing it to the night."

At this point the only place to go was further into the velvet drink. To stop now, to leave and find a taxi, to return to the room, to TV, to Virgil or no Virgil, to the real things going on in the real and earnest world, what good would that do? If the velvet drink was accompanied by her hand on my waist, leading me to the dance floor, what of it? If, when the music slowed, she drew me in close so that our hips touched, what of it? All that drinking demands is more drinking. The rest is incidental. I liked the smell of her, the unexpected swell of her breasts, the hard certainty of her clavicle where I rested my head. Someone passed us a joint. She declined, but not me. I gave it a good suck, and quickly felt as if my feet had been harnessed to doves.

Deep in my purse, my phone was singing.

chapter 5

Beverly leads Virgil into the courtyard of a box-shaped apartment complex, and unlocks, with three keys, a door on the ground floor. White metal bars give her windows the aspect of a ladylike zoo. Once inside, she relocks the door, two deadbolts and one in the knob. More than a studio, less than a one-bedroom, the apartment smells of oil paint and eraser shavings. Color speckles the furniture, as if she has yanked it from a Pointillist painting. There is a table covered with a spattered white sheet, two wooden chairs, a bed on the floor, a TV near it, also on the floor, and canvases propped against the wall, frame sides out. An easel stands in a corner, without canvas. A low counter separates all this from a dark kitchen. Virgil spies hardened orange spots on the stove. A mess, an appalling mess.

He sits on one of the chairs and listens while she puts away the groceries. She has turned on the television upon entering the apartment, to the news, braying the story of a young man found dead. Virgil listens closely for a moment. It's not David.

"Mind if I turn this down?" Virgil mutes it without waiting for her answer.

"I just have it on for the voices. I'm so often on my own." She comes to him with two glasses and the rum. "Get us started," she says. "I have to pee." She smiles at the word, a beautiful smile.

Virgil's side throbs. He lifts his shirt and touches the space between the third and fourth rib on his right side, where the lump grows. Though dense and hard, it's cool, like ordinary skin. Must be the other injury. He pours some rum into the mismatched glasses, one tall, one short. The short glass says Rock 'n' Roll, emblazoned with a black guitar, and he drinks from it. Even though the rum's too sweet, too sticky, he drinks quickly and pours himself a second. Beverly comes out stripped down to her jeans and a sleeveless undershirt.

She takes up her drink and perches on the bed. Her toenails are painted dark brown.

"Are these your canvases?" Virgil asks, walking about the room. Beverly nods and extends her hand.

"You can look."

Intricate images, every inch filled with activity, curlicues of vegetation, water, cities, mountains, forests—and people, with shopping bags, in taxis, walking dogs, throwing Frisbees, dancing, kissing, stooping to pick flowers. They inhabit a better world and know it. Virgil feels the slight, condemned to this world. No wonder they want to look at the wall.

The precision of the line impresses him. There must be forty canvases, all similar, rendered in different color schemes, some more urban, some less.

"They're interesting," he says.

She draws her knees up to her chest and circles them with her smooth, long arms. They look tan; probably they always are.

"Does that mean you like them?"

"Yes I do," he says, sheepishly. "I have to admit I thought they'd be not that good and that I'd have to fake it. But these are fine."

"I studied in Bali. It's the same style, translated into American vernacular."

"Bali! That must have been wonderful. I've always wanted to go."

"It's paradise there. It really is."

On his one trip to Asia, to Bangkok, Virgil had walked through temples as ornately decorated as wedding cakes. He wanted to lick them, they looked so sugary. It made him hungry.

"Paradise. Really?"

"Every morning, where I lived, they left offerings of rice and flower petals at my door. By midday the dogs would come and eat them. You'd find them trampled in the street. And the women would be making more for tomorrow."

He turns another canvas to face him, and considers it in light of this new information. The faces look out at him, happy and indifferent.

"They're kind of otherworldly," he says.

"I don't know what you mean by that," she says, sounding hurt.

"It's just"—he looks again, and tries to formulate words—"the world's not that perfect."

"Isn't it?"

She pours more rum into her glass and extends the bottle to him. He turns the canvas back toward the wall and accepts the drink. More of what he doesn't want.

"Let me show you my illustrations." She opens a portfolio book on the bed. Still standing, Virgil stoops to see, and she takes his hand and draws him down beside her. He winces and doubts that she will notice.

The drawings show a dragon drawn with the same precise, elegant line. The same innocence, that the world is a well-intentioned place. Hallmarks of her work, he hears himself say to an imaginary client down the line, casually advising on an investment. Bound to appreciate. Despite the flame billowing from the dragon's nostrils, something merry shines in his eyes. Next a small boy, red balloon dancing high above him, tethered to his wrist. A forest of adult bodies surrounds him, their heads cut off by the drawing's edge. The pictures continue: the fragile meeting, friendship grows between boy and dragon, regret when they part, reunited in joy. Words a superfluous waste.

The world isn't that perfect.

Is it? Has he been wrong on this count? Has he missed something major? Could she possibly know?

Beverly still holds his hand. Virgil takes hers to his mouth and kisses it. "Really lovely," he says.

"I'm glad you like them," she says, and she guides his hand to her stomach. The vortex of her navel, there is paradise.

Beverly lies back and stretches luxuriantly over her head, slowly turns her chin from side to side. Her smile comes in twitches with his touch.

He groans sharply, his patriotic tumor-bruise flaring like fireworks, cascading arcs of flame. David the son, Caroline the niece, Jane, lost Jane. Such a small circumference of love. Now lost. He didn't labor.

Should have, but here he is, and Virgil knows this place well, eyes closed beside an unknown girl.

He lifts her shirt and begins to learn how her nipples take his hope.

The rum, the rib-to-rib burn, his culpability in the loneliness that love has turned out to be—with these stinging, he disappears into Beverly's heat. This time, he thinks, maybe even says it in short breathy gasps. Show me. And once more he annihilates himself, explodes, hurls his every atom to the farthest points in the galaxy. Where he's headed, exactly. Paradise does not exist. Paradise is men worshiping their fondest wish. Projection into the void, infinite silence, space. Black, cold, a place where you dangle and float, where things that travel at the speed of light appear not to be moving at all.

"Why are you crying?" Beverly asks in the stillness that settles on the room. "That was"—pausing, her breath evens out—"amazing."

chapter 6

The third night of my third week in jail, I can't sleep again. I have barely slept since I've arrived, what with Douglas needing to caress and prod, Tyrone snoring, and the rest of the noise, actual and mental. I don't like that this is becoming what normal means to me. It doesn't bode well for shaking the Horse for once and always, although I haven't shot up since that fateful day and now the jones has begun to subside and my elbows don't itch so awfully much and I ought to be encouraged because I can call things by their right names now that I see with unmediated vision. But really, isn't that half the problem? The dreariness of things.

Sam Bauer entered my not-guilty plea to groans all around, and I await a day in the bright light of justice, set for six weeks hence. He doesn't return my calls now that his work is done, even though I call every day to say, "Come on, six weeks, are you nuts?" It seems unduly long. Tyrone laughs at me, "Wheels turn, brother," his cryptic response that I ponder through the long, long hours of the day.

"Checkers, bro?" Tyrone offers the next afternoon.

"Sure."

He chooses black, lines up his pieces like predators. "Your move."

I advance on the diagonal. Checkers. I haven't played since I was six, when my father taught me chess and it ruled my imagination.

"You ever play chess, Tyrone?"

"Hell, no."

"I could teach you. You'd be good at it."

He crosses one of my men and whisks him off the board.

"You just don't want to lose. White man don't want to lose to the black man, but you will. Our day is coming."

"I don't doubt it. What are you going to do when it does?"

He looks up from the board and smiles. "Keep you down, bro. You see how it feels."

"Like shit? Just a guess," I say, and smile so that he'll see the humor of the moment. He does and laughs.

"David, man, I know you're a smart white boy. Not like that cracker Douglas. Call your daddy. That's what you do. You are a fool."

I cross his man and end up on the king line. "King me," I say. He does, unhappily. "Tyrone, here's the thing about my father." I look around the rec room. A few men gather in a semicircle around the television, watching a soap opera. Others thumb through magazines, or toil at GED homework—I sometimes help them out with geometry problems. Through the window, through the bars, I see a cloud, far off, white milk, remote as the face of God.

"See that?" I point to the window. He looks. "The cloud. That's my father. I don't believe in his capacity to help, ergo, the call would be a waste, and worse, painful to me in confirming my worst fears, painful to him in providing yet one more opportunity to disappoint. Chance of happening: nil."

"You don't know nothing." He crisscrosses the board with his man, effectively wiping me out. "King me!"

chapter 7

It aches to dress. Virgil dresses anyway, soldiers on through the pain, his beloved pain. He is *with* it, though this isn't what he had in mind. He stammers through formalities—good-bye, thank you—eager to be on the street again so that he can start wishing he were here. He is eager to regret the loss of Beverly, a thing he can't achieve without the actual loss. That's the cycle, the familiar rhythm. He is eager for something fresh and moist blowing off the river, for a sound he hasn't heard before. He is hopeful that the one moment of unity exists, and here it is in the wincing as he zips his trousers.

"You don't have to go," she says, looking up from the bed, groggy and tousled. They slept a good hour in each other's arms.

I do, he thinks, I have to. As fast as I can.

"I mean," she continues. "I wish you'd stay. I hate a man just to leave. Would you like to know why?" Her question sits alone in the silence, and she turns onto her stomach.

He says good-bye again.

It has rained and stopped, and the wind has picked up, blowing clouds around the night sky. The clouds hold hints of orange from streetlights, but mostly they are dark moving against darkness. Some brace of pigeons wings over him. What are these fellows doing out at night, he wonders, admiring their whiteness against the gray sky. They look white to him, although he knows they're not. These impressions seem to mean something, to add up. Pigeons look white but the brain says gray, and the eye capitulates. But tonight, the heart insists, the eye will not be denied. White.

Weakened from his exertions with Beverly, he doesn't know where he is and there are no cabs. It must be very late, wee small in the morning. Paper scuttles across the street then rears in an updraft, whisked high over a roof. Trees shimmy. He doesn't know where he is.

He can only walk on. Outside a convenience store, he sees a pay phone. He dials Caroline and gets her message, "Can't talk, you figure out why," her voice a surprise. "It's Virgil," he says. "Pick up," as if she could hear him. Where is she? Why does she not hear him on this cold night? He turns onto Tchoupitoulas Street, and the name itself cheers him, sounding like a hybrid of Greek and gibberish. Could be a disease, a spicy Balkan stew, a plant found only on a single mountain in Macedonia. Wild Tchoupitoulas, a refrain from a Mardi Gras song, sings itself to him as he walks.

All this mysterium can't be good. It's the mind drifting from the do or die. No good to be wondering about pigeons or making up stories about names. There's a lost boy, there are a thousand and one details, bills to pay, miles to go before he sleeps.

But the refrain still sings in his head, a defiant scrap of joy. The street is bathed in the white halide light, the ground blanched by it, the glare of it detonating against the foundations of homes. A car drives by, a few people spill out from a doorway up ahead, he must be getting close to some pocket of civilization.

Do or die. Do and die. Or don't do and die. That's the hard fact of it. Is this fixation with the hard fact of it some kind of grief? He stops into a bar and notices how the conversation dims a notch when he sits down. By the clock over the door, it's nearly four in the morning. The bartender, his thick neck and short haircut suggesting someone who's been a fighter, stands before him, his presence a question.

"In training?" Virgil asks when the man brings him a whiskey with a splash.

"I keep in shape," the man says.

The smoke in the place must make that hard. Virgil pulls out his Dunhill's and lights up. A couple sits beside him, the woman swaying on the bar stool saying, "No, no, no, that's not right at all," and "what a asshole." She wears a coat of crinkled leather. It catches the odd-colored light and refracts it till it hurts Virgil's eye. Her hair is long and appears to be orange, with a few waves burned into its middle length.

Her eyes are rimmed with black eyeliner. Virgil likes the trashy look of her. If the man goes to the john, he'll strike up a talk. What would a woman like that talk about?

"Where you from," the bartender asks, back again after mixing up a Tom Collins and pulling a draft.

Before Virgil can answer, the barkeep walks away and takes another order. Virgil drinks down his whiskey and leaves too large a tip, glad to escape the question, the story, the sound of his own stupid voice.

chapter 8

Uta escorted me a few blocks toward the hotel, and on a corner, she stopped. "You're beautiful," she said, leaning toward me, her breath a frenzy of cigar smoke and whiskey, and we kissed. "Let me stay with you," she said. But I needed sleep. Things were spinning too quickly—if I gave in to her, I might never recover, might never get back to Virgil and amid all the uncertainties, I was pretty certain he needed me.

Or maybe I needed him.

So I stumbled the rest of the way alone, finally getting firm with her—no, no, and no. I turned right where I should have gone left and found myself on quiet, empty streets. I sat on the curb and reached into my bag, my phone the talisman of comfort. Virgil had called, sounding chilled and alone and like he might be calling from Mars. Stupid fuck. Where was he? Where was I?

A police cruiser stopped, and the cop rolled down his window and shone a light on me.

"Miss," he said. "Can I help?"

"I'm a little lost." I told him my hotel and he drove me over.

I had the elevator to myself but at the last minute, a man's hand sliced into the closing door and it opened. Two men entered, faces red and lively. Nice looking, probably football players back in high school. The one with the blue eyes and brown mustache pushed six. I reached over and pushed nine.

"Six, nine," the man said, and he laughed. "Hey! Sixty-nine."

I looked at the floor.

"Now you've gone and scared her," his friend said, he with a thicker face, pale, blotchy skin. "She'll think you some ignorant Southern boy. Which'd be about right."

They both laughed.

"C'mon, sweetheart. Give us a smile. We just a little drunk," the brown-haired boy said. One of them sniffed loudly. "And you a little high?" They both laughed again.

They made me nervous and I was relieved that they actually got off on the sixth floor. When the door slid open on nine, I sprinted to the room, and locked the door, engaging the chain.

My brain would not slow, though I willed it to. Cease and desist. No! The rogue, the rebel, it kept on, it flashed random frames captured from the last few days—the eloquent descent of a leaf through the air, my father's pinky finger with Mona's class ring from Cornell, the ridges along the roof of Virgil's mouth. It was a confusing array. I clung to the notion that it would cohere.

A banging on the door woke me. I lay in bed with my heart pounding, sure it was the drunks from the elevator, back to ravish me.

"Caroline," I heard Virgil say. "Open up."

I obeyed. He looked purple with exhaustion—face drawn, a blue pocket forming between cheekbone and eye.

He leaned on me. I pushed the hair off his forehead. Our eyes met and he saw my question before I could give it voice.

"No," he said. "Nothing."

He had brought in a cool night-air smell on his clothes. The room freshened in his wake. I listened to him wash.

"Jane didn't call?" he asked, wiping his face with a towel.

She hadn't.

"You still love her a lot," I said, understanding this as if for the first time.

"I'm in no condition to tell you how much."

In his blue-and-white-striped pajamas, he stretched out on his bed. I climbed back into mine.

"Do you want the light on?" I asked.

"No, go ahead."

I switched it off.

"What'd you do tonight?" he asked.

112

"Went shopping. Had dinner with the shopkeeper, and she took me to a bar and we danced."

"Sounds like fun."

It did.

"Virgil," I said. I wanted to tell him how strange it was that even the truth could hide the truth. It's something I thought he'd understand.

"Hmm . . ." his voice was languid and relaxed, like the warmth of a fire, the mellowness of wine.

"What'd you do?" I asked.

"Just wandered."

In the morning, he took me to the Café du Monde. His mood was jocular, energetic. It made me nervous.

"No need to forgo all the pleasures of the city," he said as we walked through the empty streets of the French Quarter. A cleaning crew, its truck laboring noisily, crept its petty pace up the short blocks. A man in coveralls jumped out of the cab every few feet and speared go-cups and wrappers with a pike. The truck belched smoke that hung in the still moist air.

We crossed Jackson Square and the sun split a cloud. Virgil suddenly grabbed me in a dance embrace and led me a few steps into a waltz.

But once the coffee and beignets were finished, his mood went somber.

"So where did you look yesterday?" I asked.

He pushed a pile of confectioner's sugar around the table with a paper napkin.

"We need to talk about this, Virgil," I said.

"No we don't. It's my problem and I'll solve it."

"We know he's not at his old address," I went on. "And Jane didn't have any other one, right?" I paused and let the question's gravity force an answer. "Do you want to know what I did last night?"

"You went to dinner with some shopkeeper. You went dancing."

"With the shopkeeper. She and I sat on her couch for four hours first and drank homemade whiskey. I smoked parts of five joints. We kissed. If you leave me alone again, I'm going to disappear into the ether. I need work. You need help. Don't close me out of this."

I took his hand and looked earnestly into his eyes.

He shrugged his shoulders. "This isn't what I wanted," he said.

"It's what you got, though."

We were at an outside table. Sparrows whisked about, angling for crumbs, but the busboys were quick with the bleachy towels, and the birds went hungry more often than not. One sparrow had managed a rather large hunk of beignet and was hopping furiously, lugging it far from the throng.

Virgil looked at me quizzically. "To the clinics, then," he said.

chapter 9

"Liberation Works," the sign over the door of the methadone clinic promised. The clinic was just off Canal Street, a busy artery running out of the French Quarter and into the part of the city where people lived but no one visited—not the New Orleans of the mind, but New Orleans nonetheless. Plasterboard covered the windows except for a row of transoms up top. A few white plastic patio chairs sat unoccupied on the sidewalk, while inside, five men with pale and shiny bodies—soft, doughy or scrawny being the body-type options— waited in stiff silence. All men. A black nurse in a crisp white uniform sat behind a sliding window.

Virgil knocked on the glass and she slid it open and regarded him unkindly. What would it take to come here day after day, I wondered—to sit beneath the harsh light, in this windowless, airless antechamber, watching men in hell, dispensing Dixie cups of heaven.

"Has my son been here?" Virgil's voice was aggressive; then he fumbled through an explanation of himself, smiling at the wrong times, leaning too far into the window toward the woman. "You need to tell me."

The nurse shook her head. A gold cross glinted on her collarbone.

"Confidentiality is a condition of treatment," she said. Virgil persisted, and she shut the glass.

He turned back toward the room and eyed the patrons. Of the five men, four were white. The fifth was a tall Latin boy, his olive skin gone jaundiced, his jet black hair swept back in an abundance of greased curls. I sat down beside him and picked up a copy of *National Geographic*, its address label torn off. The Latin boy appeared to be asleep. Virgil paced a bit, then sat down, too, beside a fleshy man in black jeans, black T-shirt, and black sneakers. Though he was bald, the vestige of his wavy hair circled the side of his head like planetary rings.

He looked straight at Virgil.

"What'd she say?" he asked. His voice was full of feverish excitement.

"Excuse me?" Virgil said in his most patrician tones.

"I've been waiting forever, man, and I need my hit. How long?"

Virgil seemed to think this over.

"Ten minutes," he said. "At least ten minutes."

"Shit. She always says that. It's been like forty minutes, you know what I mean?"

Virgil nodded.

"I'm Eddie," he went on. "Haven't seen you before."

"I'm Virgil. I'm looking for my son. Do you know him? David Harris is his name." Virgil's voice had a belligerence that surprised me.

"No, man. I don't know him." Eddie answered.

"You wouldn't tell me if you did, would you, Eddie?" Virgil said. The other men in the clinic shifted in their seats. A few stared openly at Virgil, but the atmosphere was one of apathy. This was television.

Eddie jiggled noisily in the chair. He couldn't sit still. "Hey man, you know," he said.

"Yeah, I know. Junkies have to stick together. Never mind that my son's got an abscess the size of grapefruit in this arm," Virgil indicated his left elbow. "A code is a code. I respect that. I really do. A man has to live by something, don't you think, Eddie? You know, to be a man? You are a man, right, Eddie? I mean, these days, who knows—you might just be an incredibly ugly woman for all I know."

"Cool it, Virgil," I said, but he didn't acknowledge me.

Eddie flushed to the crown of his bald scalp. "No, man, I'm a man," he fairly whimpered.

"Good. Then we can talk—man to man. Do you have kids, Eddie?"

"Yeah. Yeah I do." His voice was full of mourning.

"I bet you don't see them a whole hell of a lot," Virgil said.

"I'm not allowed. Injunction."

"I bet you miss them."

Eddie nodded and to my horror, started to cry. The other men listened intently, their eyes fixed on the floor or the rubber plant grown gangly in the corner.

"That's what my life is like, Eddie," Virgil said, and he touched Eddie's arm in a move that charged the room with squealing static. "Except," Virgil continued. "Except that my son is you, Eddie. He's a loser like you."

"Ouch, man. Ouch," Eddie said.

"You got it. Exactly right. It hurts. Every day. For years and years."

"Eddie Flynn," the nurse stood at an open door, holding a manila folder, looking around the room.

Eddie sprinted at the bright white light radiating from behind the door.

The Latin boy beside me sat forward, elbows on his knees.

"What kind of trip is he on?" he asked me, nodding toward Virgil. "'Cause I don't want to get me none of that."

I shrugged. "Grief, I guess. His son's missing. You know what that could mean." I turned toward the kid. "I'm Caroline." I extended my hand.

He took it. "Pedro."

"You have any ideas where we might—you know"—I gestured in an arc around my head—"look for him? As you can see, my uncle's a bit"—I looked over for a moment at Virgil, who sat rigidly in his seat, eyes squinting toward some dark interior destination—"he's a bit crazed at the moment. I'm worried about him, to be honest with you. I've never seen him like this."

"If it was me," Pedro said, "I'd forget that boy. He's a loser, like Tio there said." He looked up at me with huge brown eyes full of his own nervous torment.

"Yeah, but it's me," I said. I smiled.

"You got a cigarette?" He nodded toward the door.

Outside, I gave him the pack I'd picked up.

"Keep it," I said when he handed them back. "I need to quit. Again."

We sat in the plastic patio chairs, which seemed farcical in this setting. Surely the designer had never envisioned this, the cheap chairs vibrating as jittery addicts awaited a calming hit.

"You from around here?" I asked Pedro, who smoked contemplatively.

"Houston. I been drifting."

We sat quietly for a moment or two. I looked at him, trying to figure out if he could tell me anything. I read the dark bags below his eyes, the slick grime on the thighs of his jeans. This was how I always looked at people—not looking, sizing. I felt ashamed. He looked wasted and I wanted to let him rest somehow, to lay his head on my breast and sleep.

"You look tired."

"I am, so tired. No shit."

"Are you kicking?"

"Like you and these"—he gestured with the cigarette—"I need to quit."

"There's always something to do, isn't there? Never a chance to just be." I felt my own fatigue start to well up in me. "I'm tired, too."

"You look it. So you and your uncle need to find this boy? He get lost here, eh? He's lucky his Papi came."

"Do you know him?"

"I think I might." He looked down at the ground and I studied his face. Whatever he meant was opaque to me, and I wasn't sure how to proceed.

"I'll be honest with you, Pedro. I never liked him much. But he's my uncle's only child, and I care a lot about my uncle." I paused but he stayed silent. "Well, if you think of anything, call me here." I gave him a book of matches from the hotel and wrote my name on it by the phone number. "Okay?"

I went back inside. Virgil sat clutching himself, rocking. I put my hand on his shoulder.

"Shall we?" I said. His eyes, when he looked up, suggested lashing rains.

Pedro handed the matchbook to me as Virgil and I were leaving. Inside it, in thick, childlike letters, he had written an address.

The next morning, I drank the insipid coffee Virgil had made from the Mylar packet. The room was strewn with clothing and sections from the newspaper. I watched images on the television with the sound off. A military helicopter took off, ascending heavenward, again and again. I tried to guess the story. The helicopter looked old and battered, some U.S. castoff, waging war south of somewhere.

Virgil showered. I heard his deep voice hum then sing a phrase, then hum again. Occasionally he cursed, probably when some other room flushed. The hotel was old enough that a plumbing event in one place touched all others.

I flipped through the channels some more, and landed on a travel piece about the Grand Canyon. Fly-over footage at sunset, other-worldly hues of purple and rose suffused the landscape, the stone flowery magenta. I watched, gaping. I could feel heat off the rock, smell the pine through the television. I started to cry.

Virgil came out of the bathroom with a towel sarong fastened around his waist, his hair flattened to his head. He smelled dewy, and the bruise on his side looked smaller, though it was still etched in violent hues, chartreuse and a tan that looked like pus. I flipped the channel.

"Was that the Grand Canyon?" he asked. "Go back. I'll show you where we're going."

I returned to the channel.

Sunset—or maybe it had been sunrise—had dissolved to midday bright. A uniformed guide pointed to a cactus.

"We'll start here," Virgil said, pointing to a ridge on the far side of the screen. "That's Bright Angel Trail. It's the main route down, but it's beautiful. Then we'll drop down to about . . ." But the shot cut away, before he could show me.

"We aren't going anywhere. We'll never get out of here. Everything's screwed." I cried in earnest now.

He dropped onto the bed beside me and took me in his arms and we rocked together for a moment.

"We'll get there. I promise. Finish your coffee." He held the cup up to me, and held me as I sipped it, and together we watched a jackrabbit run along the canyon's rim.

chapter 10

The address on Caroline's matchbook takes them to a condemned building, forgotten, it seems, even by its executioners. Brick, turn of the century, Virgil can tell by the shape of the glassless windows, by the ornamental lion heads along the roofline. A graceful place, once.

A set of stairs leads to a basement door at the side of the building. The stairwell smells like urine. It's filled with trash. The metal door hangs from its hinges and opens with a wailing. They step into a cavernous space. Red and blue lines arc across a warped wood floor.

"Must have been a gym," Caroline says. As his eyes adjust to the dim light, Virgil vaguely detects bodies lying about the room. Small fires burn, and when he gets nearer, he sees that these are the flames of Bunsen burners, camp stoves, candles. Tiny flickerings, vigil lamps. Cooking the goods.

Caroline walks up to a couple lying on a sleeping bag, boy holding girl, each with long brown hair splayed across the shoulders of the other. They look almost angelic, beatitude of beastly bliss. Caroline smiles and says hello. "Do you know where David is?" she says. Virgil admires the question, the gentle voice with which she asks it, her ability to squat and rest her hand on the floor to steady herself. He could not touch it. He can smell what's there.

"Who're you?" the boy says.

"Caroline," she says simply, an answer that seems to suffice. The two smile on and shake their heads. They continue to move their heads from side to side like dervishes suddenly entranced by motion.

She speaks to an old woman on a swaybacked mattress, its ticking spotted brown and red. The woman cries at David's name. "Doing five," she says. "Doin' fine, doin' five. A hard place. A hard, hard place. I pray for him. Yes I do."

There is a scuffling sound and a sudden flash of light, a burst of voices. "It's my goddamn blanket."

"Caroline, we shouldn't stay," Virgil says. He thinks the light was a gun. He does not want to die here, even if David is.

She pretends not to hear him and walks farther away. He hurries after her. There is a burning-sugar smell and a man holds one end of a rubber tube between his teeth, the other end tied to his big toe. He shoots into the gap between toes, leaves the hypodermic there a moment as if he has just ejaculated and wants to linger in the body of the beloved. Such pleasure. Virgil can see the man's shoulders drop in peace. How good it looks. He would like to feel it himself. Even in the moment of oblivion inside Beverly, and the quiet point afterward where desires momentarily cease, even then he does not let go as this man just has.

"Hey," he says to the man. The man looks up at him as he takes the syringe out of his foot.

"Hey yourself." He looks well into middle age, straight hair hanging to his jowl, wire-rimmed glasses clinging to small grooves in his nose.

"Do you know David?"

"David lived down the block from me. Good God, must have been fifteen years ago. How'd you know?"

Virgil looks at the man a moment more. "Thanks," he says. Tremors start from his chest.

Caroline is talking to a young woman with a cat in her lap. The cat is eating out of a can, and the girl tells Caroline that the cat has worms.

Headache explodes behind Virgil eyes. "Caroline," he says, and finds he is whispering. "Caroline," he says it louder and a woman looks up at him. She pulls one of her breasts from her blouse and waves to him with it. Heat climbs up his body and he falls into it, a blue sea, saline and supportive. From its surface he regards heaven beyond the searing sun.

chapter 11

"It's me," I said. Virgil was asleep on his bed, evening falling over the river outside our hotel window, lights on the far shore coming on in the twilight.

"God, how are you?" Donald said. "I've been so worried—I haven't heard from you." He let that sit. I didn't say anything. "Are you okay?"

"I'm fine. Everything else has gone to hell in a hand basket, but I'm just dandy." I stopped. "Look," I said. "I need your help."

"Anything at all. I would do anything to help you."

"It's about my cousin." I explained. Virgil's fall, the heroin-addled missing person, I could hear Donald take it all in, this sudden windfall, the secrets he'd sensed but never glimpsed, now all his.

"That sounds"—he paused a moment—"chaotic. You must be exhausted."

I went silent, stifling sobs. Everything inside me was in rebellion, but after finding Virgil blacked out on the floor of the gym, and all it took to get him out of there—pulling him, enlisting the help of the strongest-looking man I could find who turned out to be too far gone to lift Virgil's legs, then waiting for a cab to come, even after I'd called and called again, I didn't see a choice in the matter. We weren't going to find David this way. Donald would know someone, he always did.

"Tell you what, Caroline," he went on. "I don't want you to worry about anything. Your cousin will be fine. I have some favors to call in. Where are you?"

I told him the hotel.

"Got it," he said. "Don't go anywhere. I'll call around and get back to you within the hour. You hear me? It's going to be fine. I promise."

"Thank you, Donald." I couldn't help it—I started to cry. "I'm just so scared about Virgil. He passed out, we were in that awful place, I should have taken him to a hospital and made him stay."

He listened, or at least was silent. "Hey, go easy now. It's going to be fine. Just rest up and let me handle this."

part III

chapter 1

This is everything you need to know about Donald. The sixth time we slept together, he wanted to give me an enema. It was a prelude to anal sex, a first for me, and I was willing enough to give that a go, but an enema. But he'd bought the damn thing, with its vaguely medicinal shape, its mineral oil, and I sat in a bath, knees to my chest, regarding it on the counter.

"I can't do this," I told him.

"Sure you can. It'll be fun."

"It will be uncomfortable." He was my boss, but it's not like I needed a promotion or anything.

"Give it a try. *Please*," he added, insisting, whining, wheedling.

"All right, all right, but this is the one-and-only time." I noted with dread that he was already getting hard.

Once I finally got out of the bath—and I lingered, wanting to see him shrivel up again, even if it meant waiting till I looked like a scrap of chicken skin—he toweled me off in a hurry, observing some ritual of sensuality. ("Try to enjoy and appreciate your lover's body"; I imagined him drawing a hurried check mark next to that one.) We were in a hotel room, naturally, because I couldn't stand to have these trysts at my apartment, and his wife wouldn't have liked it at theirs.

It was a nice hotel room, expensive, with a marble bathtub, a TV and phone near the toilet, small pink lights recessed into the ceiling that made everything look rosy. They still locked the mini-bar, though, and as an extra security measure, they clipped a little plastic clamp around the handles, so the maid could tell right away if you'd been pilfering the teeny vodkas.

We had—all of them, plus most of the whiskeys. He had asked me to strip for him. I didn't mind stuff like that; it was fun to slowly unbutton my blouse and guess when enough breast was showing, with enough still hidden, to raise his anxiety. I enjoyed how much he desired my body, his hunger, the way he bit my breasts and licked the undersides, the crevice between them, twisting the nipples as if adjusting dials on a radio, then looking at me to check the reception. He didn't roam the territory much, but I liked it. I saw other men besides him, men with velvet tongues and hands of silk. I knew what good sex felt like. This was not about sex.

I suppose it was a power trip. I got off on being his midlife crisis, I got off on knowing he was thinking about me as he lay in the bed next to his wife. It was shallow. I could say I was young, which is true, and young women are brutes in bed, but what good are excuses?

So once he'd toweled me off, he picked up the enema and led me to the bed. He rustled around in a bag and pulled out a white satin teddy. Plastic stays ran up its sides, holding it up. It looked inhabited, like a body cast.

"What is that?" I asked, laughing, wanting him to laugh. Surely this was a joke. He didn't. We appeared to be in the grip of something bigger than just an enema.

"You'll look so sexy in it." He handed it to me.

"Where'd you buy this, Frederick's of Hollywood?" I laughed again, then saw the bag. That's where he'd bought it.

"Last time I was in L.A., and you"—he blew the hair off my back to emphasize my culpability in this—"and you wouldn't come along. I kept thinking of you."

"I'm deeply touched. Let's get married." I looked at the teddy more closely. Plastic lace plunged around the bodice and tickled the bottom. It would be scratchy.

He looked at me, all eagerness. "I bought stockings, too." He pulled out white ones from the pink bag.

It took awhile to get into the teddy. It was clear where everything went, with its exaggerated curves over the breasts, the waist-slimming stays, the four garter straps hanging down like a primitive compass. But it had about a thousand little eyelet clasps, and the stockings kept getting twisted. It was a kind of Rubik's cube in clothing, a mental challenge, and I engaged myself on that level. But when it was on, my breasts, which I'd never thought small, vanished in the ambitious space allotted them. My waist, which is small, strained against the draconian stays. My thighs bulged just over the tops of the stockings like mushroom caps.

"I guess it's not . . . ," I leaned down to unhook a stocking. Donald drew my hand to his bobbing penis.

"You look so sexy," he whispered. He drew out one last item from his bag, a pair of stiletto-heeled pumps, white.

He told me to lie on my stomach and I did. He brushed the hair off my face rather tenderly, then tied a scarf around my eyes, and plugged my mouth with a rubber ball, held in place by a stocking which he tied snugly behind my head, snagging a bit of hair in the process.

I tried to say something, to spit out the ball at least, we hadn't agreed to this, but he drizzled some mineral oil on my rear, and with a finger, lightly skimmed my anus. I was alive all over at once, throbbing, wanting fingers and tongues and toes and cocks in everything. I wanted to be penetrated in every pore.

He stroked along my thighs, slowly, teasingly. I tried to buck his hand toward my center.

"Ah, ah, ah," he said, "so someone likes this."

I did not like it, but that didn't begin to express the emotion. I did not like that I liked it, I did not like that what humiliated me turned me on.

He teased my thighs some more, then I felt something cold and thin enter my anus, heard a squish and felt a gush of liquid. The enema was in.

I lay there and felt the pressure build. My sides strained against the stays, my eyes saw the pink underside of my eyelids and saliva slid out of the corner of my mouth. The ball tasted of rubber and unwashed hands. I had to get to the toilet. The bed was pulsing with rhythm. I tried to climb off it.

"A minute," he said, and I could tell from the strain in his voice that he was jacking off, probably not too far from glory. I felt him climb astride, his legs squeezing either side of mine. He pressed down on my back.

"Oh, Caroline," he said.

I wasn't going to be able to hold it. I tried to rise again, and he pushed me back. I felt him entering my backside, and I lifted my ankles, trying to scratch him with the heels, then reared up and let everything go on the quilted bedspread, while he ejaculated in a hot smear across my thighs. I knocked him off and stormed to the bathroom and locked the door.

I showered for ages. Then I wouldn't come out, just sat beneath the heat lamp, a towel wrapped around me, watching the tiny television. Late-night talk show, hammy jokes, a singer with a knack for leaning into the bad camera angles. He knocked on the door, he implored, he apologized—he'd gotten out of hand, he'd never do it again. There was an awful tone of gratitude in his voice, a way that this exchange had made him mine, as if he'd bartered his soul in it. So who did that make me?

Then he had to go home. I could practically hear him cry when he said it, but I didn't come out. And he left. Alone in that hotel room, I stayed up all night, ordered room service three times, it was on his card. Fuck him. Fuck him very much.

Virgil slept while I remembered this, the tears warm down my cheeks. Why had I continued to see him, to sleep with him, hell, to work for him? Now I was waiting again, for his call, all too familiar. What had I been thinking? If I could have pulled the words back in and stuffed them down my throat where they belonged, I would have. I surely would have.

Despite my cynicism, I had spent some of my hard-earned emotion on this man—a ridiculous portion of hope in the early days, earnest delusion that he would leave the wife and be mine for real, surely I was that compelling. Yet, despite the fact that he had proven incapable of anything other than sexual disloyalty to the woman who bore his child, and despite the lashing grief this caused me, I had been able to separate all that from work. If anything, it gave me the upper hand. Whereas others tiptoed around, did his bidding in the fawning way you do when the boss is unpredictable, I forever had the goods on him and knew no fear.

Disappointment, yes. Fear, no.

Disappointment was what I expected now. His track record in the moment of crisis was dismal. It was a measure of how lost I felt that I'd called at all. Or a measure of other things—my lack of resources, my loneliness. Nothing I cared to catalog.

Virgil shifted and moaned in his sleep. His eyebrows scrunched together, wincing, as if the tension that follows pain could protect you from the pain to come.

I moved to his bed and sat beside him, stroking his hair. His head felt damp, swampy with fever, his cheeks oddly cool to my touch. I touched him all the more—there had to be some healing in the mere fact of finger on skin, human to human, outside the contingencies of the blood common between us.

The fearsome moment of the present reared up in front of me, its purity, the piercing beauty of things stolen from time. The mole just outside the upper, outer spiral of his right ear. I actually saw it. Then the phone rang, Donald no doubt, the cavalry, the blaring of bugles.

chapter 2

The call was not Donald. It was a man named Simon Boudreaux, calling from the hotel lobby. Could I please meet him in the bar?

When I went down, I met a light-skinned black man, his face freckled like a robin's egg, his hair coppery rust, his eyes alarmingly green. He was tall, and had a large chest straining at the buttons of a plaid shirt. He was one of Archer Demwalt's men, he said, in an alchemy I couldn't fully grasp.

It was a circus-themed bar, with swirling clown faces and snarling steeds carved into a wood canopy that overhung the liquor bottles. Boudreaux was the only man there, it being ten in the morning. He drank a Bloody Mary, and his palm around the glass made it look freakishly small.

"I don't understand what Arch has to do with it," I said.

Boudreaux shrugged his shoulders. "We picked up your boy."

I gave him a puzzled look. "Picked him up?" He showed me his badge. "Where was he?"

"Central Lockup. No place for a lady," he said, and he smiled a very charming smile.

"But we called there."

"You didn't know he'd changed his name, I'm betting."

"Shouldn't we go get him, then?"

"Sure, sure. But Arch is an old friend. At least, he will be when a few years pass. Right now let's say he's marrying well. And there's something he wants you to do."

"I'm all ears."

He took another pull on his drink. "They make a good bloody here. You want one?"

Very badly. "Why not."

He signaled the bartender.

"What-all you put in that mix? Hear? You can tell me, I won't tell no one," Boudreaux asked the barman.

"Eye of newt," the bartender said. "The usual voodoo mix." They both laughed at this, like it was some long-standing joke between them.

"Do you have a cigarette?" I asked Boudreaux. I wanted a little time to size him up. A big man, a tough man, a man who got answers and found things. I tried to imagine his apartment. No wedding ring. Probably divorced. A high-rise, with a distant river view, paper piled on the desk, the kitchen table. *TV Guide* folded open over the armrest of a chair. A monster bed for those lucky times. I wasn't much to him. I couldn't see my angle.

"Simon," I said, as he lit the cigarette for me. I drew in deep and blew the smoke between us, creating an atmosphere. "Tell me something about yourself."

He shot me a glance and laughed. "No you don't. Don't go flirting, little one. You don't know what you're liable to find."

"I don't care what I find. I'm just interested." I met his gaze and tapped the cigarette against the rim of the ashtray.

"I am a very good dancer," he said.

"That so? What are we talking here—funky chicken, fox-trot?"

"No, two-step, the waltz. Zydeco. I hold you close and take you for a little ride. Then you will not know which direction is up." He smiled the lady-killer grin again, and I felt slightly slayed. "You a girl who's always trying to play, no? I've met you before. I think I married you one or two times." He took one of my cigarettes and lit it. He leaned down to look at me. "I see that mind working inside your eyes. You got something you need to take care of and you trying to figure old Simon out. What can he give me? Sometimes, chère, you got to give first."

"I'll buy you a drink," I said, taken with this unexpected loquacious perception. "I thought you were just a dumb old boy from down South."

I called the bartender and had him mix us another round. And we were fast friends. I told him all about the funeral, about my mother, my uncle and my cousin. I told him about Donald and Demwalt and work and running away, how good it felt to run away.

"I thought I would think. Like—'om,' meditate on the cosmos and figure out my place in it, make a little sense of things. But guess what. I've just looked. Smelled. Tasted. That's it, from Illinois to Tennessee to Louisiana. I haven't learned a thing."

"Who's this father, then? You don't love the man? You don't stay to see him buried?"

This father was first of all a smell to me. Pungent skin smell, against cloth, his robe. A thing I held to my face, so that when I breathed, it was the air.

"Don't you do it, too," I said, hurt. He waited for me to go on. "Don't you tell me there's only one way to love. I know what I feel. Or don't. I know that I felt nothing that night, not even when I looked at him, laid out. 'Peaceful.'"

That was the composed image. On the inside it was bottomless. No beginning, no end, just endless falling. I felt as if every lie I'd ever told was swirling around me, my atmosphere. How could I stay and breathe those lies? He was my father. I loved him deeply and in small ways. I loved his hand holding mine at the tidal edge of breaking waves. I loved his eyebrows, thinking through the cross-word puzzle, the sound of the sports section shaken open, Bach cello suites mournful in the air. All those details. I loved each one. My grief was remembering.

The things a Bloody Mary can do.

So Simon Boudreaux and I sat at the Carousel Bar, and drank our way through the late morning, into the early afternoon. I could have done it for days, and he didn't seem to mind. He got more and more silent as I spoke, as if we were teeter-tottering, his silence balancing my appetite for language, my sudden flight into revelation.

Then I quieted. "Really now, what does Arch have to do with this?" I asked.

"Maybe you want your cousin now," he said after I'd spoken long enough.

"Maybe I do," I said. Everything so vaporous in this life.

We drove in a Delta 88, an old one, silent despite rain splattering the windshield, white vinyl seats, maroon carpet and dash trim. Squeaky clean. He clicked on the radio and Diana Ross was in the middle of "Love Hangover," the bass line pumped in torrents up and down the fret board. Simon drummed his fingers on the steering wheel.

"How long's it been since you seen your cousin?" he asked.

I thought a moment. I had no idea. "We're not exactly close-knit," I said.

"Mr. Demwalt posted the bail, but you the one got to pick him up and take custody. You know what that means?"

"Sounds official."

"Yeah, you got to keep him with you a while. You got to take him out of the state. He's a troubled boy. I don't know if you know. But he is."

"What does Arch have to do with this?" I asked. This detail was starting to nag at me. Donald hadn't said anything about this when we spoke.

"Mr. Demwalt can do this, no problem. He did it for you."

Simon took one hand off the wheel and plucked a document from his breast pocket. He nodded toward it, for me to read. My name was typed in as David's custodian. Why not Virgil? There was a rider with conditions—I was to go to Dallas for the two weeks until the wedding to get the damn thing planned. Please sign at the X.

"Do you mind if I make a call," I asked, pulling my phone out of my purse and dialing Donald's number.

chapter 3

We sit on the stools that ring the circular bar, and the whole thing is turning. It's a carousel theme, and it's totally corny and funny looking and as soon as I see it I have to go in there. I am pissed to be with Dad, but it's a hell of a lot better than sitting in jail itching my elbows. And Caroline, well, she might be a teen angel or dream come true or one of those other things you hear about on the radio.

She comes with me to the bar, I can see she's going to be the good-cop parole officer who'll be cool with me, but only because she wants to make sure I don't do something stupid. But man I'm so tired there is nothing stupid left to do. I am so tired I feel it cell by cell, like each one of the thousands of little fuckers that make up the me of me are on strike, wielding tiny placards. Send David to Hell! That's what the signs in my cells all say. And the little freaks are yelling, too, so it's real noisy about now.

"Mind if we just sit here?" I say to her. She nods. Whatever, it's cool. She orders a vodka and tonic and drinks it fast. I have a tonic water. I don't really like alcohol. I don't like what it does to me, makes me all sop eyed and tearful. I'm what you'd call a lachrymose drunk, and I'd prefer to be bellicose or varicose, anything but what I am. I hate to cry, so what do I need something that actually makes me cry for?

The bar is pretty empty. It's only like 2:30 in the afternoon, and all the drunks are sleeping off last night's bash or out eating something real greasy so they can do it again tonight. I hate how repetitive alcohol is, too. That's another drag about it. But hey, who am I to talk, right?

"I don't mind if we go to Dallas," I tell her, because she looks all distracted, and since she'd been talking about it with that guy on the phone, I figure that's probably what's on her mind.

"Yeah?" She says this like she's grateful.

"You're pretty for a cousin," I tell her, and she laughs.

"I used to think you were such a bore," she says. "Guess I was wrong."

"I am a bore. I just do heroin, that's all. Nothing too interesting in that."

I stretch out my right arm in front of her. I'm wearing a T-shirt and some old corduroys, feeling pretty scrungy, actually. The vein that runs smack down the center of my arm pops up and vibrates expectantly. I have a small abscess just south of the bend in my elbow, a purple bubble. I don't think she likes the look of it, and who could blame her, it's ugly, ugly, ugly. But I have come to love my veins. I know them well, I know which ones speed the delicious slow break of pleasure to me, what a thing it is, a slowing down and a speedy rush at the same time, it's so good, to relax in a way like you never do, not even when you fall asleep. Maybe it's like what a baby feels, a really lucky baby with a warm bed and mom and dad cooing over it, a mobile hanging upside the head twirling in the long darkness.

Maybe it's like that, but I think it's probably better. Imagine the complete cessation of tension. Come on, really imagine it—take a moment. I'll be one of those guided-meditation guys. Close your eyes and release the tension in your toes. Didn't know you had tension in your toes, did you, but you do. That's the damnable thing—there's all this tension that you didn't even know about. And the sweet thing, the sweet, sweet thing, is realizing you had it by its sudden absence. All gone, bye-bye now. Sweet, sweet, sweet. Wicked witch o' the West was right. Poppies. Hate to say it, but maybe death is as good. That would be my best guess at an analogy.

Here's the part where I'm supposed to disavow all this drug doing and say how bad it is, but I don't think it is, necessarily. Essentially it's neutral. It's the actions that can be bad. Like what I was saying about alcohol—I don't want to be this cry-baby drunk, because to me that's a bad action. Or you get in fights or you steal stuff—those are bad actions. But they're not the drug per se. Most junkies like me aren't bad. Weak—yeah, I think that could be fairly said. You succumb to something powerful, and you think you're going to imbibe in the power, to be lifted up by it, but it doesn't work that way. It's like you're a little piece of wood, and it's a big ocean. No matter how sharp and pointy a badass piece of wood you are, the ocean is still going to bash you against the rocks. But it doesn't make you bad, unless you're bad. Unless it's given you to do bad things. Am I making sense?

And then I realize that I'm not actually saying any of this, I'm just looking at Caroline like I expect an answer and she says, "What?," as in "What, moron?" I know the tone.

"Nothing. I was just thinking, that's all."

"Care to share?"

"Share to care," I correct her and she laughs, which makes me happy. I am so glad to be here, in this hilarious bar, smelling and looking like capitalized shit, but free and in the bosom of thems that loves me.

She sits with her arms crossed across her front, looking like tension incarnate. Makes me wish I could turn her on. I think everyone should know the possibility of not being tense, it gives you a new perspective. Now that I'm going clean, my hope is to remember that I have been without anxiety and call forth the memory when needed. So I try to radiate it over to her, like a contact high, David Harris the great Svengali of relaxation technique, from drug to mind, now that's a cool idea. Maybe I'll do that, have an exercise video and an infomercial shot in Hawaii.

"Why didn't you call your mom?" Caroline asks, and again, I don't know if I've been talking or not. Seems like it, like the lips has been moving and a cacophony of sound has left the body, its waves no doubt altering the universe to its subtle fibers.

Why didn't I call? Shit, Mom is so loving and nice to me, always, without fail. It is the thing I know. So why should I hurt her? It seemed that the disappearing David was the course of the warrior, the better part of valor, as they say.

"You hurt her just as much."

Shit, so I was talking. "Caroline," I say. "You don't always think your clearest when you're coming off a three-month high and you discover that you are in a Louisiana jail. You may not know this, but that reptile brain stem back in the back of your head turns out to be exactly enough in jail, you can just shut off the frontal lobe all together, in fact, it's better, things go easier for you if you do."

She calls the bartender over and asks for a second vodka and tonic.

"I wish you wouldn't," I say to her. I don't know what kind of drunk she'd be, but the tension coming off her is like mustard gas. "Let's just go."

"Go ahead," she says, nodding to the barman. "I need to think through some things."

I don't want to just go to the room and sit there with Dad, and the streets present perils for a boy like me, so I stay. She does what she said, she thinks. She draws flowers on a napkin, then takes one of those calendar-everything books out of her purse, the kind people who have lives carry, because they need to jot things down in the midst of those lives to remember later on. I admire that, the needing to write and remember, and all it implies about the interconnections between Caroline and whoever it is she thinks of as she jots and doodles.

I myself would have no need of the calendar-note jotting device except as a way to stay anchored to the notion of time—as in, today is Tuesday, as if that actually meant something. I would need a calendar that was like one of those cheapie toys they used to sell at the grocery store—a piece of cardboard, a carbon and some plastic over it, and a penlike thing, a stylus. You could draw squiggles to your heart's content and then lift up the plastic and it's all gone, ready to be drawn upon again, perpetual tabula rasa. I like the way the drawings just disappear. I would want it to have sound effects, too, so that when you lift the plastic and the illusion of this day as separate from yesterday or tomorrow disappears, it giggles or in some way indicates that we are engaged in a mutually-agreed-upon illusion, and isn't it a gas?

The barman is a short, thick guy who looks as if he has toiled many the hard hour for his shirt-bursting physique. He has close-cropped hair the color of nothing. It simply is not a color and I stare at him a while, trying out metaphors and similes to see if I can nail it. Dishwater is accurate, but it requires the caveat that the dishwater has already had the dishes soaking awhile. This is not the water when first streaming from the tap, generating so much excited bubbling in the soap. This is the later dishwater, a drab and distasteful element, full of rogue garbage, shards of green onion drifting onto your hand like the near-drowned.

"You need something," the barman says to me, and his nameplate reads "Chet." I guess I'd been trying too intently to understand Chet's hair.

"Chet," I say, "I need a Coke. Very badly."

He whips down a highball glass and spins it like a six-shooter. "That's too easy. Ask me for a hard one."

"I don't drink."

"Bar's the wrong place for a man like you."

This is rife with interpretive possibility, but I doubt Chet has it in him to go over the permutations with me. He doesn't strike me as an analyst.

He places my Coke in front of me, with a straw bent at its elbow. I sip and let the bubbles work their magic.

"What drink do you mix the most of?" Caroline is deep in her ruminations, and I watch from the corner of my eye. She vibrates when she thinks.

Chet points to the staves of the draft beer pulls. "Your number one drink order, courtesy of Mr. Bud Wiser," he says, and bangs down the Bud pull, cupping his hands under the stream. "Every bar's bread and butter. Cheap to buy, quick to pour, excellent markup."

Caroline looks up from her napkin etchings.

"How do you two know each other?" Chet asks.

"We're cousins," she says, and she wraps her arm across my back and kisses my cheek. "Just picked him up out of jail today. I'm so glad he's all right."

140

"Whoa, brother," Chet says. "Damn, too bad you don't drink, I'd stand you one." He looks around the bar distractedly, then brings over a menu. "Anything you want. Big steak, plate a onion rings, you name it."

I read at the menu, and the words "mashed potatoes" present themselves, sounding like something I could eat.

So I order that, and a slice of cherry pie. And they taste not at all dangerous.

"Do you know about my father?" Caroline asks me.

I chew and look at her, waiting. Her dad is a nice guy. Mild, quiet, a moral presence. He's like a fireplace. You just know that after the huffing and the puffing blows the house down, he'll be there, standing up, same as ever.

"He died," she says.

I put down my fork. The pie gleams too brightly, its undulations of cherries and the gelatinous goo that contains them looking for the life of me like viscera.

"God," I say, and I start to cry, instantly, just like I hate. "He did?"

"Yeah, he did." We both sit there, she hard as rocky blacktop road, me sopping wet with my own salted sadness, but the two things are the same, her angles, my spongy receptivity, exactly the same. She puts her forehead on my shoulder.

I'm not as affectionate a person as it seems like I would be, I mean, physically affectionate. It's not the first thing that comes to mind. In fact it's so far down the list that it's safe to say that it doesn't qualify as coming to mind. But her forehead, the gesture of it, you know, like she's bowing, that gets me.

"So Dallas is all right with you?" she asks.

"No better place."

"Let's go tell your pop."

Chet stands Caroline her two drinks and offers her a third, but she says, "Better not, but a cup of coffee would be great," the thought of which makes me cringe.

"Caroline, I don't like the way you treat your body," I say.

She laughs. Everyone does, health advice from a junkie, yeah, right. The ultimate hypocrisy.

"I'm serious. You're suffocating your every cell with all this shit," I indicate the glasses, coffee cup, and ashtray holding the burning husk of a cigarette. Chet isn't big on clearing stuff away, unlike most barmen, who tend as a class to be compulsive neatniks. I suppose they want to eliminate the potential totting up when you order the next drink—oh, I've already had three, I—fill in the blank—do/do not need another. Yeah, it's probably that rather than the neatness.

She smiles at me, and the smile isn't derisive. Her eyes are dark brown, so it doesn't seem correct to say they burn, but eyes do that, no matter what color. Sometimes they burn. There are different kinds of burn, too, and I don't know for sure what this one is, but it feels warm.

"Duly noted," she says, and she squeezes my hand.

She folds her napkin drawings into the calendar book, puts the pen back into the loop attached to it, everything in its place. Then she hops off the stool, and looks at me, smiling and softer than I've seen yet, and it seems that whatever she does, there's a liveliness that you have to follow. You just have to, because not to do so is to miss out.

chapter 4

When we get to the room, Caroline knocks before entering though she has a key. My father stretches across the bed on his back, his arms bent around his head as if shielding him from blows. He starts when we enter, and the movement appears to hurt. His shirt is off, and I can see on his left side the blue brown tendrils of a vicious bruise.

"Hope the other guy looks worse," I say.

"What other guy?" Dad says. He sits up on the bed now, and he doesn't look well.

"The one who gave you that." I point to the bruise.

"This is just my own stupidity."

"Virgil had an accident," Caroline says. She's in the bathroom with the door open, rhythmically brushing her hair.

It's been three years since I've seen my father. The last time was the summer before I dropped out of Brown. I lived with him in his sprawling Lake Shore Drive apartment, a three-bedroom doozy on a corner, windows everywhere showing off the vastness of Lake Michigan. It terrified me, all that nothing out there, the empty space above the water. I have a bit of *horror vacuui*. You could call it agoraphobia, but that implies fear of the people in the open space, whereas for me, it's the void, the white noise, the gray space before sleep that is too close to oblivion for comfort, and therefore to be avoided. Which makes heroin such a telling choice of drugs. I've thought about that.

My father looks older, which of course he is. But he looks more than three years older, and this news flash about an accident puts that into context. Experience can age you faster than time.

"What happened?" I ask.

Dad shrugs. "I fell."

This answer raises more questions than it answers and I feel immediately tired. To know the story will require kneeling and prof-fering. He can be so niggardly, parsimonious with words and what they signal—thoughts, emotions. I start to ask, "From what?"—and hear the sarcasm seep into the vocal tone like squid ink.

I don't think I can do this—either the supplication or the fight.

"From grace?" I say, and there's the sarcasm.

"He smoked a joint and fell from a tree," Caroline says, hair brushed and smooth. "For Christ's sake, Virgil, say hello to your son." And with that prompting, my father rises and takes me in a kind of an embrace.

She opens the mini-bar, breaking its plastic seal, alerting tomorrow's housecleaner of the transgression. Takes a Jack Daniel's and a can of Coke from the fridge, then a bag of peanuts from the counter.

I do not like this.

"You smoked a joint," I say to my father. An incongruous thought, this geezing creature puffing a fat one, then falling from on high.

"You know," I say. "Drugs are dangerous."

"Oh David," he says. "Let's not do this."

His tired tone, the constraint of pain audible in his voice—these seem grossly unfair. Fine, now that he's the-down-and outer, he can preempt the righteous outrage he's showered on me. *Throwing your-self away.* How many times have I heard that?

"It's too late," I say, and I lay myself out on the other bed, sprawling in my pain as he sprawls in his.

Caroline orders up a cot, and room service, and we three lie on our separate beds watching Galapagos tortoises soldier across barren islands on TV. Virgil sleeps and, from time to time, moans.

I watch Caroline when the program gets dull. She smokes lazily, letting the cigarette burn long branches of ash between inhalations. I think she just likes knowing she can inhale, which a cigarette makes palpable, as if breath, too, is hers to choose.

* * *

"You shouldn't do this."

This is my father's voice, hushed, as gray light begins to push at the windows, dawn dawning. I had been asleep, sweating mightily so that the sheets are soaked, but something in his hiss, his anger broke through the cavern of sleep.

"I have to do it, Virgil," Caroline says. "He got your son out of jail. I owe him."

"Not everything that's owed gets paid. I am worried about your soul, darling, your sweet, immortal soul."

I lie still, too stiff to be sleeping.

"My soul is not at stake in this."

"It's supposed to mean something when you run away. You haven't run away from anything."

"So now I'm the petite bourgeoise. Disappointing, eh?" Her voice has a hot edge of anger, then she laughs. "You old hippie."

I open my eyes just as she gets up from her bed and kisses him. Then she sits on the side of his bed and strokes the hair back from his forehead. I shift in my sheets.

"I worry about you," Dad says. "I want you to live."

"Is that it? Is that everything? Because I am living."

He's silent awhile. "This moment matters. Don't think it doesn't. You're choosing something here."

In the morning, then, we take to the open road, which in the south doesn't feel all that open. The air is too thick, slowing your car with its humid drag. But we drive west toward Baton Rouge, through swamp country, oil-colored water all around. I sit in the backseat like the family pooch, my head close to the window, looking at all the ways to live the world offers up. Clapboard and slats and brick and tar paper. Possibilities.

Caroline drives and sings to the radio. I think about what I thought I saw last night, that kiss. On the lips, the cheek, the neck? Why is location the court-appointed interpreter in the language of kisses?

Dad leans against the passenger door, a heap of morose coal shov-eled into the seat. Look at that, I'd say. Did you see that? C'mon, pops, look at the world, the blessed, blessed world.

No dice. Asleep, encased in his pain, whatever. The man is not here.

Caroline is, though, and she seems happy. She drives fast and well. This is a two-lane highway, and there isn't much traffic. But from time to time, we draw up behind some behemoth from days of yore, wide, long, speckled with rust or shiny with care, either way. But slow. Slow, slow, slow, slow, slow. An old man driving, his arm out the window, fingers holding the roof. A blurred tattoo on his forearm, an ancient anchor on the now-leathery hide.

"Why can't this guy plan his own wedding?" I ask.

"Rich men don't trust themselves," Caroline says. "It's a power thing. Guys with power can't actually decide anything, they simply approve or disapprove."

"People with money live off the backs of others. Why should he drink your blood?" So Dad's awake after all.

"Oh Virgil, he's not drinking my blood. I could do this with my eyes closed."

"My point exactly."

I do not like them arguing or kissing, or anything, probably. I would rather we all stay blandly nice, ever so kind and dead. That's a sick thing to think, but it's hard to come back to reality and see what muck there is in life.

So I hang out in the largesse of the day, its sky, its shifting light. This day like no other. Caroline's cell phone rings four times before we even stop for lunch, and she answers it. From the long pauses between her *yeses* or *I don't think sos* or *show me when I get theres*, it's easy to see she's at work. She always has an answer. She never sounds annoyed. She never lets him down. The things money could buy.

chapter 5

It is a huge house with white columns on an expanse of empty land. Two shrubs on the left, two shrubs on the right—it's that precise and that dull. This is where we'll be staying, where the wedding will take place, and there's not a hint of cover, just a white house baking beneath flat hot light. And the bride is supposed to transform this place into a garden, a paradise of lush life amid dust and an overlarge sky. The job is hopeless. I want to tell her this—run for your life, get thee to Hawaii, or Vermont, so she'll have some notion of green, of verdant life. But I keep my mouth shut, because Veronica is the most beautiful collection of corpuscles I have ever seen and I am quite literally struck dumb.

I have never been in love. Not once. Douglas, well, he doesn't count. I did have sex, once, with a girl I knew at college. It felt good, but queasy making. And that's how I feel stepping out of the car with its dead leather seats and unnatural atmosphere. Caroline looks after my father, Arch huffs and puffs, ordering around his uniformed staff. He doesn't look after me, as I'm a man and generally speaking, men don't fear getting out of cars. So I step out on my own dear feet, into the large air that is the same as God, all too vast, and disappear and start to shake to know that I still exist.

And there she is, squinting down at me, from the back of a gray horse.

They set us up in a guest house by the aqua kidney pool, Caroline and me each in the bedrooms. Arch has a doctor on hand for my father, who's staying in the main house. I should be there, too, but I'm not. There's also a large, open living area separated from the kitchen by a counter. Everything is blue or white or rattan. Plants with wide leaves intrude from the corners of rooms. The living space opens to a patio and the pool, and the doors slide away so that there is no separation between inner and outer, a fact I ponder, with a bit of dread for later tonight when the shadows shift and noises I've not heard before begin to sound.

Caroline comes in and she's speedy, happy in a way I haven't seen before. It's nerve wracking to be around this brand of happiness that's entirely derived from activity. She writes lists, she whispers to herself, shuttling in and out of her bedroom getting things arranged. A pile of faxes and mail awaits her on the table, and she alights for a moment, reading.

After a minute of silence, she starts and seems to realize I'm there.

"I didn't mean to scare you," I say.

She looks me over. "We need to adjust your wardrobe, kemo sabe."

I don't respond to the squares and angles of the house. Square windows on larger square planes of wall, all of it sitting on a square of land. I feel as if I am seeing it through a silvery distance. I can see it's a place I don't want to be. For one thing, she's right, I'm not dressed for it—still wearing the sweat-soaked corduroys and thin T-shirt.

She takes me to the mall, with its marble floors and music of the spheres and vaguely perfumed air. All is calm, all is bright. I hum the carol. Caroline selects khakis for me, and a pair of jeans. White button-down shirts and polos. All fragrant with the new. She makes me try them on and come out and show her. I let this happen, happy for her tutelage. She knows better than I do what I should appear to be. Whatever it is—Ivy League, old money, fine breeding, it seems—that is who I'll become, disappearing my scabs beneath white cotton sleeves, sopping up my inner oils with the love of a good soap. Make myself over, invent a David who is not who I am, a David unacquainted with his own feces. Because this is what Caroline needs for a few days, and I feel I have it in me to give it to her. I may have it in me, anyway, and I'm curious. Who am I in a new set of duds?

So I submit and am saved, because salvation and surrender are one. Her vision of me will create me. She leads in this dance. All I have to do is turn, one revolution at a time.

*　　*　　*

At dinner, I am seated beside Veronica. Large tropical flowers bloom on the wallpaper, a ceiling fan turns, wood slats cover the window. I am supposed to feel regal, I guess, a colonial rajah circa 1904, but the slats are closed and the wood is dark and it feels like we've gathered here to sit out a bombing, and in the morning we'll walk out to a world offered in holocaust.

I remind myself that that's just how it feels, not necessarily how it is.

We eat ostrich steaks. Arch—he wants me to call him that—raises ostriches on some portion of the flat square land that is not the same as the land allotted to cows and bulls and calves. Never mind that cutting into it is like slicing into my own thigh, or that I am eating death. I tell myself to ignore this. And I bite, I chew, as if I knew how to do these things.

There's a salad, too, which I like: tomatoes and a green leaf that's charged with pepper. Veronica says she made it, and smiles when I tell her, stammering, struggling with each damn word, that I like it, I like it a lot.

I don't know why she makes me so nervous.

Not true, I know.

Her hair hangs down her back and it's exactly the color hair should be, sunlight through wheat. Her waist tips in just above the hips and flares out again at the ribs. Her legs are short and strong, and when we pulled up, she leaned down from the horse to look at us with her hand to her forehead, and her hair fell across her shoulder. For these reasons, and because her voice is like water moving over rocks, I have a hard time talking to her.

"Won't you have some more?" she says, proffering the platter of ostrich. Juice runs down the plate, a mix of red and brown. I focus on the brown. It's gravy, that word will be my anchor, but I see the red, too, which must be blood.

Veronica's hand is shaking. Stop thinking now.

"I'm like a vegetarian," I whisper by way of apology. "But can I offer you some?" This just pops out, and I take the platter and hold it for her.

"Don't tell Arch," she says, "but I am, too." She winks at me. "I've got a garden out back. Come see it tomorrow."

This I know: I take orders well.

chapter 6

Arch had suggested a breakfast meeting where he and the bride would "brief" me on the wedding. I was back at work. A woman in a maid's uniform brought a basket of bread and croissants, warm and swaddled in a maroon napkin. She tilted the basket toward me and let a pair of silver tongs hover until I indicated the croissant.

"Well, darlin'," Arch said to Veronica. "Why don't you start? You're the bride, after all." He laughed with a heavy heartiness. I smiled politely.

We were seated in the breakfast room, a semicircle of windows looking out to the rear of the house over the equestrian ring, and beyond that, barns and fields. Horses grazed, necks to earth, a palomino, a bay, a dapple gray, an Appaloosa.

Veronica was extraordinarily beautiful. Her hair was tousled, she had on a little mascara, but not much else in the way of morning maintenance, that I could see. No pores punctuated her olive skin, her forehead was high and smooth and gracefully rounded.

"Well, I'm thinking I'd like to ride up on King of the Wink," she said. Her voice was throaty and arresting. She spoke quietly.

"King of. . . ," I said.

"Her Arab stud," Arch clarified.

"Yeah," Veronica said. "That's him." She pointed to one of the horses grazing in the distance. "I'll introduce you later."

"Okay," I said, after a long pause. She didn't seem to have any further input. "How about colors? Have you selected any?"

She looked at me blankly.

"It's customary," I began, feeling like Margaret Mead. "Usually you select a palette, and it brings everything together. Bridesmaid's dresses, flowers—they all coordinate."

"I see," she said. She picked up her cup of coffee and took a long drink. "White and gold are nice." She had on a thick bracelet and lifted her wrist up to show me. "Like this. Shiny, beautiful, rich."

White and gold and an Arab stud.

I thought for a moment, taking a bite of croissant, though I regretted the choice instantly, as it flaked all over my pants. I brushed at them, which only made things worse.

"This is kind of an abstract question, but give it a shot. What would you like the wedding to feel like?" I paused and looked at them. They were seated across a round table covered in chintz. The tablecloth matched the curtains, which hung in voluptuous curves. I flashed on Rousseau, the woman in the jungle being consumed by vegetation. Arch and Veronica were looking at each other a bit puzzled.

"I mean, do you want it to be formal or informal, colorful or sedate? That's all I'm trying to get at."

"What do you think?" Arch asked me after a moment more.

"Well, to be honest, it doesn't matter, since it's not my wedding. The point is what would you like, what impression do you want to create, what would feel comfortable for you, what would help you celebrate your joy?"

"*Celebrate our joy*. I like that. Let's put that on our invitations," Arch said to Veronica, indicating to her that she should write it down. She didn't look at him, and didn't write a thing.

The blessed day was less than two weeks away. Invitations? Either Donald had screwed up big time, or these two were the most hapless pair of socialites I'd ever seen.

"Really, Caroline, I'd like to hear what you recommend," Veronica said. She spoke so seldom and slowly and softly that I found myself commanded.

"Look, I don't know what's unique about your love, so how can I recommend what your wedding should be like? As a rough guess, and this is based on the most superficial observations, I'd suggest something that feels country French. Your house has a mix of formality and casualness. It's full of color, and it feels like a bustling place. So formal seems out of place. But I don't know—you tell me."

"You're right about the house. We wanted it to be a place people could be. Not just visit, but be themselves when they got here. I'm glad you picked up on that," Veronica said, and now she smiled. "I'm kind of a tomboy. The only thing I really care about is riding up on King. The rest I'm leaving to you." And with that, she stood up, wrapped her arms around Arch's neck, and walked out.

Arch followed her with his eyes, wistful, abandoned. I didn't blame her for running. Who could stand a gaze so full of need?

"Let's talk about the venue," I said. "Is it a church? And where will you hold the reception?" I wanted to be all business so that Veronica's departure would not echo.

"Honey, it's all right here," Arch said. "Church is under God's roof. And this here's the reception hall. I'll show you 'round."

Arch drove me to a grove in his off-road truck with its two sets of tires to any normal car's one.

"This is the place," he said when we disembarked. "This is where I want to kiss my bride and solemnify the whole works. I don't want to be in a goddamned building, this is a thing for God to see, what's going to happen to me and her. Your man Donald just didn't seem to get it."

Here comes the bitch session, I thought. He'd been spoiling for it ever since I arrived. There'd been little drops, like the first pattering of rain before a deluge. Donald didn't know his flowers, Donald didn't get back to him quick enough with prices, he didn't think of options, he just did what Arch asked, whereas what Arch wanted was for you to come back with that plus more. Donald should have known that.

"Donald doesn't usually deal with event planning. That's my specialty."

"Well he's damn lucky to have you, darlin'. There ain't no two ways about that. I don't know why you stay with him, actually. You could do a whole lot better on your own. Hell, I'd help you get started. You could work in-house for me. I'd move you right on down here."

"Whoa, down, boy. Do I look like a Texan to you?" I presented myself: black jeans, white T-shirt, sandals. I had to admit I didn't particularly look like a New Yorker anymore, and I regretted the invitation to peruse.

"I don't know what you look like," Arch said, quietly. " 'Cept you look all right. What do you think of Veronica?"

"She's pretty," I kidded him, raising my eyebrows. Let's just shift any sexual tension right on over to the old stallion.

"Come on, girl. What do you think?"

"Arch, I've hardly said two words to her. I'd say she's got great manners."

We walked a little farther along the road. There was a glade of pines and poplars, and a creek about four feet wide flowing noisily that eddied around an outcropping of land. He'd chosen well. This would be what I'd want if it were me. I felt a pang at the thought.

"Hey, I sure am sorry about your father now. Donald told me he was a judge and all. I didn't realize."

I felt dangerously close to tears, something about the smell of pine and the sound of water and the solemnity of love and death. These could bring it on.

"Thank you," I managed to say, then I walked ahead of him. "So Arch, what if it rains?"

"It won't. Never does this time a year."

"God has a freaky sense of humor. Can we at least set up a tent?" I looked at him, but he was shaking his head. "Plan B, Arch. That's the name of the game."

Arch squatted down and picked up a twig.

"Caroline, honey," he said, looking up at me, snapping the wood. "I am the founder and proud CEO of a two-billion-a-year company. I know about contingencies. And I've learned that sometimes there shouldn't be one. If it rains, if that's God's joke for me, then fine. I'll laugh my head off. And I don't give a good goddamn if not one single, solitary guest stands witness. But me and the preacher and that woman, we're going to sanctify it right here. Got it?"

I nodded.

"Now. She wants to ride up on that dapple gray she's so crazy about. Can we do that?" He regarded me a moment. He had blue eyes that looked too light and clear to hold any power. Yet they managed to generate heat through their focus. I felt myself squirm. "The answer is no, by the way," he added.

"What's the matter with the horse? We could braid flowers into its mane, small pink ones. It would be gorgeous."

"I don't want the damn horse. You got to get me out of this. You do that, and honey, you can name your price. Anything you want. But I got to warn you—Veronica's a stubborn woman, and she's got her fool heart set on riding that horse. I think she'd marry him if she could."

I walked around the glade and sized it—we could have about twenty people here if we didn't have chairs. Maybe ten if we did. Chairs, small white ones, would look fabulous.

"I don't see what you have against the horse," I said. "You're always saying you want this to be the showstopper wedding. What could be more dramatic than to have your beautiful bride show off one of her most renowned talents?"

"She don't want to barrel-race him," Arch said.

"You want people sitting while you take the vows?"

"They can swing from the goddamned trees for all I care. Don't go changing the subject on me. No horse. Got it?"

I had it, though I was pretty sure the horse was integral to my overall design scheme. Pretty damn sure.

"How many people do you want at the actual ceremony?"

"No horse, Caroline. And something small—only 'bout a hundred or so."

"You need to trim that—they won't fit." I started to walk down the road, toward the house.

"It's a longer walk than it looks," he said. But I waved my hand behind my head and didn't look back.

The air felt sweet against my cheek. It smelled of apples, or grass coming up, a green scent that refreshed me. The doctor had seen Virgil and was horrified by his condition, but wasn't telling me something—I was certain of it. I felt guilty for saying yes to this trip. My impulsiveness, my greed for experience had made a mess of things. This thought kicked me with its big black boots as I walked along. I sought refuge in the breeze, the clarity of the light, the expanse. I could see Arch's house and the buildings around it—the pool house, sheds and barns and garages for all the equipment, animal, mineral and vegetable, required to make this concern go. It puzzled me that a man who spent the better part of fourteen hours a day managing a computer-chip firm would want to spend his off-hours managing all this. It looked like one decision after another, and I was weary of choices.

The road wound along beside the creek, hard-packed dirt. This would present logistical challenges for staging the ceremony. I judged it to be at least a half mile from the house. Too far for most of the guests to walk—women in their finery wouldn't want to, the great-aunts and elders of the church wouldn't be able to. So we would need—golf carts. Gold and white, and when she said gold, she meant the Vegas kind. I imagined festooning the carts with gold lamé ribbons and my heart sank. I could make it look beautiful, to specification. It just wasn't my notion of beauty, and I wished there were a disclaimer I could attach to the bottom of everything: Not my idea.

But where did the line between idea and execution lie? Weren't these ultimately my ideas, if I was the one bringing them to life?

Grass wavered in the breeze, deep green on top, silver along its underside. There was the rusty smell of creek and a splash of corn-flowers.

chapter 7

"These are heirloom tomatoes," Veronica tells me. She holds one toward me. I cup my hand around its red and green striations and smell it. Acid. Green acid.

Inside the hothouse, whitewashed glass dims down the harsh light. It rattles when there's a breeze, but other than that, no sound reaches us from outside. Tricklings and tremolos from the irrigation system, and a smell of loamy soil. It's another world here. The greenhouse has two rooms—we're visiting with the vegetables just now.

"Heirlooms—like your grandmother gave them to you?"

"No, silly, the seeds are old varieties that were lost for a while."

"I once was lost, but now am found," I sing. I can't help it.

"I love that song," she says. "It was written by a slaver. Did you know that?"

I didn't, and she tells me a story about the man bringing slaves across on his ship, and in the middle of the ocean, he realizes the suffering he's causing.

"So what did he do?" I ask. "Turn around? Back home, no harm done, or go ahead and then never again?"

"I don't know," she says. "What did you do, David?" she asks and her look is sidelong magic.

I step away and kneel to look at another plant.

"Green chilies," she says. "Very hot. Great in omelets."

"You must be excited with the wedding so close," I say.

She picks a yellowing leaf off the chili plant, her fingers close to my temple. I am still kneeling, as seems fitting. She studies the plant, gently turns its leaves upside down and runs her finger tip along its veins.

"How long have you been engaged?"

"I've known Arch forever," she says. "Look, here's a chili baby." She holds the nascent pepper toward me. It shines. "But we just sorta decided to do this." She gestures toward the roof, as if it meant *wedding*. "On the spur of the moment, you could say."

The second room of the greenhouse is filled with orchids, and I have to say, they creep me out. They look edible, but poisonous, the thick creamy petals and long woody stalks, like something a witch would use in her stews.

"My daddy grows these," she says. "Aren't they ugly?" She smiles at me. This room is darker than the other, and smells more dank.

"So you were in jail, you bad boy. What'd you do?" She stands close to me and gives off too much excitement on this topic.

"I don't want to talk about it."

"Now you know how I feel about this wedding stuff."

I ponder that for a moment. "I can't believe that."

"Doesn't matter what you believe, now does it?" Her eyes are sea green, foamy, direct. I want to swim there. "David, I'll make you a deal. We won't talk about jails or weddings, and we'll get along like a house on fire."

We step outside again. I start to leave.

"Don't," she says. "Not yet. You need to meet King."

When we near the barn she breaks into a run, all the way to the stall where the horse I saw her on that first time is waiting, his head hanging out the half door, gray fringy mane gently curling on his neck. He shakes his head. His nostrils are pale pink with black and gray spots that start in the skin and then become fur. He has square pupils and though Veronica has her arm around his neck and speaks to him in sweet tones—"Aren't you a proud old boy?"—the King has his eye on me.

"Ain't he a beauty?" she says, nuzzling him. "We been together ten years now. He don't like to run much anymore, but I'm still awful sweet on him. He's gonna carry me to the altar, aren't you boy?" She kisses King's nose.

"Really? You're going to ride him in a dress?"

She smiles wickedly. "Don't tell a soul this—and especially not that busybody cousin of yours—but I'm not wearing a dress. White jodhpurs and a white hunt coat." She squeals with pleasure. "My momma's the only other one who knows. She's sewing them for me."

She takes an oval grooming brush and goes into the stall, circling his coat with broad strokes.

"Hey," she says. "You wanna ride him? He's a gentle old beast."

I want to do anything she asks, but I do not want to climb up on the back of this animal glaring at me with naked violence in his square eyes. He'll trample me in a stallion's dance then eat sugar from her palm.

"Maybe another day. I should get back now."

"Why? What'd you have to do?"

I shrug.

"Suit yourself," she says turning back to King of the Wink. "But I got questions for you." She smiles and I drown a bit more. "And I mean to get answers."

Back in the pool house, I sit on a chair and flip through channels. Sun off the water casts white, wiggly shadows. There are 132 channels, including a closed-circuit station just for FirmShare, Arch's company. Programming includes highlights from last year's Christmas party—there's Arch dancing with Veronica. He's in a tux with a cummerbund that looks like blood, she's in a black velvet sleeveless thing that sparkles. They dance like they took lessons. I can practically see him counting the steps. But he's smiling like gangbusters, a million teeth to the average joe's measly mouthful, and she, of course, looks great. Graceful, at ease, distant but warm.

Now it's a speech to shareholders. Sober gray suit, dark blue tie. Half glasses on his thin nose, reading numbers. They must be good ones—big and getting bigger. Much applause as the camera pans the room. What home is complete without a press kit on the coffee table? Not Arch's. It tells me that FirmShare employs 21,578 souls worldwide. That's really a lot of people, all depending on this ostrich-raising buffoon for bread, butter, and soup on Sunday. He is four years older than me. I have exactly no one depending on me, not counting me, I guess. But I don't depend on me. I am other-directed. It takes a village for me to make it on a daily basis.

I scan the TV to see if she's in any shots. There, front row. Dark gray dress-jacket thing, purple scarf like a silk waterfall. She gazes down into her lap. I'd vote for him, despite misgivings, because four years of him would mean four years of her.

chapter 8

Through the window Virgil sees the day's brightness. He nods off against his will. Sleep is for sissies. He is strong enough to rise, to join the voices he hears occasionally, workers calling out to one another. He would dearly like to work, to labor at something, to plant a tree. That would satisfy him. Physical work, unassailably moral, a show of faith in the future.

But he is in bed, dozing like an old woman.

The doctor insists on this bed rest, having sussed out Virgil's condition. Virgil knows he has been an obstinate fool, a stubborn old coot. Should have stayed at the emergency room. Should have gone home, bed rest, tea and biscuits, bland food and daytime TV. Should not have sat in an inhospitable automobile for days on end, should not have indulged a disinterested lust. Should not have found David? No, hard to say that one.

I deserve a call, he thinks. There's a phone beside the bed, white and cordless, looks like human hands have never touched it. The whole room looks that way, blindingly white. Thick white carpets, his bed smothered in a white cutwork duvet and a cairn of pillows encased in white crocheted shams. The walls contrast all this ethereality in a buttery ivory, but the bookcases are white, the desk, the guest chair, the marble around the fireplace, white, white, white.

My kingdom for a color, he thinks and looks through the window to the yard. He can see the sky, a blue so faded it's almost white. The tops of a stand of poplars twirl in a breeze he does not feel, green silver, a thousand handkerchiefs waving at him, all the darlings of the world bidding him fond adieu.

He and Jane ended it in a restaurant on Michigan Avenue. She did not raise her voice or cry. She simply looked at him tenderly with her silvery eyes, so large, so deeply set, perfectly framed with the dark eyebrows—and said, "I believe I've had enough." He had affected the understanding cad, chivalrous beneath it all. Yes, of course. The house, of course. Custody, of course. Who was he to fight such demands? Too many late nights with Charlene. Was that her name? Sydney? There was an Agnes, too, around that time. Agnes who'd been a nun. My God, how she'd cried. Agnes, not Jane. Jane cried when David was feverish once. And probably at times Virgil didn't see, probably about him. He had probably made her cry.

He reaches for the phone. The nurse enters to take his vitals. And they feel taken from him—blood pressure, temperature, pulse, twice daily, as if the pulse might slip away in the interim, or his blood against the walls of his veins fall to imperceptibility. She is a young Hispanic girl in blue scrubs, crepe-soled shoes, a plume of long black hair down her back. Her touch is warm on his wrist. Virgil smiles at her, but she concentrates on her watch, counting each beat of his heart.

"You look better today," she says, her English accented.

"Yes?" Virgil has not seen himself in at least a day. He has not shaved and the stubble itches. "That's good to hear."

"You'll be up in no time. Are you here for the wedding?" She puts her stethoscope on his chest and the cold of it makes him jump. "Take a few deep breaths for me," she says. She strokes his back lightly. It tingles. He wants this touch.

She takes the stethoscope off him and says, "It sounds like there's fluid in your lungs. You need X rays."

"No," Virgil says. "I'm not here for the wedding."

The nurse looks at him, exasperated he thinks. The social chatter isn't the important stuff. How could he forget that? You need X rays, man, X rays! Beams breaking through the cells to show the bones, the dark patches of his lungs and whatever gurgles inside them. It hurts to breathe, though he won't divulge this tidbit. It's his own damn business how breathing feels.

This is how it will be then. Efficiency and cold metal against his skin. The warmth of her hand modulated by the cool professionalism of her touch. Lying back on this mound of white, knowing the day is hot but not feeling it—shit, this can't be the last of it. He will recover, he will climb again, and fuck. That too. Who was the last? Quick, quick, quick. Beverly. But before that. Quick. A woman named Maureen. Delectable high arches. Virgil lies back on the bed and wants to be hard, but he isn't. He wants to be here for the wedding. But he isn't.

Just outside the window, from a low branch he hears chirping. The nurse washes her hands in the adjacent bathroom. Water running and chirping. He hears these things.

He has fallen before. Lost his small purchase, slapped at rock in the panic of descent. He once lost it on an overhang and dangled there, the harness gouging his scrotum, until his partner hauled him up. And he'd hauled up others. Falling happens when you climb.

He dozes again then flips through the latter-day chat shows. Large women, usually, talking to herds of illiterates. He imagines their dinners of hamburgers and fries and soft drinks, layering around them all the comfort of fat.

"I can't believe you're watching that," Caroline says. She looks like the goddess of spring to him, despite the black pants and gray sweater.

"What would you prescribe, doctress?"

She ponders a moment, smiling a small smile, almost private, for internal consumption. "Seven Hail Marys, two Our Fathers." She puts a large binder down on the bed in front of him. "Which cake?"

Virgil looks through page after page of outlandishness. Cakes shaped like mansions, golf clubs, clown heads, rosebushes, horses. Not just a horse's head, but a free standing, four-legged beast, saddled in buttercream, a blanket of frosting roses draped on its neck.

"A Derby winner," Caroline explains.

"I like it," Virgil says.

"So does Veronica. I think she'd marry the horse if she could."

"Well, it's a tough choice." He smiles, and she gives him one back, more than family, warmer than work. The real McCoy.

"Have I told you what a beautiful woman you are? Have I told you how happy I am to see you? Have I told you the one about the traveling salesman and the farmer's daughter?"

She sits on the bed beside him and bats the pillows around.

"Arch is a controlling pain in the ass," she says. "I'm sorry for Veronica."

"Why is she marrying him?"

"Beats me. She's got her own money."

"You can always use more. Especially when you're rich."

"I suppose." She looks toward the window, then back at the pillows, the bed. She is never still. "How are you?"

"Bored beyond belief."

"Think healing thoughts, uncle dear. Have you talked to David?" He shakes his head, wishes she hadn't mentioned this. "You should, you know. You need to."

"Jesus, Caroline. Who's a controlling pain in the ass now?"

She looks at him with genuine hurt, then gathers up the binder of absurd cakes, decadence made manifest—can't she see that?—and takes her own sweet breath of unconscious vitality out the door. He wants to sing out to her not to leave, not ever. He wants to tell her that she won't always move with such ease. There will be aches.

"I'm sorry," he says. "I'm so sorry."

chapter 9

After leaving Virgil, I found Veronica—where else?—at the barn. She was brushing down King of the Wink's flank with an oval brush strapped across her hand, smoothing him with her free hand after each stroke. His coat rippled silver, with spots resembling lunar landscapes, gray on gray. All subtlety.

"He's beautiful," I said.

"Ain't he?"

"I keep seeing him with pink roses braided into his mane and tail."

"That would be pretty. But I ain't much on pink. You ride, Caroline?"

"I went to horse camp for a few summers. Happiest time of my life."

We were together in silence a while. Hay and saddle soap and leather tack tinged the air. A dog slept in a shaft of sun shining through slats in the barn. Dust circled in columns above him in the light.

"Arch doesn't want you to ride in the ceremony," I said.

She rolled her eyes. "I know."

"Do you know why?"

"Not a clue. Maybe you can illuminate me."

"I'd say it looks like he's a jealous man."

Veronica's hair was pulled back in a long ponytail and her face shone from the exertion of brushing down this large creature.

"That's the smartest thing I've heard you say," she said. She put down the oval brush and now worked over King's coat with a pair of wood brushes, one in each hand, that clacked together when their arcs intersected across his stomach. "My question to you is how you gonna convince him? He's a stubborn old dog."

"He said the same thing about you. Except he didn't call you a dog. He's too in love with you for that."

"You think so, huh?" She didn't sound insecure. She sounded knowing, and like whatever she knew had scorched her.

"That's how it looks to me," I said.

"Well," she said after a long pause, and she paused again. "Mostly love's a thing you steal." She circled the coat again and the brushes punctuated her words. "That way you control it." She turned to the horse and started to comb his mane with yet another implement. "So you see, I'm riding this horse. And Mr. Archer C. Demwalt the one, two, third can kiss my sweet ass if he doesn't like it. He needs me more'n I need him."

"How's that?"

"Come on, Caroline. You know. He's a boy, and a boy needs a captive wife. I'll get a lot of freedom there. I know you know." She put down the comb and looked directly at me now. "I think you and I are about the same thing."

"Except no billionaire is making it legal with me."

She shrugged. "You're not trying is all."

"How 'bout this. I'll tell Arch you agreed, then you can do what you want. Break the rules. Hell, it's your wedding."

"No thanks. I'm not going into this thing a liar. That's your job." She turned back to the horse and cooed low and throaty. King of the Wink had soft brown eyes, and he dipped his head and snorted.

chapter 10

I nod off in a sunny patch on the velveteen sofa. That word nod, a danger word. I mean that I dozed, napped, a cat addicted to the warmth. Addicted. God, listen to me.

The sofa faces a wall of glass framing the pool, and white shadows of the water's motion ripple on the floor. A bird sings lullingly. Don't be scared. Be at peace. I can't believe where I am, and even in my dozing, I keep an eye half cocked in case this turns chimera on me. These things happen—what's the line, I could be a pair of ragged claws scuttling? I could indeed. Already have, in fact.

I am on the lookout for the smell of urine on the concrete floor where I slept my first night in jail, after Douglas finished his ministrations. I'm alert to the shivers of that particular life, the chills that won't subside, the mattress lumps, the sleeplessness of cold aches, jonesing and fear, my whole cosmology crashing at once. Not to mention the company of men who will smack me for my knowledge of large words, who cry in the night and discuss the Rapture or the wrath of Allah or whatever vengeful fantasy they can wrap their mitts around. In these moments, like a sap, Sunday-school residuals jump eagerly to mind. Samson brought that crash on himself, elected his destruction. I don't have the fiber to make that choice, but the crash came all the same.

When I wake, my T-shirt is tacky with sweat. Disgusting to be so sticky. Sleep and its attendant succulence makes me feel way out of control. I take a shower and the water scalds me clean. My body is pink with pain but I don't want to get out. I don't want anything but to shoot up. The thought of Veronica back there in the barn makes me hard. What tawdry nonsense sexuality is. There is soap in the shower, and I use it and get some relief. But it's temporary; the thought comes back. The real thought, the one behind thoughts of

Veronica or the other scrims life uses to deflect our attention from truth. Craving is a thought. Though I feel it along my arms, in my stomach, those are echoes. The source material, the gong itself, is up top, packed into the cranium.

Stop all other thoughts. That's what this thought is about, that's why it's so huge and strong and arrogant, why it needs so much space and attention. It's a jealous god, this craving. It is going to protect me from all the piddly-shit thoughts, from counting pennies to make the mortgage. It is going to immortalize me, make me bigger than I am. I am a thin guy, though tall. And I've always been thin, it's not just a drug thing. I was all points and angles as a teenager, my long neck like a sharpened pencil rising from my button-down shirts. Damn if I'm not back in the same wardrobe. Maybe Caroline's vision of me isn't so great after all, maybe she only sees me as I was, not the me of me, the mighty me. Veronica, I think, sees it. And I'm stirred again.

I towel off and prowl around the guest house, the towel my skirt. The refrigerator contains some soda pop, and fruit and cold cuts, and there's a plastic bag of bread on the counter that the cook brought down this morning. Just made it, she told me. She smiled a lot, a large woman with hair like chrome, plumpness pushing her apron. I will have a sandwich. Thus will I crave less.

I slather mustard on the bread. There is also mayonnaise, but I distrust its whiteness, its texture. It's a tasteless bit of froth, but mustard stings your mouth, so it's all right. Then the cold cuts: thin slices of something red—more ostrich? I can't put it between the bread. I can't even touch it, so I leave it out. A fly lands nearby.

With the two slices of mustardized bread, I open the doors out to the pool and stretch myself on a chaise. That cook slices her bread mighty thickly, and biting into it is like biting the softest pillow. It's perfect, except there's too much mustard. The bread is overpowered. I stand up to go scrape some of it off and the towel falls from me, but I go in anyway, and get rid of the yellow stuff.

"Knock-knock." I hear Veronica's voice and see her peering into the glass door that opens into the kitchen. She has now seen my rear.

I dash to the bedroom and hear her let herself in.

"Were you skinny-dipping? Scandalous!"

"No," I stammer as I jackknife myself into a pair of jeans. They're new and stiff and unyielding and I fall on the floor.

"What in the Sam Hill are you doing?"

I don't answer. I don't want to go out. I have become permanently blushed.

I push myself out the door.

"Sorry."

"What for?" she asks. She pulls chunks of bread off the loaf and feeds herself, then does the same with the cold cuts. "What'd you do today?" She hoists herself up and sits on the kitchen counter, continuing to eat.

"Do you want me to make you a sandwich?"

She brightens.

"Would you?"

I make up the sandwich I couldn't eat, slice it on the diagonal, plate it, and serve her.

"You do that nice."

She takes the sandwich and flops down on the couch, leaning deeply into its curves, its shining pillows. "Milk?" she says.

Milk it is.

"You were buck naked, weren't you."

I resume my status as a red thing. "I don't know what got into me. It's just, it's the first time I've been warm."

The jones creeps back into my elbows. I want to rip out my veins. I blame them, with their grotesque appetites.

"What're you all squirmy for? I won't bite." She bites the sandwich with an audible chomp.

"It isn't you. It's, well, me."

"So I see. You didn't tell Caroline about my bridal outfit, did you?"

"Why would I?"

"You two are as close as raindrops in a puddle. I don't want anyone to know till the day arrives and I ride up on that beautiful animal, and blow up my life. Ka-boom!" She throws herself about on the couch like a rowdy kid. I get the feeling she's been drinking or something. I'd guess drinking. cocaine would be a choice, too, for a girl of her means. But she doesn't strike me as the type. Probably did it once or twice, because she could, a certain unearned promiscuity. But not more than a couple of times. And she's certainly not a heroin girl. Much too speedy for my preferred bliss.

"You did something," I say.

"What do you mean?"

"Drank a bit," I suggest, and I look at her with a question in my face.

"Might have. Why shouldn't I? I'm a-gonna get married to one rich fella, why shouldn't I celebrate that joyous fact with a few of my personal favorites?"

I went back to the kitchen and began to make coffee. I hate to combine two dehydrating substances, but she needed it.

"David, why don't you like me?" she says.

"I like you fine. Who wouldn't?" Coffee drips through the machine, filling the air with a smell of metal and heat, of things burning. Not my smell.

I bring the cup to her. She's crying.

"Oh come on now. Drink this."

I hand her the cup but don't—can't—sit down. I cross my arms in front of me, grasping my elbows, and I start to scratch. And I don't stop. Scratch, scratch, scratch, I tear into that guilty flesh, red and scabbed over with white flakes, white shelves of me that no longer feel, except that something in them reaches down from their own death into the living me and the only way to eradicate it is to scratch. A petal of blood blooms in my elbow.

"Dang, boy," she says. "Don't scratch so hard." She gets up and wobbles toward the bathroom, and returns with a washcloth, a white one, soaked in hot water, and she swabs my arm. She holds the cloth against me and the red disk widens among the strands of terry.

"Silly one," she says, and her voice is practically inside me, almost my own. I recognize it, I have heard it in the depths of nodding. It's the voice that says *more*.

On her breath, the air is wine and cinnamon.

"I should go," I say.

"Where you gonna go? This is you."

I should go, this isn't right. Your proximity unsettles me. I should go, I should go, should go. I am back to grabbing my elbows. She touches the cloth to me again, then rubs it across my forehead.

"I know all about you, David Harris. Saw your file on my father's big old oak desk back home." She rubs my forehead again and the bread inside my stomach opts out of digestion. I vomit on the rug. "Poor silly duck. I'm gonna put you to bed."

And she does. She leads me to my room, and leaves while I take off my jeans. I climb into bed as fast as I can, which—let's be honest—isn't that fast. But I don't want her to see me in my underwear. When she comes back, she has a bowl of warm water and a new white cloth. How wonderful her world is—the blood disappears, and the cotton of these cloths, irresistibly high.

"You're so lucky," I tell her.

"Oh, yeah. Sure am." She has folded the cloth and it rests on my forehead, held in place with the light pressure of her palm.

"How come you're so sarcastic?" I ask.

"Don't talk now. Rest up. Cook's making vegetarian for you tonight." Before she leaves, she kisses my cheek, and her lips trail across mine for the softest moment.

chapter 11

Why he has to come to Texas to have the best gumbo he's ever tasted Virgil doesn't know, or why should it be that Arch plays a surprisingly soulful Cajun fiddle and sings on key in an affecting baritone—these talents seem unfair in a man with so much money, the man who gets the girl and all the toys. While the rest of them sit about in their chairs sated, Virgil eats. More cornbread, more gumbo, more salad, more sweet potatoes. More beer, though the doctor has told him to abstain. Alcohol impedes healing. Healing is not an option. Ergo, reckless old coot.

Arch starts a waltz, a sad and pretty thing. Virgil stands and bows to Caroline, extending his hand. She accepts and curtsies and follows his lead like a shadow, fitting her motions to his, flowing and trusting the way the best partners do. The cook stands in the doorway to the kitchen with her hands together as if praying. She smiles without boundaries, a thing mere lips cannot contain.

"I'm going to hold you close now and really dance," Virgil says, and he pulls her in and exaggerates the turns. Caroline wears a white blouse and black skirt and a circle of pale jade around her neck, hanging from a black ribbon. Virgil's eye travels just below the jade. Her skin is so white.

"About today," he says.

"Never mind," Caroline answers. "You're exhausted."

"No, I'm sorry. Don't let me pull that."

David and Veronica sit near one another, watching the dancers, David looking pained. Dad the fool again.

The waltz ends and everyone claps. Veronica gets up and stretches, says good night. David's eyes follow her. The boy has a crush.

"Wait," Virgil says to her. "I want to make a toast."

"Well, then, just go 'head and do," Veronica says.

Virgil raises a bottle of beer and looks at his son, his niece, at the rich boy and the beautiful girl he gets to marry, at the cook who still stands in the doorway and the woman behind her poised to clear things away whenever the ruckus ends.

"I have been reminded, these last few days, lying in that room with not much to do but look at air, I have been reminded that you don't learn much in life. In my life I've made a bit of money, and at the time that seemed special. I've climbed some mountains and while I was doing it, nothing else could come close. That was living. But when you climb, you fall. You fall into dark holes, you dangle off cliffs with nothing around you but blue sky and hard rock. I've done a lot of things wrong in my life, given in to too many impulses without learning a thing from them, disappointed people, disappeared without a trace. There are things I've done that I would give anything—any piece of my flesh, any limb or organ you could name—I'd give anything to change the way I've gone through time. But it doesn't work that way. You don't learn that much in life, but you learn a little bit. And I want you two," he indicates Arch and Veronica. Arch has stepped over to her and holds her waist from behind. "I want you to practice hanging in there. When you fall, it's panicking that kills you. What you two are doing, that's a scary bit of business. So when the hard times hit, don't panic. Just hang in there. And forgive."

He slumps down into a chair and raises his beer high again. "Here's to you. Thanks for your kindness."

Arch picks up his own beer and says, "That's about the gloomiest goddamn toast I ever heard. But I thank you." He pulls on the beer and bangs it down on the table.

"I thank you, too," Veronica says, and she kisses Virgil's forehead. "And now, for real, good night." She kisses Arch with a flourish.

"Yee-ow!" He yells, and hands the fiddle to the cook. "Play us a fast one. Maisie's the best."

Maisie steps into the room, pounds a tempo with her foot, and begins pulling and scratching. Out comes an evanescent sound, "Turkey in the Straw," but as if sung by a choir of tomcats, low and guttural, sexual and strong. Arch holds his hands out to Caroline and begins a two-step.

"I don't know this one," she says.

"Don't you worry, honey, I'm driving."

Virgil sits opposite David, and watches as Caroline moves stiffly at first, then with fluid energy as the steps enter her body, becoming hers to play with. Virgil moves to the seat next to his son. David sits rigidly, holding his arms, his head cocked down.

"You all right?" Virgil asks.

"Hell, yeah," David says. "It's just, you know"—and now he looks up at the ceiling—"it's just everything."

"I love you, David," he says, but the music's loud, and Caroline lets out a whoop that Arch answers, and probably, David hasn't heard.

chapter 12

The next days flew by in a whirlwind. I was on the phone nonstop, calling in every favor I had, waving Arch's money like a magic wand, making a wedding appear where there was no wedding before, resplendent in white and gold.

I have games I play when I do such things. How quickly can I close the deal is one. The florist held out. It's too sudden, I can't source the flowers. The bouquets were to be nothing but white blooms—roses, plus lilies of the valley and gardenias, really fragrant, all tied together with elaborate gold ribbon. I had designed them in ten minutes at 4:00 A.M. the morning of the impromptu hoedown, when I awoke, restless, to the sound of distant lowing. David was up, too, watching cartoons in the living room, so I sat with him and sketched this out.

"You all right?" I asked him, and I was too distracted to have heard the lie in his answer.

"Oh yeah, fine."

"What do you think," I said, showing him the sketch. He smiled at me.

"Purty, real purty."

We stayed up together, silent, till sunrise, all crimson and peach across the lightening blue sky.

"Jesus, have you ever seen anything so beautiful?" I asked. When I looked over at him, after a long silence, he was crying.

That morning I shared the menu with Arch.

Sit-down four-course meal for 250. The menu had to walk the line between elegant and edible, which in this part of the world, I came to gather, meant unadorned meat. The appetizers could be groundbreaking, but the entrée needed to be the best red meat yet to be barbecued in these parts. Ostrich and veal, and vegetables from Veronica's garden—the fruits of the ranch, secretly augmented by the local organic farm, as hers was more in the realm of hobby than cornucopia.

"I don't know how you do it," he said when he saw it. "Why aren't you married, Caroline? I don't get it."

"Too prickly."

"I don't believe that. Look how beautifully you've done everything."

"Listen, Arch. There's a difference between giving the client what he wants and making choices for your own life. Don't get confused here. It's beautiful, I hope, because it's what you've asked for, to the letter. That's my job."

"Okay, hold on there, don't get your back up." We were at another breakfast, the two of us as usual. Veronica had stopped in for a quick gasp of coffee and a roll, clad in breeches and T-shirt, heading to the barn. We ate on the terrace, which overlooked an equestrian ring, and watched her take King through his paces. She had set up a steeplechase course, with water traps and sharp turns in the jump pattern. King of the Wink executed each leap like Pegasus.

"You know, Arch, I don't mean to say anything, but she doesn't seem that interested in the wedding," I said.

"Well, hell, Caroline. Any fool could see that." He smiled at my relief. "I figure she's like that horse—just needs some room to run around. I give her that, and I just might have the best wife around. At least I'll have the woman I want, 'stead of half the men I know, married to their mothers or the first woman who said yes, or some young thing, got a hold of them by the gonads."

"You're not worried, then."

"Hell, no. A baby or two, and she'll forget old King of the Wink." He snapped his fingers to indicate, I guess, the simplicity of the human heart.

"You're a wonder, Archer Demwalt."

"Oh, shush now. I'd say the same damn thing to you if I knew you well enough."

"Good thing you don't, then." I didn't believe in the curative power of babies, or any other easy answers to matters of amour. It seemed a matter like snow to Eskimos—love was simply not word enough for all the things that love could mean.

"You should let her ride to the ceremony. I can tell you this: she's going to do it with your permission or not. Let her, and you build some loyalty. Fight it, and you're starting your marriage as a war."

He looked thoughtful for a while, down into his coffee cup, and then out to the ring where Veronica posted up and down, trotting King along the perimeter fence.

"Marriage is a war."

He had my attention now.

"You're a woman, and God love you, that means you want peace. But I know some different things. Did you know I was a pilot in Vietnam?"

I hadn't known.

"Yeah, true fact. I shot napalm at trees, burned villages. Now I'm not saying that was such a great thing, but I learned a thing or two there. Sometimes in a fight, you got to make it hotter for people. You have to go against the conciliatory grain to win."

"Earth to Arch: we didn't win in Vietnam."

"That's not my point and you know it."

"You want to break her."

"She's a horsewoman. She understands." He folded his napkin. My shock at this introduced an awkwardness between us, instantly available as a scent we couldn't ignore. "I'm in my office all day. You call if you need anything, honey." He leaned down and kissed my cheek. I turned my lips to him and he kissed me there, too.

"Arch," I said. I wanted to bite him, to draw blood.

But he was striding toward the garage, his cell phone appended to his ear.

chapter 13

The backseat of the Mercedes has deep bucket seats of glove leather. The exterior is navy blue. We have a driver, Veronica and I. She has declared that I need a bathing suit—"You can't keep swimming in your birthday suit," she'd said. "The staff is scandalized." The staff. So here we are, the two of us cruising so quickly and without bumps that it is as if we aren't moving at all, the way airplane travel feels. She leafs through a fashion magazine, folding down corners of pages.

The mall has a marble entryway, and glass doors fifteen feet tall, brass handled, opened for us by men in uniforms. We enter into a cosmetics area. Waves of florals and sandalwoods and musk notes gallop out to meet me. I sneeze. Veronica has on a short skirt, boots, and a long coat, looking a bit retro, like Ali McGraw in *Love Story*. I expect her to drop dead of cancer at any moment, after giving up a promising career as a pianist. That's love.

Except, of course, she's the preppy, and I'm the scholarship case up from poverty.

"Your dossier said you went to Brown," she says.

"I dropped out, though."

"Brown's a good school."

By now we're in a wide corridor of commerce, part perfumes and cosmetics still, and part jewelry, each category an island unto itself. There are reefs of cases in which diamonds glitter, and a central podium where a tall slim girl pushes the buttons of a cash register.

"Why'd you drop out?" she asks. She leans over each jewelry case. I want to see what her eyes see, what she makes of so much sparkle.

"Wasn't that in the dossier, too?"

"I want to hear your story."

I look at her. "Where are the swim trunks?"

"Oh David's gonna get all petulant now." She pinches my cheek.

"Don't."

"You left because of mental instability. That's what the file said."

"Well, there you go." I feel tears rising in me. The smell, the lights and glitter, the sight of a woman with unwavering blond hair chiffoned around her scalp and the eyebrows in contrasting shit brown—I want out.

A slim saleswoman approaches us, exotic, maybe from Somalia or Ethiopia. "Can I help y'all?"

Veronica indicates a diamond necklace she wants to try on, stones shaped like luminous teardrops.

"When I was fifteen," she says, holding it up to her neck, "I used to come here and look at these and think, someday I'm gonna walk in and buy one." She turns to the clerk. "I'll take it," and she hands over a charge card bearing Arch's name.

"Oh, right away, Mrs. Demwalt. Would you care to wait in our preferred-customer lounge? I think you'd be more comfortable, and I could bring this to you."

"Fine."

The clerk leads us to a doorway behind a side salon. She whispers to the hostess.

"Mrs. Demwalt, it's a honor. What can I bring you?"

"A bottle of Veuve Clicquot and a selection of men's swim trunks. The bottle should be corked—and bring an ice bucket."

The woman hurries away.

"I was just the daughter of a cop." Veronica laughs.

The room has no windows. It's papered with a wickery covering the color of asparagus. Veronica sits on a couch, and I take a Louis XIV chair in white crushed velvet. Gauche. She looks relaxed and beautifully in her element, and I work hard to avoid connecting the two observations.

The champagne comes and Veronica opens it and pours us each a glass. I shake my head.

"David, have some fun."

"It's not fun. It's poison."

She laughs. "Honey, it's liberation." She holds up her glass and clinks it with mine.

We drink deep, but I drink faster. And she refills me. Pronto.

Substances disappear time, and we drink and laugh and evaluate the merits and demerits of a variety of swim trunks. Her diamond necklace arrives in a velvet box, but she ignores it.

She selects the sky blue swimsuit, long boxer trunks that I imagine will pull me down to the bottom of the deep end and hold me there till the last bubbles gurgles surfaceward.

"Let's go," she says, and her slightest motion, her very breath it seems, stirs the minions. Your car, your packages, sign here please. She hands the champagne bottle to the hostess. "I need a bag for this."

One is procured. The Mercedes awaits.

"I need to go to my apartment, Enrique," she says to the driver. Dallas, with its mirror buildings refracting the vast, terrifying sky, passes silently by outside the window.

"How can you stand all this?" I ask.

"What?"

"The size of things."

She looks puzzled and takes the champagne out of the bag. "Have some." She holds the bottle to my mouth and tilts, and doesn't lower it until champagne cascades down my front. "You hog," she says.

Soon the car moves through tree shaded streets and stops in front of a squat two-story building.

"I'll call when I'm ready," she says to the driver, and then she looks at me, a look that says 'come on then.' No nonsense, hard stuff, sharp angles in her round, soft eyes. Yes ma'am. But I feel a little wobbly from the drinking. Or from the extravagance, the foolishness of it. I don't need swim trunks and these had cost $250. She surely doesn't need the necklace.

But then again, it's not about need.

She is already up the stairs unlocking her door, a large white door inlaid with red and black Chinese characters.

"What's this mean?" I ask.

"Do I look Chinese?"

Veronica's apartment begins in mirrors. Mirrors make the vestibule walls and reflect a side table with a red marble top, on which a black vase holds long red roses, roasting beneath a spotlight. Dramatic but not beautiful, not a joyous start. The living room is white and glass, so it feels bigger than it is, more open, which makes me nervous.

She disappears into another room, and I mill about. Normally I would look at a bookshelf or a music collection, but she has neither. There are photos on her glass desk—King of the Wink, with and without her on his back, a big one of Arch in a silver frame. The word "official" pops to mind, the official picture of the official boyfriend, larger than any other photo, prominently placed, everything on the up and up.

"Come here a second, will you?" she calls from wherever she is. I walk down a hallway past one room filled with clothing in boxes and on hangers. "Here I am," she says.

It's her bedroom, immaculate, all white again, except for the large four-poster bed of oxidized copper. She lies on top of it and what do my wondering eyes behold, beside her there, a hypodermic and a bag of Horse, and the rest of the kit and caboodle.

"Oh, no," I say.

"Oh, yes."

Not this, I say, or at least I think it very intently. *It would be wrong for me and certainly wrong for you to start.*

"I'm getting married in a week," she says. "Don't you think I should walk on the wild side at least once?"

Something tells me she's walked there at least once before.

"I need something to remember you by," she says, close to my ear, her hot breath thrilling to the small hairs that make sound.

Her windows are double paned and vaguely green in tint. Trees shroud us, and I have a sense that we are high up in the air, far away from the noisome concerns of the ground. Exempt. She looks at me with her liquid grass eyes, perfectly round, perfectly lashed. I will drown there.

I tie her arm with rubber tubing. She has moist towelettes and I swab her elbow where the vein is already rising. She takes the needle like a kiss.

A small dab of blood seeps from her elbow, her inside out, and she swoons. "Oh, my," she says and she lies back. "Now you."

Now me. I had said to myself and to others, which is the same thing, when I was in jail, that I would not be doing this again. I believed that I had taken my final exam in heroin and that for failing, I'd been incarcerated, internal reality matched by external circumstances, as is always the case. We do create our worlds, thought by thought by thought.

But the exam is infinitely trickier, more lovely and promising, irresistible.

I do not take the needle so easily, my veins being old warhorses hardened in the battle for oblivion. At last I find one on my left foot, between my third and fourth toe, far from the brain, far from the heart, the pleasure centers. She watches me shoot into the crack. And on it comes, waves breaking slowly, slower, slowest, then stopping mid-curl, all life suspended.

"How do you feel?" I ask.

She hums "Have Yourself a Merry Little Christmas."

"I'm having one," she says.

The great thing about turning on is the disappearance. The troubling hesitations, the moral qualms as well as the more metaphysical barriers between self and other—all gone. We lie together on her bed. Metallic cherubs—precious metals, gold, silver, copper—bless us from the wallpaper that circles the top of the room. The ceiling is painted sky. So this is heaven.

Could be, could very well be.

I stroke her forearm, and it is the most astonishing texture. Skin. Smooth, soft, pliant, warm with the blood of a human, containing the her of her, a border, a beginning, an end, terra incognita.

We lie in the emptiness, the quiet, the absence, looking at the tarty painted ceiling sky, far superior to the true nothingness above this house, above this world. This one has visible borders, a safe rectangle boxing up the infinite. And beside me, a woman I love, our untouching bodies bound in pure intimacy. I have entered her as steel, and delivered a man's blow, pure bliss.

That it is night I can tell from how the darkness outside matches the darkness within. Veronica snores lightly at my side. So we have slept. It might be eight or midnight or some evil early hour of morning, its stillness ruffled by devils winging through mind and air. Either way, I don't care for the moment. I feel full, as if I'd gorged on turkey and stuffing, football and parades—homey satisfactions, binged and binged again. The coverlet clings to my sweaty cheek. I'm thirsty and my tongue tastes of salt.

"Veronica," I whisper. "We should go, huh?"

She doesn't stir. I touch her on the shoulder. Her breath quickens and she makes a small worried sound, a child dreaming. Her hair lies in a wing across the pillow, high contrast in the silver light streaming in through the window. I touch it, its infinite softness. A place I could die happily.

But she doesn't stir, and I don't have the heart to wake her, or kill myself in delectation of her. So I lie beside her, trying to time my breaths to hers, but it's no use, hers are even and long, unspeakably relaxed, and I feel rising in me the shallow breath of lawyerly worry, as if my life's complaints have sworn out complaints and lined up inside my brain, each to plead its case this very night.

Complaint one: Another man will marry this woman. This man does not see beyond the striking beauty to the simple girl within, the cop's daughter. That phrase of hers rings in my ears, her laughter at the dumb luck of it. I have nothing to offer her, no VIP salon at Neiman-Marcus, no cash on the barrelhead, nothing but an affinity for substance that won't suffice as a foundation to lasting love.

Complaint two: Heroin tastes too good, too full of oblivion. It frees me. I have been out of the cage, and now, in this post-liberation moment, the bars resolidifying thanks to the mercurial magic of the mind, now freedom's residue haunts me, wind in willows, storm-lashed fronds tapping the window, come play, they sing, come back. We miss your molecules in the air around us.

Sod off, you fucking fronds. You don't know me.

Which leads to complaint three: What do you do with what you learn on drugs? No separation, for instance—what do I do with that priceless bit of knowledge, that the lovely woman beside me, so mysterious in her beauty, her thoughts veiled from my limited capacities for comprehension, this creature the same as me? Preposterous. Yet I hold it to be true. Now what?

By the time I get to number four, I am awash in tears, snot mixed in, salinity scorching my cheeks. To love or not be loved, to know things or dwell in ignorance, to abstain or drink deep—either way you suffer. I see the gray of the trackless gray area, stretching out, fog on fog, ad infinitum.

"David, I'm falling," she says dreamily, lifting her head slightly, then dropping it as if discovering its weight.

"You're safe," I say. "Absolutely safe."

"I don't know where . . . what," her voice seeps into the pillow as she turns her head away.

"Whatever," I say, and touch her hair, now spreading across her shoulder, flowing toward me like heavenly lava.

Under the blankets, we remain silent as if sleeping, but I sense she's awake, and I certainly am. I may never sleep again.

"When is it safe to do more?" she asks.

"Umm," I think a moment. "Pretty much never."

"Don't go puritanical on me now. Not you."

"No fooling, Veronica."

She turns on her back and stretches her arms up over her head. "So what I want to know is"—she rolls onto her side and draws a finger down my cheek—"tell me about jail."

"It rhymes with quail," I say.

"David. Come on. Are we just going to be people who did drugs together?"

"And loved each other from afar," I offer.

"Why don't you love me up close, right now?"

"You're about to get married."

"Which means I'm not married yet." She reaches under the covers and puts her hand on my penis and begins to pull, resting her intoxicating head on my chest.

Nothing happens. I mean, not down there. Plenty is going on in my head. Just zero in the lower regions.

"I don't think it will work, sorry to say."

She lifts her head to look at me, then pulls more vigorously. No use.

"A downside of the drug," I say.

"That's one hell of a downside." She holds up the covers to look. "How dare you," she says to my crotch. "You'll just have to please me some other way."

I have no idea how. There's only been the one woman, that one time, and we'd only done it the baby-making way. I put my hand tentatively on her shoulder.

"I have no right to a woman as beautiful as you," I say to her ear, beginning to succumb to the hair, the touch.

"Some things are just given." She guides my hand to her breast, which I circle with my fingertips and am rewarded with her nipple rising to my touch.

She shows me how to do more things that please her, and the sound of her joy humbles me. I would do anything to hear it again. She kisses me and holds me and says, "You learn fast," but although I want to be inside her, my own insides are in collapse. I let myself be held.

"Really," she says. "What was it like?"

"Wonderful," I say, and nuzzle her.

"I mean that thing that rhymes with quail."

"The opposite of this. The absolute opposite."

"Did you get raped?"

"What?"

"I hear that happens a lot."

"No, I didn't get raped. Look, Veronica. It's over. I'm lucky that it's over, and I want it to stay over, so I think that talking about it is like not what I should do."

"You're wrong about that. It'll never be truly over until you talk about it." She thumps my chest softly with a finger to emphasize the point.

"Did your shrink tell you that?"

She rolls away. "Don't talk to me like that."

I'm sorry. But I can't say so.

She gets out of the bed and gathers her clothes.

"Don't. Not yet. Not all angry," I say.

She looks at me with hard eyes.

"I'm sorry," I say. "I know you're trying to help. I have a kind of a hard time with intimacy."

"You think I don't?" She sits back down beside me.

"Why are you marrying that guy?"

She pulls one leg of her hosiery up her right leg. " 'Cause he wants me to."

"Great reason."

She punches me on the arm. "Who knew you were such a sarcastic little prick."

"I don't think you should. I don't think you want to."

"You're wrong and right."

She dresses the rest of the way. I can't help but watch, and she performs for me, pointing her toes into her shoes, gyrating into her skirt.

"What'll I do with this," she says, tapping the baggie of Horse. It makes a crinkly, wave-break plastic sound.

Feed the winds with it. Snow it down the sewer. Sprinkle on pond, attach to asteroid. Anything but what you want. Decide who you are. Close your eyes and look at the shape of your life, see it there in the months ahead, in the years—see your life. What is its shape, its color and vibration? What are you going to feed—the inner or the outer? Decide. One more shot, and it's all outer, it's flu when you're not sick, it's your whole life's worth of longing, everything you've ever wanted, yearned for or hoped, shrunk to a pinprick and a plunge.

"Give it to me," I say.

To my amazement, she does. Though not right away. I have to shower first. When I emerge from the bathroom, she's on the phone in the kitchen. I strain to hear. Had I stained her, left a mark? She laughs sharply, a little snort.

I love her forearms, their tawny color, their ropy strength. I'd told her that, yes?

Maybe not. Maybe never.

But in the car, a different one, her own, a white Mercedes, some teeny-tiny Barbie-sized model, white leather innards, too much damn white in her life, like perpetual heaven. In the car, she pushes the baggie at me, not turning away from the dicey traffic.

"You keep it."

chapter 14

"I triumphed with the orchids," I told Virgil. He sat with me in the pool house watching television while I tied bows from yards of frothy gold ribbon. "Three dozen at below-market price." Someone on the screen said something hilarious, and I laughed with all the other laughers, whom I couldn't see but sure could hear. Virgil did not laugh. He didn't seem to notice to what the screen people said or did. He flipped through a *Smithsonian* he'd scared up somewhere. His briefcase, beside him on the couch, held out files, each demanding that he pay attention, but he didn't. Instead, he drank a Jack and Coke. Just the Coke for me. The bottle stood on the glass coffee table. Something about the glass on glass scratched at me.

"Supercalifragilistic," he said.

More hilarity exploded into the room.

"Did you see that?" I asked.

I enjoyed the rhythm here, the feeling of being part of an important enterprise—Archer Demwalt's life. Imagine that with three exclamation points, and you'll get a sense of what it felt like. What would it be like to think yourself so important that the running of your life required a staff of eighteen, simply on the domestic side? People constantly came and went to and from the ranch, arriving by helicopter or Lincoln or Jeep. He met with them all, fed them, appeared to listen, hustled them out, then inevitably hunted me down to pursue some point of nuptial arcana.

"Surely I missed nothing," Virgil said.

"You're too judgmental," I said, my blood suddenly rising. "You should lighten up."

"Said the spider to the fly," he said. "Caroline, what are you doing?"

I held up a bow for him to inspect.

"I didn't mean it literally," he said. He rose and went to the bathroom, and returned with a hand mirror, which he held up in front of me. "Take a look."

"Fuck you," I said, concentrating on my bow. "I'm working."

"Oh, right. Working. The vaunted GDP wouldn't be the same without you. Give it a rest, will you? You make me tired."

"You've been mad at me since we got here. What's the matter with you? Can't you see—"

Someone knocked on the door. Virgil rose with an exaggerated sigh to open it.

"The lord of the ranch," Virgil said, letting Arch in.

"Hey there, you two. Sorry to intrude." He said this stepping broadly into the room. Arch had a knack for taking up space.

"Can I offer you a drink?" Virgil said, pouring himself another.

"Why, sure. Don't mind if I do." He watched Virgil pour the Jack Daniel's. "Easy there. Gotta be clear for tomorrow." Virgil poured a bit more in, and a dab of Coke.

"I'll take one, too," I said. Suddenly it looked good.

"To Caroline," Arch said. "The lady who does it all."

I groaned. We clinked glasses.

"Lord, look at those bows," Arch said. "Veronica's gonna be so pleased." He picked one up and adjusted it slightly.

"You wanna tie them, Arch?" I said. "Quit micromanaging."

"Sorry." He took a pull on his drink and looked around, slightly worried, as if he'd lost his keys, or couldn't decide how to tell me something awful.

"Where's David?" he asked.

I had no idea, which made me nervous. "He's not feeling well."

Arch appeared to think about this a while. "Sorry to hear that." To Virgil he said, "Must run in the family."

Virgil raised his glass to that and said, "To health."

Arch ranged around the room, adjusting a plant, then a small statue of a horse. He seemed to notice the television just as another bomb of laughter detonated.

"This is still on," he said, lighting on the couch for a bout of inertia. The story seemed to grab him hard and pull, and he began chuckling.

Virgil stood by the counter, which formed a divider between the living area and the kitchen. He nursed his drink and looked over at me, lobbing daggers.

"So, Arch, is there something I can do for you?" I picked up the bow I'd been working on and finished tying it.

"Oh, yeah. I wanted to check in on the flowers. How'd that work out?"

He didn't look away from the television, and it hit me, with a bit of dread, that he simply wanted to hang out. He was lonely.

"Well, as I told you this afternoon, the orchids are ordered. That leaves the lilies of the valley and the peonies, but I think I've got a line on them. We'll know for sure tomorrow."

He laughed more at whatever had just been said on television, and drank his drink down. "Mind?" he asked as he poured himself another. "Anyone else?"

Both Virgil and I offered our glasses.

"Now, what?" he said to me.

"Why don't we go over it at breakfast?" I said.

A commercial came on, a car climbing up a glistening mountain road. "What do you think, Virgil, should I get one of those?"

"Do you need another car?" Virgil asked, seated now beside me. He rested an arm along the length of the couch, suggesting by proximity that it was around me.

"What do you do?" Arch asked him.

"I find money for people and make it legal for them to keep it."

"Makes you a useful man. So what are you doing wandering around with this filly?"

"My niece was in need of a change. Out of my undying love for her, I decided to be that."

"You're not a married man, then?"

Virgil poured more Jack into his glass. "Was once."

"What happened, if you don't mind my asking?"

"Just why are you asking, actually, if you don't mind my asking?"

I threw the bow onto the heap of shiny ghostly gold.

"You gotta excuse me. I'm just a curious person. Like to know who's enjoying my home."

Virgil drank a bit more, and we all three looked at the TV. I had muted it during the commercials, and now the show was back, the actors fretting and strutting in silence. It was supposed to take place in Seattle, but it looked like anywhere.

"I hate to tell you this on the eve of your wedding. But an adulterer is enjoying your home. Chronic. Couldn't not love other women, and rather understandably, my wife wasn't too thrilled."

"Virgil, now, I respect a man who tells the truth." He drank a little. "I do think a man should keep his pecker in check once he's married, though."

"And before that?" Virgil asked.

"A man is a man."

"Oh for Christ's sake, you two," I said. "Spare me the pissing match."

"Well, anyway," Arch said. "Love the sinner, hate the sin, as my grandmother would say. Always a shot at redemption in this life, don't you think?"

"You'd have to ask Caroline about that. She's the religion expert of the family."

"That right?" He nodded at me. "I wouldn't have known that, but I'm not surprised." He drank a bit more. "What's he talking about, honey?"

"I double-majored in college—art and comparative religion. I've read some books."

"Very interesting," Arch said. "I'd be curious, you know," and he was shy in a way I had never seen. "You know, to hear what you think. You believe in God, actually, a sophisticated New York heathen like yourself?"

"My mother's a minister. I can't help it." It was fine to believe in God, but talking about it was another thing.

"That's just family inheritance. My granddaddy was a Pentecostal snake-handling son of a bitch, complete with tongues and holy rolling. I hope God isn't impressed by that flimflam. It doesn't have anything to do with the heart."

"Faith isn't only about the heart," I said.

"How 'bout you, Mr. Adulterer—you know a God?" The Jack seemed to be loosening Arch.

"I'm the heathen. Caroline is the only spiritual person I know," Virgil said. "I love that about her. In fact, I love her. I mean look at her, isn't she beautiful? And smart? And capable?" He tossed a bow at Arch. "She's way too capable, if you ask me."

Arch and I looked at Virgil, who smiled at me fondly and foolishly.

"Well, hell, don't we ever get to say what we mean?" he asked. "Or is that against the rules? Arch, Veronica's a lovely woman. You deserve a great life together. Don't do what I did. If you love her, love her, no matter what."

"I intend to. For a man in your cups, you say some all-right things."

"I'm not in my cups," Virgil said, suddenly belligerent. "I'm—" but he didn't finish. Instead, he clicked on the sound. And we three watched awhile longer. The show raged on, and I felt more aligned with Virgil. The pacing, the stylization of movement, of voice—as archaic as a silent film, but a mirror to the now.

When it was done, Arch stood, stretched, and moved toward the bathroom. I heard him flush, then rattle the bedroom doors, first one then the other. The bows sat at my feet, twenty-eight so far, all perfect, I had to admit, eleven inches across, fifteen inches vertical, lovely looping wings. I tie a damn good bow.

"Hope David feels better," Arch said, when he returned. Then he said good night and left us.

"He looked in our rooms," I said.

"Watch out, the loyalty oath comes next."

"I don't like that."

"They're his rooms, honey." He edged a little closer on the couch and reached across to touch my arm. "Let's dance or get drunk or do something stupid," Virgil said. "I miss you."

"We're already drunk. And you're still weak."

"Oh, Christ, Caroline, let me worry about my own damn body." He snapped the TV off. "Truth or dare?"

"Dare."

"I dare you to kiss me like you did that night."

"Truth."

"You already said 'dare.'"

I drank the drink down quickly and poured myself another, then got up and turned on the radio. All I could pull in was Mexican music, heavy on the accordion, too lively for the moment, boisterous like Sunday football.

"I dare you to dive into the pool," I said.

He got up and dropped his pants, his underwear, so that he stood in socks and shirt. The shirt he removed at the lounge chair outside. His dive was perfect, a trim nick into the water, streamlined, graceful, powerful. Rendered absurd by the socks.

He came up sputtering. "Burrah! Your turn."

I was already barefoot, so I stripped down to bra and panties and dove in. The water was silken. I slipped off the underwear and dove under again. I love being underwater, the heaviness of my hair, the grace as it wavers from side to side. I wish it were the way we always moved.

He climbed out and went back into the house, still in the socks, and retrieved the bottle of Jack, taking a long swig from it. "It's too sweet," he said, and handed it out to me. I swam up to it, in full mermaid mode now, and took a deep pull.

He sat at the edge of the pool, kicking lazy circles in the water.

"Your bruise is almost gone," I said.

Looking down at his rib cage, he smiled and stroked my chin.

"Caroline."

"Yes?"

"I want to tell you something."

"Okay." I waited. He didn't say anything, but took the bottle again and drank a bit more. "What is it?"

"Cherish the mundane, right?"

I smiled and pulled him into the water by the ankle, and we kissed and dove beneath the surface, which is probably why neither of us saw David when he came in.

chapter 15

The greenwood. I sense the green deep within the barky husks of trees as I walk by the creek. Inside the trunk it's there. I can practically see its hue—corn silk, or the green that inexplicably appears between orange sunset and blue night. If I try, I'll hear throaty sap rise, speeding nitrogen to branches and leaves, the showy outer limits.

This wood and I are aligned. We're analogs, metaphors. Two alive things, two things growing. Even the expanse of the sky, usually so terrifying, appears more kindly today. I appreciate that warmth emanates from the blue, from the far-distant sun.

Veronica rides in the morning light. I stand by the ring and watch, but she doesn't wave. Last night never happened, apparently. She posts up and down, increases her speed, and old King soars over the jumps. The sight of them, together with her failure to see me, scares me. So I walk away to listen again to the things she said to me, replayed like a symphony requiring multiple performances to fathom. I walk because I don't want to see Caroline this morning, having seen her last night swimming naked with my father.

Creekwater trickle and creekwater play of light. Gold streaks, oblong squiggles, rectangles gone bad. I don't see what I can hold onto, just now, with geometry bent beyond recognition, or simply expressing itself in a form too subtle to be calculated. The old standbys, dropping like flies.

My jacket has an interior pocket, and inside it, touching my heart, the bag of Horse has a pulse all its own. And a voice. Her voice. I remember thinking that I'd bring it with me to pour into the creek. But the powder must have gotten wind of my homicidal tendencies, for now it sings to me in its most alluring tones, at once motherly and wicked.

David. Da-a-a-vid. My name never sounded so good. The release of a lover's ecstatic breath (a sound I now know). Crackle of hearthfire. The lost now found.

"David." It's her. I stop. She rides up, weaving King in and out of the poplars. "Didn't you hear me call you just now?" She rolls her eyes. King sniffs suspiciously. His nostrils flare and his eyes look wild. A thing that free has no business on this earth. He will surely learn that.

"What are you doing," she asks.

"Smelling out the greenwood."

This seems to baffle her.

"Never mind. It doesn't matter," I say.

"Do you have that stuff I gave you," she asks, and she flashes a sly compadre look.

"No."

"Well, why don't you go get it?" and she pauses, a girl about to reveal a luscious secret. "I was thinking it would be great to do a little and then ride."

Doesn't sound too sound to me. "Didn't you see the warning label? Says 'Do not operate heavy equipment.'"

She narrows her eyes. "It's mine, you know."

I shrug my shoulders. "Possession is nine-tenths of the law. Don't you hear the greenwood, Veronica?" This seems to irritate her. "Come on." I reach up and to my amazement, take King by the bridle and hold him. "Listen."

We're silent. The wind works in the trees, the undersides of new leaves go silver with its caress.

"You don't need this," I say, taking the heroin from my pocket.

"You lied to me."

It wasn't much of a lie. I squat down by creek. She sees what's happening and jumps down from King.

"Give me that," she says.

I pour a small amount into the clear flowing water, but she snatches the rest from me, climbs back up on the horse, and rides away.

chapter 16

I drove into Arch's office in downtown Dallas to discuss the flatware situation. He'd set me up with a beeper, which seemed silly given my cell phone, and the one beep I'd received so far said simply: "Flatware, eleven sharp." It was followed with a call to the phone, and a set of instructions: when I arrived, I was to drive three-quarters around the block to a small garage marked "Private." There, I'd show the attendant my FirmShare badge, which had some designation declaring me an industrial-size VIP. Joaquin, who manned the garage, would park the car—"Tell him you'll need it in forty-seven minutes." Joaquin would then escort me to the private elevator that went directly to the executive suite.

And it all happened exactly as described. Exactly. The elevator was paneled in dark oak, as confidential as a confessional. It impressed me, this elevator hoisting such ponderous wood up and down all day. No music intruded on the upward journey. I had on dress shoes and a skirt for the big-city visit, and my heels sank into the pile of an Oriental carpet. He designed all this to suit himself, and I couldn't let go of that. It fascinated me—this ability to impose order based on unflagging will. It was the same force that compelled me to do his bidding, no matter how stupid, graceless, or without taste.

The elevator opened to more Oriental rugs and wood floors, light walls with dark paintings of fruit and hunts in the Old Master vein. Which Old Master? Didn't matter, though one receiving special prominence was a Rembrandt. In it a rabbit hung against a door.

Arch's receptionist led me to a conference room. Through its window I saw Arch in mid-meeting.

"Should I wait?" I asked the woman.

"No, he wants you to join them."

Entering, all six men—and it was only men—rose.

"Don't you look pretty today," Arch said.

"Don't I, though," I said, making a gift of my laughter, so the men could laugh too. They needed it, in their Egyptian cotton shirts fresh from the cleaner, sweat stains growing beneath their arms. The room was airless; it smelled like war. There were four white shirts, including Arch, one pale blue, and one rather daring in dark gray. He was the rebel, the interesting one, the one who painted or plucked musical strings or in some way expressed himself. I sensed an ally, and sensed, too, that I might need one.

The gray-wearing man had salt-and-pepper hair that curled in stylized waves around his head. His eyes were hazel and arresting in volume. Fine skin. A looker. Something nice in his look, too. A human.

"I'm Caroline Davies," I said, extending my hand to him, diagonally across the table, about as far away as he could be from me, but what the hell. His was the hand I wanted to touch.

"Harper Benson," he said. "In-house counsel, mostly though, I count beans." He smiled, and that was a glorious thing to see.

"Actually, all these fellas do," Arch said. "They're helping out with the wedding."

"So you're the ones writing the checks," I said, twitching habitually into the coquette.

"We wanted to talk over some of the arrangements," one of the men in white said. He had introduced himself, Ted or Ed, I wasn't quite sure. I looked at him and didn't speak, didn't smile.

On the table were copies of the spreadsheet I kept, listing the various items that went into creating a society wedding and their associated costs. It was a Bible of sorts, a bird's-eye view of this creation, and it was what Arch and I worked from each morning in our "strategy sessions," as he called them. The number at the bottom was large, but there were no surprises.

"You have down two hundred chairs"—Ted or Ed began—"with custom-ordered damask slipcovers, rented for three days. Last time I checked the wedding was set to last one hour, the reception four. Talk to me about the time element."

I took a drink of water from the glass in front of me. There was also a bowl of fruit in the center of the table, and one of the bananas looked appetizing, so I peeled it and ate it. Ted or Ed watched impatiently, which I wanted.

"Mr. Demwalt specifically instructed me that all setups had to be accomplished the day before the wedding, and the teardown would take place the day after. He said—Arch, correct me if I'm wrong here"—and at this, I took out my notebook and read verbatim—"'I don't want a goddamned ruckus fraying my nerves.'"

I also took from my files my negotiation log, which documented the starting price and the steps by which we arrived at the final cost. This I kept for my own information, as it was helpful down the line in assessing the fairness of offers and counteroffers.

"You'll note from this document"—I handed it across to Ted or Ed—"that I was able to get Mr. Demwalt an excellent price on the chairs as well as on the labor costs."

He took a quick look at it, then handed it down the table. It stopped with Harper Benson, who read it a long time.

"Well, all righty, then. Let's move on to the flatware," he said. He read from the spreadsheet: "Rental Flatware," the item said. "4000 pieces @ $3000/hr; $30,000."

"Would you like to take us through that one?" one of the other bullyboys said. They sat in a line around the table's other side, arrayed in a semicircle of inquisitors. Arch sat at the head of the table, a little aloof from the proceedings.

"It's sterling silver with gold doves on the handles."

I saw a few of them roll their eyes.

"And it's being rented for ten hours," another one said, the one in the blue shirt, bloated with overly pink skin and receding blond hair, a small nose. The kind of man on whom fine features were wasted, good breeding material if you could stand the notion of him naked. I wasn't feeling nice.

"I didn't catch your name," I said to the bloated man. I smiled at him. I decided I'd seduce him, because he was ugliest.

"I'm Chuck," he said. "Chuck Gallagher."

"Are you married, Chuck?" A large gold ring gouged his finger.

"Two years now."

"And you had a fine wedding," I said.

"Oh, yes, ma'am." The "ma'am" thrilled me, signaling, as it did, the heart of his southern fear.

"Well, then you know how important details are," I stood up and walked around to their side of the table, taking up a teacherly position behind Chuck Gallagher and the Ted or Ed monster. "And if the details of your wedding were so important, then imagine how important they'd be at Mr. Demwalt's. Everyone in Dallas will be there. Do you want them looking at the flatware and thinking: Brass? I don't. My job is to make sure this wedding is executed with the utmost taste, to relieve Mr. Demwalt and Ms. Fitzmorgan of all anxiety on that account."

I wandered now to the head of the table at the opposite end from Arch, and looked down its expanse at these chimps. Four of them, Chuck Gallagher included, leaned on their elbows, looking at me as if I were stripping. And I was indeed performing. Only Arch and Harper Benson sat back. Arch had his hands clasped behind his head, a grin on his face. And Harper, who was nearest to me now, looked down into the depths of his own lap, where one palm rested on top of the other, open.

"You see, Chuck, taste has a price. And it's absurdly high, especially when you write down all the numbers, as I did in preparing this document for you all." I picked up the spreadsheet and pointed to it, as if they hadn't seen it before, exhibit A. "But the damage done by going cheap, to a man of Mr. Demwalt's reputation—the cost of that is irreparable."

I now stood in front of the room's window, and felt the sunlight on my back.

"Ms. Davies has been quite eloquent," Harper Benson said, "illuminating us on the exigencies of wedding planning."

I'd read him all wrong, I heard in his tone of voice. He was a kindred spirit, but of the evil sort.

"But in conversations with Mr. Demwalt—"

Arch broke in. "Will you all stop being so formal? Since when was I my daddy?" He glared around the room. "Caroline, honey, I'm sorry to call you on the carpet like this. I don't know my head from a hole in the ground when it comes to this stuff, and you always make me look good. But we got an eyeful of the figures and these fellas about shit their pants. And hell, I gotta listen."

I let that echo a moment—he had to listen, it wasn't his choice.

Harper Benson jumped in. "I don't notice on this spreadsheet—and it's been meticulously put together. We were all very impressed." He paused and smiled at me, as if he'd just bestowed an A+. "I didn't notice the fees you and your outfit will receive."

"We have a standard contract with FirmShare. I'm surprised you haven't seen it." I stood directly in front of him and held his gaze.

"I probably wrote it, but it's been awhile. Remind me."

I had a contract in my bag, but that would mean scurrying back to my side of the table, and that didn't suit me. I turned my back and looked out the window. Dallas gleamed, clouds rolling across its glass buildings. I didn't know how to play this one. We had a standard percentage deal above costs. Everyone in this room knew it. But I wasn't padding expenses. This was the price of late planning, the price of being known as a moneybags. My stomach jumped. For a moment, I smelled my father, heard him clear his throat. I tried to channel his impartiality.

"Ms. Davies, are you with us?" Harper Benson said.

"Our contract is fifteen percent," I said. "I'll be happy to work within whatever budget you decide is appropriate. It's entirely up to you. Please let me know. In the meantime, the wedding is five days away, and there are details to attend to." And with that, I returned to my side, picked up my things, and let myself out.

Arch followed me out.

"Hey now, darlin'," he said. "Those are a sorry bunch of pricks and I'm gonna have it out of their hides."

We stood by the elevator. I could feel the receptionists and assistants, good-lookers one and all, checking us out. I felt an urge to tell him about New Orleans, about the crack house and Uta, to give him a big whiff of my life. That's what he wanted. I gave him a sidelong glance. He was gleeful in his repentance, crocodile tears all the way.

"Arch, honey," and to my astonishment, I stroked his cheek as if he were my son. "Don't try to break me. Because you can't." I slapped him lightly, all in good fun. "It's your wedding. All I do is make it happen. But it's supposed to happen pretty goddamned soon, so I suggest you work this out, or you'll be heading to Vegas for the blue plate special at Little Kirk o' the Heath."

Harper Benson walked up behind us, and when the elevator doors opened, he entered with me.

"That was his idea, you know," he said after we'd descended a few floors.

"His who?"

"You know who. The big man. He needed to see what you had." He laughed conspiratorially.

"It's Harper, right?" I asked.

He nodded.

"Well, Harper. It's his wedding, and it's his money."

"You handled it real well." He paused, waiting, for me to fill the void, the nice girl afraid of silence. But I had no need to talk. "Just like he said you would," he finished.

The elevator landed at ground zero.

"Would you like to have lunch?" Harper asked.

"I would," I said, and watched while his eyes brightened. "But not with you."

Joaquin brought the car around—it had been forty-seven minutes. Arch knew his stuff.

I drove a long way out on the expressway. The towers of the city stayed behind me, and the earth rose in brown green plateaus. It made me miss the road, the aimless wandering that had seemed so dull. I cranked up the radio, listening to the exhortations of a preacher, beware the whore of Babylon, then to the plain talk of common folk, advocating the death penalty for a rapist, the details of a case that had been all over the morning paper, not clear at all that the boy had done it. My father had tried any number of capital cases, almost always coming in with a decision that undermined capital punishment, quite predictably, though at least once he'd played against type. Through it all, I couldn't remember a time when he'd been angry, as I was now, listening to these idiots call for blood. He was a measured, moderate man. He studied hard, then did his job. But the detail, the telling detail about him, was that he had amassed the power to make decisions.

My mother might know about this. It crossed my mind to call.

I pulled the car off the road, easing it slowly onto the shoulder beside a fence made from uneven blond posts and barbed wire. It was Arch's car, a steel behemoth, and I climbed down, and looked out over the empty land. I felt carsick suddenly, but the air steadied me.

Of course Arch had cooked up that little scrimmage. A fight, a loyalty oath, just as Virgil predicted. A betting pool with the boys. Not a problem at all. What had me ill was not caring that I'd spent $30,000 on flatware with doves on the handles. And that after hard negotiation. I'd gotten them to halve the insurance requirement, and to price it in bulk rather than per piece. Surely this skill had other uses.

Small dust clouds twisted across the landscape, dancing with the distance, farther and farther away. The breeze assaulted me with its heat, its grit, its astringent smell of sage.

chapter 17

What sounds like fucking, from behind the door of David's room, surprises Virgil. It is mid-afternoon, and he is restless, lonely for Caroline, off somewhere buying something white or gold, the details of which she will bore him with when she returns long after supper.

His disappointment is boundless and unnamable, so taboo that it only registers as vague self-loathing.

His side aches and he longs for his home, his bed, his dishes, his routines. He stops by the door. It's definitely fucking, and though King of the Wink is not parked outside, his smell of barn and tack and sweat permeates the very fibers of the pool house.

There's another smell, treacle sweet, burnt sugar, caramelized skin. Where there's smoke, he thinks, and he would like to go elsewhere, anywhere elsewhere. Get thee to a nunnery. Exeunt, as the ancient stage directions direct. The thane of Fife had a wife—all sorts of worthless Shakespeare cascades through him, none of the wisdom. I met a motley fool in the woods.

He coughs, makes a noisy turn about the house, slams a cabinet in the kitchen from which he has taken a tall glass and poured himself a tall bourbon. The glasses are dirty at night, and in the morning they're clean. The miracle of the self-cleaning highballs, he thinks. My sins washed away, or at least discreetly hidden.

Someone around here is keeping these secrets. Or not.

The polite stomping has worked, for suddenly the noise stops, and the house, for a moment, is as still as a set trap.

He will need to disappear for a moment to let Veronica leave. He finishes the glass of bourbon, and it hits him hard, following too closely on last night's drunken swim. His side aches like an ancient branch breaking off. He feels tired and as if he has been away, as if things have happened in his absence that affect him profoundly, that he is now powerless to influence or amend. Sunlight swallows this room, with its openness—the living area and the kitchen aren't separate, facilitating an easy, breezy way of insouciant living. It's all about flow, he can just hear the real estate agent cluck. Or maybe it was an architect. Perhaps this was an old potting shed, the pool a swamp filled with frogspawn. Someone had a sun-filled vision, realizing that that's what rich folks ought to have, and voilà, the wand was waved.

He tips a tiny bit more into his glass, swallows, and makes a noisy exit.

Caroline is pulling up in the obscenely large luxury truck.

"I wouldn't go in there just yet," Virgil says, opening her car door and leaning in to hug her. She returns his embrace tightly. "Take me to your leader," he says, affecting a space-invader voice.

He gets in. She looks questioningly at him.

"Never you mind," he says.

It's an automatic transmission, yet it has a pretentious gearshift on the mound between driver and passenger. She maneuvers it to the R position. "Okay, master of mysteries, where to?"

"Off the Res."

She backs them up—the drive leading to the pool house has a herringbone brick surface, and some delicate creeping plant, baby's breath perhaps, etches the space between bricks. No doubt there's a nose-hair trimmer just to manicure these tiny leaves.

"It's decadent here," Virgil says. "In case you didn't notice. Did I ever tell you my feelings about decadence?"

Caroline is in a good mood, she smiles over at him, ready to laugh.

"It's like VD or gonorrhea, something easily cured with primitive penicillin, quaint almost, but left untreated, quite disfiguring nonetheless. We have an advanced case here."

"The world has gonorrhea," she says, much to his surprise. Though her voice is light, when he looks at her he can see the seriousness of the statement.

"I'm sorry you know that."

They cross off the property, beneath its white metal gate that spells out "AD III." The light is shifting from merciless midday interrogation to soft sunset romance. Birds rise from a ditch beside the road, several hundred small brown bodies lifting at once. It takes Virgil's breath away.

"Tell me about your day," he says. Her knowledge about blight has cheered him. She is his again.

"You know, just the usual, trying to interpret the chicken entrails in order to make an auspicious choice of rental flatware blending silver and gold. Precious metals only need apply, but please not to cost too much." She takes a breath, as if drinking deep. "Why don't they plan their own damn wedding?"

She is quiet a minute, then starts laughing, and Virgil does, too. He reaches across the chasm between them and touches her hand at the top of the steering wheel. He does love her, however wrong and absurdly. Her fingers are long and soft, warm, they sport rings that mix stone and metal in complicated patterns. She presses a button— one of hundreds on her side of the car—and rolls down the car's many windows at once. The sepulchral stillness inside the beast—this car like Jonah's whale—ruptures with the screeching natural friction that exists between tire and road.

"Why couldn't I go inside," she asks.

"Not the right moment." He looks out the window, more birds rising, swooping, turning in fascinating parabola, he can see the equation as they move. "And because I miss you."

"Anything else?"

To the right, outside Virgil's window, there is nothing but pasture. In the midst of it, perhaps a hundred yards off, a vast pond shimmers gold in the late day light. Cattle mill around it, some kneeling to drink, others walking right into the water, steam rising off their mottled bodies.

"Nothing you need to worry about." He looks again and a rise has obscured the pond and its sociability. "I love you, Caroline."

He thinks she smiles.

chapter 18

Sugar smacks. Veronica now calls the kisses she gives me this, laughing like an ancient tree when she does so. It freaks me out to see how old she is, really, beneath her youth. She's ancient dust and she's blowing away. Arch is a wind machine, a windbag, if I were inclined toward the conventional metaphor, but he isn't really that. It's not that he's a bore or a pedant or a prognosticator or a know-it-all. He's a force. He doesn't see what he's blowing down, just as a tornado has no feel for the country flattened at its forward edge.

I don't know that I love Veronica. She scares me, her appetite for Horse is profound, it's like she just discovered oxygen. "Breathing is so cool!" She's right, it is, and I'm glad she knows this now, because it's helpful to know. But what matters is knowing it when you're not high. I told her this, except of course it was lost on her because we were both so high.

So I had been crying. That is, until someone came into the house. The sound of another human instantly ended my sentimental bummer jag. Residual snot cools on my cheek and I feel too weak or lazy to wipe it off. Really, I hope she'll wipe it off, so I snuffle.

"What's the matter, Mr. Bucko?" she says. She props herself up to look at me and she does wipe away some of the tear-stream. It's not a genuine win, though, because I had to prompt her. But still. She touches her fingers repeatedly as if tears were a total novelty.

"I don't know if I love you," I say.

"I bought you a new bathing suit," she reminds me in a singsong voice. *Bathing suit* never sounded so melodious, so like prayer.

"Do you love Arch?" I ask.

"What do you have to go and bring him into this for?"

"Because it's important to me to know. Do you love him?"

"You're such an idealist. God love you for that."

"So you don't love him, and I'm like a country rube for thinking that you should if you're going to marry him." I grind that word *marry* down hard. It's a rock, and I throw it at her head. Sticks and stones.

She lies back and looks at the ceiling. "It's not so simple."

"I don't think you love him, or you wouldn't be here."

"Think what you want. You're the one who cares."

She turns onto her side, away from me, and cold winds blow between us, the long night of arctic winter summoned, needed. My desires run amok inside me, I want to keep asking her until she tells me that she doesn't love him or that she does, until she says something. It's hopeless. My want will always be on the far side of her. And I will never know what she is, even though—I suspect, I flatter myself—I know her better than anyone.

"Why don't you marry me?" I say.

"You don't love me, remember?"

"No, I do now."

"David, do we have to keep talking about this?"

"Yes."

But neither of us says anything more. She gets up and starts to dress.

We have to keep talking about this, because if we stop, she'll marry him for sure. But my tongue is tied up by my eyes, which drink her in, the straight line of her thigh into her beige breeches. I'm as desolate as I've ever been, which, not to be dramatic or anything, is saying something.

"You want to hear about jail, don't you," I say.

She looks at me with distant kindness, a kindergarten teacher used to the crushes of five-year-olds. "Not now, I don't."

She kisses my forehead and exits, and the day fills with silent heat.

chapter 19

Veronica riding. She drops the reins and raises her arms high above her head. The horse trots, she posts, up and down, bouncing higher. They circle the ring and she whoops like a large flightless bird. A car drives by a little too fast, a beat-up Camaro, four on the floor, man, and its mufflerless engine roar spooks King of the Wink. King veers a little toward the fence then a little toward the center of the ring, where a course of jumps has been set. He knocks a post. The fence rail falls down and bounces. Veronica tilts left, hanging out of the saddle. Her arms are still outstretched, but not in joyous abandon. She tries for the reins. King changes his pace, hesitates in front of a pond that's gouged out of the dirt, almost moves a step backward, but one leg is in the hole. When she falls, there's a look of surprise on Veronica's face. King's falling, too. Veronica's right foot stays in the stirrup, and as King runs and falls, he drags her about the ring, over the posts, and he lands on her pelvis.

I see this as I walk toward the ring, thinking I'll talk to her, get it right now that I've come down and see things more clearly. It's no good what we're doing, and I know why now, and when I explain it, she'll understand. She took the last of the heroin with her, though there wasn't much left.

"Veronica!" I yell, and now I run toward the ring, and others run, too, from different directions: the housekeeper, groundsmen, one on his cell phone calling God knows who.

I make the fence, shinny through it, and run to King and grab him by the halter, try to raise him. "Easy, boy," I say, surprised at how gentle my voice is despite the run, despite the sight of this woman unconscious, body jagged, dirt mixing with blood. At least she's breathing. I release her foot from the stirrup and bring her leg slowly to earth and cradle it on my knees.

Of course I am crying. The sky is soft, glorious gold. A brace of doves moves quickly across it, their songs like darts dropping on top of me.

I watch her chest rise and fall with deep, even breath, and try to time my rhythms to hers. The baggie of smack peeks from the pocket of her blouse, and in the moment before all hell breaks loose, I take it from her and stuff it into my pants.

Then hell does break. I know it from the smell—sudden sweat, fear bursting from the body.

I still hold her foot, though a groundsman tries to push me aside, a take-charger. He takes her pulse and says, "*Muy rapido*" under his breath, and a siren sounds in the distance, growing louder, drowning out the birds whose songs I have been listening to for her, so that she would know she's still of this earth.

Caroline is suddenly beside me, out of breath from running. I strain to pack the relevant information into my gaze—yes to the heroin, yes to the lovemaking, yes to all the questions about the scope of the transgression. It's more than an accident. It was an accident waiting to happen, something the two of us constructed. I can see that clearly now. Maybe this was her way to get out of the upcoming nuptials, or to get a little something from Mr. Arch that she didn't get just by being the most beautiful woman on this part of earth. But that's my own rage coming into it, swaggering around in these moments of assessment.

"Are you all right?" Caroline asks me. She means am I high.

"A little bit," I say.

She stands up and muscles into the center of the throng. Her presence vibrates firmness, and it quiets the noise.

"You called Arch?" she asks the groundsman with the phone, who nods. "Good, good. Now give her a little room. She's been hurt, and the paramedics will need some space." The paramedics trot up, big men, heroes in navy blue jumpsuits with white and red insignia on the arms that say "AD Enterprises." Of course Arch would have his own paramedics. The man thinks of everything.

I relinquish her foot and try not to be noticed for the junkie that I am, but too late, one of the heroes looks at me and sees how dilated my pupils are and says, "Want to tell me what you're on?" in a loud accusatory voice. Caroline steps in and whispers to the man, and his demeanor changes.

Veronica has probably broken her pelvis, so lifting her onto the gurney takes an agonizingly long time. Veronica's arm twitches and she screams, "You motherfucker!" but they hoist her up, then roll it over the gravel and dirt of the ring. She calls out "David!" one time, but Caroline holds me back when I start to run for her.

"Better not," she says, and she squeezes my arm in a consoling way.

I do not feel consoled. The woman I love calls me and I can't run for her? I break free.

"David, don't let them know," Veronica says.

They lift her into the ambulance and I climb in, too, but one of the heroes says, "Who are you?"

I don't think they like me much and it bothers me. I could be her brother or someone important—how the hell does he know who I am or am not. So I tell him, "I'm her brother," and he lets me stay.

Once they've strapped her in and start moving, the hero says to me, "So you crazy kids had yourselves a little party." He has affixed an IV to her. "I should hook you up, too. It's a detox solution."

I say, "No way, needles scare me," and he laughs.

"She's going to be all right, isn't she?" I ask.

"That's for the doctors to figure out." This answer does not reassure me and I start to cry, feeling for all the world like the guilty party. Then I remember that I have the bag in my pocket. There's probably dust in the fabric of my pants by now, and damn if this doesn't seem like shit creek once again.

It's funny how when you know someone's going to be important to you, you always think it means they're going to be good. Like with Veronica, I knew the minute I saw her that she was something. Like a chime had sounded, the hour struck. That has to do with her beauty,

I suppose. If she'd been less dazzling, I might have felt the vibration for what it was. A warning. *Danger: Cliffs ahead.* Doesn't mean I wouldn't have jumped. Cliffs sometimes require jumping in order to be cliffs, and people sometimes need to jump in order to be people. But still. I saw myself heading back to prison, and oddly, it was Caroline I felt the worst for, because I knew she was the one who'd gone to the trouble to get me out. Freedom is not for everyone. That's something I could tell her. But what would she do with that?

chapter 20

"Would you mind telling me how you got this?" Arch asked David, holding up a small baggie that was mostly empty, except for a film of white powder. We were in Arch's private study in the big house, paneled dark, the slatted wood blinds drawn to half-mast against the blinding light outside. Veronica had been airlifted to the hospital with a broken sacrum. It was likely she would not ride again, so ultimately Arch won the battle on that one. I watched him now.

"Cash money," David said, a mouse to Arch's lion. His skin shone.

Arch had on a plaid buttondown shirt and khakis, tennis shoes, a fabric belt. His eyes were so blue, so boyish. I don't believe he'd played with chemicals much—maybe he'd smoked a joint back in the frat days, but I suspected he did it with a secret sense of moral outrage, a prig at heart, feigning groovy.

"So it's yours," Arch asked.

"Of course it is."

"David," I said, "maybe you shouldn't say anything till we get you a lawyer."

David shot me a look of daggers. "It's my life, Caroline."

chapter 21

Space howls. The eyes of Texas nighttime sparkle down on me, its voice whispers from trees and ditches, a voice of laughter and footsteps. The laughter isn't kind; nothing is funny. Veronica calls in a reedy whine, high lonesome, my beloved banshee. I see the helicopter lift her up into that sky and away in the direction that is now my direction.

I stand at the intersection of two highways, preparing to hitch a ride with whatever comes my way, waiting the good wait in the immensity of this night, not like any others, this night when I forsake liberty, this night of flight.

Flight will be my life. I might call my mother from the hospital, wish her well and all. I'd call Caroline but it will be too complicated. Arch will set the dogs on me, or whatever gentlemanly version of that is in vogue these days—he'll make a phone call and one fine day, a tall old boy in pointy cowboy boots will put his hand on my shoulder and that will be that. I can see it plain as day, which is saying something on a dark night like this one. It's a sorry thing that I won't ever marry that girl, but we're more married now than she'll ever be to Arch or whoever else comes along.

Night air, cricket-ridden. Fluttering wings near enough to feel the wake they kick up, entirely too close against my neck. Howling all about but I don't know if it's outside or inside. Knife edges, points pointing, blades smiling glinting smiles, my blood the desired offering.

I am lucid despite the jones and this interests me. I scratch my elbows out of habit, the itch a comfort. There are many kinds of jones.

Sweat sweats from me. Were there a moon, I would shine, but as there isn't, I simply ooze. It doesn't cool me. There is a curve where the top of Veronica's rib circles down toward her navel. I trace it over and over with the finger of my mind.

Parallel yellow dots approach from way down the road, the way I came, maybe a ride, maybe not. I step toward the asphalt and the car slows.

It's early early at the hospital. Veronica's brother, just flew in from Philadelphia to see her, and I look pathetic enough and it's late enough that the attending nurse looks down long enough to let me pass. Veronica's room is unshared, except with machinery. It's large, with what is very likely an extra sunny window, though just now there's only darkness on the other side of it. The bathroom light is on, and it reveals the outlines of several flower arrangements. I can't help but think of Caroline, all the florists she's talked to in the last week. A few balloons bob from one of the bouquets. Their Mylar shells catch odd angles of light, breaking it into orange shards. Machines ping and pong the rhythms of her aliveness—pulse, respiration, the subtle humors. A tube is affixed to the septum of her nose, and her hair cascades about the pillow like tributary rivers flowing from their source.

My source.

I look at her closed eyes and I cry without reservation.

"I shouldn't . . ." I wish I had a token to leave with her, but maybe the broken back will do. "I have to go, see? But I had to see you and tell you that I love you and I always will." Her eyes are just as shut as if I hadn't spoken.

I step into her bathroom and rinse my face. Her toiletries surround the sink, alabaster tubes that smell of gardenia. I take one. Sometimes inhalation is enough.

Time to go coastal. Walk a redwood forest, fragrant needles underfoot, evergreen spires lifting leafy arms as if to pray, as the old poem goes. Sleep in a fire ring, a hollow. And who knows, maybe Hawaii after that. I could stay clean, I could work. I could stay clean. There will be a truck. I'll get a ride. Life is nothing if not motion.

chapter 22

Bags packed, Virgil loaded into the car, me ready to go—that was when Arch beeped me. "Don't leave. Need to talk." So we waited. Wedding detritus littered the pool house, divided into what was returnable from what wasn't. I'd called and canceled all sorts of things, smoothed over ruffled feathers with a generous slathering of Arch's money. I assumed that was the final agenda item he needed to discuss, so I typed it all up to give him a clear picture of where he stood.

He arrived in his big black truck with the darkened windows, shiny as a crow's wing, and took me into his study. Television news flickered silently on a large TV built into the wall, and Arch's eye went to it often.

"I wanted to tell you that I'm not pressing charges," he said. "Against David, I mean."

"I appreciate that," I said. We sat in silence a minute. "I don't mean to look the gift horse in the mouth here," he winced at the word *horse*. "But why?"

"Let's just say I learned some things." He began to write out a check.

I looked blankly at him, my negotiator's stare coming in handy. Then I dropped it. What was the point? "Come on, Arch. Just tell me. Don't keep secrets."

He looked at me awhile. "If you hadn't of brought that cousin of yours, we'd be on track for a wedding this weekend." Pain broke in his voice. He looked over to the television. Stock prices rolled along the bottom of the screen, telling stories of riches found and lost, of aspiration and ideas and good or bad management, a thousand tales encapsulated in the cryptic numbers. "Do you think she loved me?"

The phone rang and Arch pounced on it. I watched the television. FirmShare's symbol rolled by, its price up a notch. Arch listened to his phone, said, "Uh-huh," and hung up. Then he pushed a check across his desk, made out to me, not the firm.

"I can't take this. Settle it with Donald if you need to, but, well." I left the check on his desk.

"Don't quibble. I pay people when they work for me. Some projects, you know, get canceled."

The check sat there, fat with zeros.

"You should have let Veronica ride in the ceremony," I said, and I tried to say it gently. I wanted him to know. "Women can't be broken—and if they could, why would you want them?"

"Your cousin might say something different on that score. He broke her good."

I didn't know what to say to that, though I didn't imagine it was so simple.

"I'm so sorry," I said.

"Just get out of here, will you?"

He pushed the check at me, but I left without it.

part IV

chapter 1

Through the open windows, Virgil's car filled up with sun.

"Where should we look?" I said. "He's probably heading to Houston—get lost in a big city. That's what I would do."

"Could be," he said.

His eyebrows pulled toward one another in the gesture I recognized as thought, and I loved him for it. I loved the way a few hairs of his brow had gone renegade, fool tendrils balanced on air. I loved the mercurial geometry of his face, the problem shifting just as the solution came into view.

"You haven't been loved nearly enough," I said.

"Who has?"

The road felt good beneath me. It showed us the basics, and the basics were all I wanted. Taking care of details, making things lovely for people came at too high a price it seemed, so there was enormous relief in simply judging the distance between painted lines.

Somewhere past noon, we decided hunger was upon us. We stopped just west of Amarillo, in a town that seemed to be nothing more than the intersection of two streets, a stoplight hovering above like a benediction. We ate at the counter of a diner, men in Wranglers, well-worn boots, grimy Stetsons, old men who seemed to be bent over their coffee turning out to be just bent, crouching to their trucks once the cup was empty and the feed loaded into the bed. They tipped their hats to me when they left.

I ordered a BLT. Virgil ordered a chef's salad, but when it came, he avoided it like an old toy and seemed content with a cup of dark coffee, a cigarette, no nonsmoking regulations to tread on us here. I reached into my purse to find my pack, and found a piece of paper. David had left me a note. His handwriting was beautiful, very precise lettering. It said simply, "Thanks anyway." He had also sketched a peace sign.

"What do you think this means?" I showed it to Virgil.

He looked at it a long time, then out the window at the blanched street. There was a sound of low conversation—a few of the older men were seated at tables, half reading the paper, half talking to one another. The waitress stood with them, holding a pot of decaf aloft as she spoke. A horse was tethered to a streetlight outside.

Virgil stood. "Excuse me," he said, and he walked to the rear of the diner where the rest rooms were. He'd taken David's note with him. There was a local real-estate section on the seat beside me and I took it up, reading through the listings—240-acre ranch for sale, cattle included. I scanned the obituaries in the same section. Erma May Thompson, beloved mother of ten, survived by eight children, and twenty grandchildren. The living survive the dead, survive their passing, survive their living selves, too, sometimes a requirement to make it to our own final rest. I had no idea what it meant to survive— had I survived my father, or simply worn him out with my dissatisfactions, my bratty certainty that I knew what was beautiful and my insistence that he see it. There's no loaning another your eyes. Even when you point to the first star in the velvet dark and you both see it and sigh, there is always the gap, another's beauty an ongoing mystery. But the sigh, the sigh was a thing shared.

How about my mother—what was her survival like? I took out my phone and dialed, but there was no cell service here.

We connected up with Interstate 80, then swung off it again to take the small roads to Flagstaff, where we'd booked a suite for the night. Virgil was all for going in style, he said. Something outré. So I'd called around and priced out the town, settling on the deluxe suite at the Canyon View Lodge with whirlpool and fireplace and complimentary turndown of sheets. This was the crescendo—let there be drums and cymbals to drown out the din of disappointment, I thought. But I could love a crescendo all the same.

"What's your fondest hope," Virgil asked me after we'd stopped for coffee and *huevos*—our toast was now tortillas.

"To live close to the bone," I said. I wanted the elemental truths, the once-and-for-alls. I wanted certainty, and knew it was out of the question. The shape-shifting nature of things had the better of me—the father who had seemed so solid, so omnipresent, turning out to be as ephemeral as the column of ants proceeding down the sidewalk on an August afternoon. Both remembered, but it seemed the one should have more substance than the other, and it wasn't clear at all that he did. "To stay hungry. To know love." I was riffing now. "To appreciate beauty and to communicate it. And you?"

"To die with a peaceful heart." And he lay his right hand across his heart as he said it.

The sky opened up azure above us, and the ground to either side of the car transformed to ochre. Arches and towers rose out of the red earth haphazardly, phantasms of cosmic imagining, a monumental child at the beach, dribbling geologic sand. We stopped and I photographed odd moments, a cow biting up the few clumps of grass in front of a rock formation. A dog strolled up to me out of nowhere, eager for my pats. He rolled onto his back, the long black-and-white fur contrasting with the orange dirt beneath him, his red tongue lolling.

Virgil sat with his legs out the passenger door, almost rocking himself, his fingers interlaced around his crossed knees. He smiled in a private way, and seemed more relaxed than I could remember for some time.

"We've done well," I said. "We've hardly argued."

"Why argue? Beauty is always right."

The sadness in his humor hit me, and I snapped his picture. The camera wouldn't be able to comprehend the light of the moment, him leaning back into the shady interior of the car, his ankles basking in the sunlight, and his expression would be a cipher. I bent down and kissed him, on the cheek.

"You're very dear to me, old man."

He stroked my cheek and smiled, and he looked old indeed.

Wind kicked up, and we drove on, then exited onto a dirt road that promised the San Juan River. The road was rutted and sandy, and our car seemed relieved after all the concrete, though Virgil looked pained—literally, wincing with the bumps. But when I asked how he was feeling, he said fine, this was lovely, and he looked out the window, hiding his face from me. Was I supposed to turn back? Was that the dance we were in—was it a test of my judgment? I proceeded farther down the road, across a sandy wash, and then we found a steadier track that led down to a willow glade and the roiling green of a loop in the river.

Parking in the shade, I hotfooted it to the long flat rocks on the riverbank. I rolled up the legs of my pants and soaked my feet, looking upriver and down at the swirls and ripples that articulated currents and obscured obstacles for those who had the vocabulary to comprehend. How the world does talk.

"Isn't it beautiful," I called, turning toward the car. Virgil was hunched down and didn't move when my voice finished, so I ran back to him, suddenly panicked. He had leaned down to change into sneakers.

"How is it?" he asked.

"Come see." I held my hand out to him, and he grasped it and I led him to the shore.

A little downriver, and up a hill that rose precipitously from the water, was a triangular rock formation. A crow swooped low across it. The breeze off the water shook the long limbs of the willows, it fluttered my hair playfully as I entered the water and swam against the current upstream. I let myself float down past our beach, splashing at Virgil when I passed. He waved at me, and smiled, and I drifted a little longer in the embrace of sky, stone, and green, green water.

The perfect moments always involve water. You walk by the East River with a lover. You bodysurf beside your brother in the clear curve of a wave. A creek teaches you the nuances of spring, its symphony of timing—the ice melts, the frogs spawn, the branches bud. That split second, drifting past Virgil, splashing, seeing his smile, and then floating on with my eyes full of sky, was perfect. But as perfect things do, the moment passed. I drifted downstream a long way, then had to swim back against a current so vigorous that I wondered if I were strong enough. A raft drifted by, and I tried to stay below the surface to my neck to disguise my nakedness. When I finally returned to our rocky bank, dripping and out of breath, hot dry air prickling my skin, Virgil was sleeping with a porkpie hat over his face, his chest exposed beneath his unbuttoned oxford shirt, khakis rolled up to mid-calf. I lay down beside him on my stomach, and let the warmth of the rock seep in.

chapter 2

We picnicked in the shade, and the wind kicked up, blowing a fleck into my right eye. I closed it and let it tear, but still the feeling of some tiny irritant persisted, and to open the eye was to experience the world through watery redness. My pupil must have dilated wildly because I couldn't handle the brightness bouncing from leaves and water and rock. "I don't think I can drive," I said. The wind blew through our sandwiches and the potato salad, filling them with river grit.

Virgil drove us out of the bottomland with remarkable aplomb, undaunted when the wheel caught and spun, or by the branches that suddenly banged against the windshield. He laughed and winced and soon we were back on the main road, two lanes stretching either way to empty infinity, to rocks and sand and shrubs the color of winter branches. The burnt quality of the landscape touched me—it made things like exoskeletons seem sensible. A hard crusty covering was the right response to this place, and yet I felt soft, a font amid the desert, my eye tearing and closed, so that I viewed the world cycloptically, swiveling my head in order to see past my nose. Why doesn't the nose interfere with our two-eyed vision? Now with one eye, it was like a sextant helping me take bearings.

"Dinosaur tracks, 500 Feet," a sign said, hand painted in sprawling red letters across weathered plywood.

"Are you up for it?" Virgil asked. I nodded, and we turned onto the side road. A child's wailing reached us when we parked. I saw the small girl being changed beneath the blue plastic tarpaulin that was set up. The girl's mother ministered to her bottom, and a few other people sat in the tarp's shade.

A man came up to us. "Welcome to the Navajo nation," he said. "Would you like a guide?" He wore tight Wrangler jeans and a plaid shirt with pearly snaps. His belt buckle was an enormous oval of brass etched with crossed rifles.

The wild dry wind blew up inside my sundress and sent its skirt billowing. With one hand over my eye and the other struggling with the renegade cloth, I found the walking hard. So at first I didn't see the footprints. Raymundo, our guide, went on about how the land had been fertile, a lush garden, near an inland sea. I stumbled behind them. Virgil looked intently at the ground.

"My God, Caroline, do you see this?" he said to me, pausing to let me catch up. He knelt and pointed to what looked like yet another pockmark on planet earth. But this one had a distinct three-pronged pattern, as if some mammoth chicken had scratched this way. You could see where the claws dug a little deeper, you could guess at the heft of the creature, at its scaled body and fey hands, the screech that would issue from its pointed beak. Other imprints crisscrossed the terrain in crazy zigzags, remarkable arcs of ancient motion.

Raymundo looked at me funny. "What's the matter with you, miss, if you don't mind my asking."

"I have something in my eye."

"I can remove it the Navajo way, if you'll allow me." And before I could say no, he stepped over to me, took my head in his two thick hands and held open my right eye. Then he puffed up his cheeks and blew into my eye. His breath was hotter than the day and smelled of campfires and sweat. "How's that?"

"No, I still feel it, I'm afraid."

Raymundo again blew his fiery breath across my cornea, but to no avail.

"I'll wait at the car," I said. "The light is getting to me."

By now I felt exhausted from the sense of irritation, and all the tearing fooled me into thinking I was sad. So I sat in the car and hung my head, not sure if the sadness were truly mine or an affliction summoned forth out of the wind. One of the women from under the tarpaulin approached me.

"Are you all right? Why don't you come sit with us. Raymundo will be back soon with your husband."

"My uncle. All right."

When I stumbled, she caught me by the arm. "You mustn't cry," she said.

"There's something in my eye."

"I'm Sally," she said. "This is my daughter Anna Maria." The little girl who'd been crying smiled at me. She looked about two, with deep dark eyes and small gold hoops in her ears.

"What a beautiful girl," I said. Sally smiled at her daughter.

There were metal camp stools with dark blue canvas under the tarp, and we sat. The other women who'd been here went to the stalls displaying turquoise jewelry and fetishes carved from different stones, though there were no customers. A radio clicked on from one of the stalls, and a voice in Spanish crackled in the air around us. The one woman still beneath the tarp was quite elderly, in a velvet skirt, two gray braids down her back. Her eyes were sky blue with cataracts, and she smiled at me when I said hello, then went back to drizzling different-colored sands on a board in the pattern of a bird.

"Let me try," Sally said, and she, too, held my eye open and blew. Her breath smelled of licorice, tinged with whiskey, which startled me. "No?" Then she took a gallon jug of water and instructed me to lean over with my eye open, and she poured the water across my eye in a gentle stream. It felt cool and wonderful, but the speck continued harassing me like a harpy. I shrugged my shoulders, and gestured no when she offered to pour more water.

"You can't see what's ahead," Sally said, gesturing with her chin toward the plateau. "We're blind, though vision fools us."

chapter 3

Despite the fire in his ribs, Virgil fingers the ridges of the tracks, massaging the earth like the skin of a lover. The tracks could be missed so easily. He can't get over them, what they mean, the truth they tell, of huge creatures and this ground, soft and giving, thousands of years ago. He can see only the few years of his life, and that seems large enough. Raymundo squats beside him

"This land was a burial place for our people," he says. Virgil looks up at him, wondering if his condition is that apparent. Does he give off an odor? "They were wrapped in blankets and left in the crevices in those rocks"—he indicates an outcropping connecting to a higher plateau. "The bodies faced the sunset. Justice comes from the west."

"Do you believe that?" Virgil asks.

"If it comes at all," Raymundo says, laughing the matter away. Who can know? Virgil might well say the same—in years of toiling with the law, he'd seen it work more to bolster the lot of them that's got, and Billie Holiday's lilt comes to mind, her sleepy eyes. So the Bible says, and it still is so. Of course, the law and justice weren't necessarily one.

"You ever live anywhere else?" he asks Raymundo. What would a life spent in this heat, among this caked earth be like?

"Studied geology in Albuquerque at the university. Went to work for an oil concern, saw lots of places doing that, but it wasn't good. So I come back here two years ago. It's good to be in a place you know. Where you from?"

"Chicago," Virgil answers, and the thought of it with its bracing wind and thick summer air is like the periodic table of the elements. He knows about it, but it has no impact on his life. "I'm a long way from home."

"Maybe, but the land suits you."

This compliment cheers Virgil enormously. At this tender moment,

it strikes deep into the rich and suddenly fertile soil of his heart. Foolishly fertile. What use, what use?

"I'm dying," he says to Raymundo. He faces out to the plateaus
again, imagining his body there, waiting for justice, feeling the wind.
Raymundo puts a hand on his shoulder.

When he returns, Caroline sits sketching a woman beneath the
canopy. The blue plastic crinkles in the howling, dusty wind. They
chat in lively tones, Caroline holding her eye shut, the occasional tear
dripping onto the paper. He will need to drive, and he adjusts himself
to this thought. But the drawing is subtle, sensitive—it's kind. She has
a spare style, economical, and he watches her torque a single line into
a tendril of hair floating about the high cheekbone. When he looks at
the woman, he sees Caroline's handiwork, floating as she described.
He taps her shoulder. This excursion has tired him.

"We should push on."

Caroline gathers up her materials and rips the sketch from the pad.
"Please accept this," she says. The woman regards the drawing and laughs.

"Shall I drive?" he says, drawing the keys out of his jacket pocket.
Even in the desert heat, Virgil feels undressed without at least a light-
weight jacket. Raymundo waves as they leave.

Normally Caroline likes the windows down, despite the heat. Arti-
ficial environments creep her out, she says. But she slumps down in the
seat holding her hand over her eye, looking thoroughly exhausted, and
doesn't complain when he leaves the windows up and turns on the AC.

"We'd better get you in to see someone in Flagstaff," he says.

"It's just a speck of dust. I'm sure it will get out soon."

"We'd better go see someone," he says again, a statement of fact.

"I'm sorry I can't drive," she says.

"It's okay to let someone else take care of you from time to time."

"Yeah, so I hear."

"Just don't make a habit of it," he says. The joke's the thing. Caroline is loved through humor. He should write up a report, for her permanent record, that could be handed on to the next swain. Absurd to

class himself as one, but he has a lover's insight, if not the tactical knowledge to back it up. How wrong was it to have loved kissing her?

She turns on the radio and flips through the dial. There are long gaps between stations, then suddenly an explosion of mariachi horns and accordions, a blast of holy-roller sermonizing. Can I hear you say amen? Amen. So close to amends, Virgil thinks. Can I hear you make amends? Amends are inaudible, microscopic, unseen forces at work.

Virgil looks at the gray tarmac with its golden lines and it seems perfect to him, an illumination of the world's most subtle impulses. Balderdash, of course. Highways were built by immensely practical men. To see in them the universal truth is to desperately fabricate that truth. But don't they follow ancient tracks—animal pathways worn down by the hunters who followed? There are layers at work here, he is sure of it. He enjoys the simplicity of driving, of a sick girl beside him, of being needed one last time. Actually, he will be needed again, just as he was needed before. And like those earlier times, he won't be there. What will that be like, not to be on this road, or in his bed or showing up for work. Not to use a telephone ever again. To take up no space, except as thought. He wonders about heaven, what it might feel like to have wings in the unlikely event of angeldom. Would they strain his lower back? Texture? Are they silver? Of a material known to man? Is hell really a hot place? Desire is a hot thing, and hell is built of it, so he presumes the answer is yes.

Caroline has settled on the mariachi music, and its robust harmonies, its oom-pah-pah emphasis on the *corazón*, fill the car. Twilight deepens and through the windshield, starlight, star bright, appears the first star Virgil has truly seen in a long time.

chapter 4

Even after a shower, which I let stream hot over me for an hour, blasting
the grit from each pore, the feeling of irritation persisted, so I agreed to
the doctor visit. An outpatient facility took me, the last patient of the
night. The examination room could have held a respectable swimming
pool, and around the perimeter were cabinets and counters tricked out
with stainless-steel containers of steel-bladed implements, cotton
swabs, the stock-in-trade of healing. The doctor dimmed the lights to
look into my eye with his pointy hand-tool–cum-flashlight.

"I don't see anything," he said. He was a young man, blond and tall
with a look of mountain wholesomeness about him—skin a golden tan
tinged with peach at the cheek, eyes clear and hazel. He had an
earnest warmth that comforted. "I'm going to flush it."

He took a rubber bulb and filled it with liquid from a metal tray.
"This has a dye in it. It'll make it easier for me to see what's going on
in there. Hold your eye open for me." I held my eye in exaggerated
openness, and he squeezed a cool whoosh across it.

"Where are you from?" he asked. He had me lie on an examination
table that he raised with a foot pedal.

I told him.

"I can't even imagine New York City, what that must be like."

"Noisy, but fun."

"I guess." He didn't sound convinced. I heard him rattling more
metal over at a distant counter.

"You're from here?" I asked.

"Little farther north, close to the Canyon. Real pretty country."
He bent down over me and I smelled his minted breath, his spiced
aftershave. He wore a thick gold wedding ring, and I thought of how
some lucky woman would kiss him under similar circumstances. He
was lovable. "Oh, I see now. Your cornea is scratched. Probably what

happened is the speck scraped it, then cried itself out, and what you're feeling is the scratch."

The notion of something tearing the surface of my eye scared me. "Is it bad?" I asked.

"Your eye is one of the fastest-healing parts of your body. Here's what we'll do. I'm going to put some salve in it, then fit you with a really glamorous-looking patch. Leave it on overnight. You should be a lot better in the morning. Then we'll set you up with seven days' worth of drops. It should be healed by then, but all the same I'd like to see you back in a week."

"I don't think I'll be here." And I explained about the trip.

"Well, doesn't have to be me. I won't take it personally. But see someone in a week."

We filled my prescription, wandering around the pharmacy waiting for it, the glamorous eye patch very interesting to feel—soft, yet present. It was hard to make sense of the world with just one eye. Distances became hard to gauge. But I enjoyed it now that I knew I'd be better in a week.

How impersonal healing is, it seems just to happen. Or did it have to do with his telling me it would be so, and my unquestioning belief in the power of his coat and all it implied—the years of schooling, the priestly knowledge of my body's ways and means.

Virgil guided me tenderly around, his hand on my arm, my seeing eye. We both enjoyed the furtive stares the cashier gave us, her eyebrows gone, and the skin a bit lighter where they'd been, new ones drawn on, blue black, inky shine. "You take care, okay?" she said to me. I told her I would. I felt light and happy.

"Home, James," I said.

We ordered room service by the trough—pasta and pizza and red wine and ale and cake, and ate on and off for hours. The room's fireplace had a timer—each fire lasted twenty minutes. We lit the flame over and over.

There was just one king-size bed beneath the peaked roof. I had long since dropped my reluctance to share space, and we lay now side by side, flipping through television channels, alighting on music videos full of silent-movie gesture and bravado, on cartoon chickens getting the better of bumpkin chicken hawks, reruns of things I'd watched as a girl, the effluvia of modern life, the obsidian mirror of what we took to be ourselves. We both lay on our backs, propped up on the copious pillow collection, laughing at chintz curtains, chintz chairs—the mighty chintz of it all. He poured more wine into my glass and held it to my lips. I drank, but some washed down my chin, and he delicately licked it away. Then he lay his head on my breast and I wrapped an arm around him and he kissed me there, too.

He kissed awhile longer, losing himself in me as he now felt lost to me. The warmth, the nearness, how good it felt. How good it felt to be loved. I knew this was love. But I lay with my eyes open, watching the pattern of the fire on the ceiling, wondering what a flame really was—all I know of flame is that it's hollow—and I felt tears sliding from my unpatched eye.

"Virgil," I said. I nuzzled his hair, so soft, smelling faintly of patchouli. "We can't. It's not right."

He stopped and there was a sudden calcifying. He petrified on the spot.

"It's not right to love you?" he asked.

"It's something we'll both have to always live with."

"True whether or not . . ."

He rolled away, the bed the last frontier, forty acres and a mule. The fire turned off and we let it stay that way. The television still shimmered, though we'd muted it, and on screen gyrated a man with a white electric guitar, the camera fawning at groin level, he kneeled and extended a fist toward us, a hideous specter in red, white, and blue leather pants, harbinger of things I'd rather not know.

"I love you, Caroline," Virgil said, from the remote west of the bed. "I want to love you."

"Then love me. But understand, Virgil, I have been loved in some rough ways, and I don't want that anymore. I don't want to spend the next six months or six years or six decades recovering from tonight. Or six minutes. I don't want to give up one minute of my life regretting the way I love you."

I got up and turned the fire back on, then sat beside it, contemplating its inexhaustible gas-fed flames, missing the crackle and smoke and occasional red spark of burning wood. Mona came to mind. I wondered if in instances of grief, like my self-repairing eye, healing simply happened, an innocent bystander of time's passage, or were some things unrecoverable? She could tell me, if I could formulate the question. How does the minister minister to the flock in the hour of her sorrow? I should not have missed the funeral.

"I'm sorry," I said.

"No need," Virgil said.

"Not about that." His assumption that the apology was for him irked me. "You know, about my mother and father."

"What about them?" He sounded tenderly interested, and this capacity to set aside his own hurt and just listen touched me. I climbed back onto the bed in his territory, stretching myself out within it.

"I guess it's the gap, you know, that's just there between people, and with some it's wider and deeper than with others."

"Yes, I know." And was silent a minute. I listened to the depth of his breathing and thought he'd fallen asleep. "But you know," he continued, "the gap is the past. Nothing more than that."

I clicked off the television and the flames danced us to sleep. Later I woke from a dream in which I'd been a seal, speeding down the oceanic depths to where red magma ruptured the seafloor. When I woke my heart raced, my head light—I had the bends. His presence slowed me, and I wrapped an arm around his waist and held on until dawn.

It was 7:00 A.M., 9:00 in Chicago. I could call home. My phone was charged. I looked at it in its cradle, the green ready-to-go light shining optimistically into the space above the phone like a halo. What would I say?

"Hello," I said. "Mom?"

Mona was silent a moment. "Caroline, is that you? Where are you?"

"Flagstaff, Arizona. How are you?"

"Oh, you know. All right. How are you?"

"Oh, you know." I couldn't believe I was saying that. "You know, tired. It's been kind of a wild trip."

"Well, it would be, with Virgil and all."

We were silent awhile and I liked the sound of her respiration on the line.

"I shouldn't keep you," I said. "But I wanted to say—"

"No, it's good. I'm glad you called. You're all right?"

"Yes, I am. I'll call soon, okay, when I'm done."

"Yes, okay, do," she said. "I love you, honey. Be safe."

"I love you too, Mom."

When I hung up, I sat with the last of the cigarette dangling between my fingers, ash falling onto the windowsill, birds calling to me from the trees, sunshine caressing me over the horizon, the day beginning with all that implied.

I thought of David wandering in the wilderness, of my mother and myself, a certain loneliness tying us together, of Donald, far, far away in the kingdom of concrete, of Virgil moaning in the night. I thought of how we're all lodged together in this pain, but sometimes we sit close together and gather warmth from one another, herd animals underneath our sophisticated pelts. I sat looking out on the day, marveling at its shifts of light, each change a miracle, a moment here now, gone now, on-off the rhythm of the universe ad infinitum.

chapter 5

Small birds drop in and out of the airy abyss, black chirping dots bathed in orange gold pink, the rock behind them lustrous, another day in eternity. Virgil sits as close to the canyon side as he can bear, funny to feel this vertigo when he has been tethered up thousands of vertical feet. But today he clings to the sure, solid earth, cross-legged on its silken red dirt. Caroline sits at the edge, legs dangling into the void. Her arms back behind her pitch her face upward and she smiles.

"Holy shit," she'd said when they arrived, she driving again, both of them relieved for that. And she was right, of course. This place at this time is the holiness of every day and all places. Each day's breaking is epic. Each place, mysterious.

This is where you go to remember that.

Reaching down the canyon walls, the sun chronicles angles of time and pressure, rocky transmutations. And there is still time enough for this canyon to get deeper, for the water at its base to shrink or expand depending on the snowy caprices of the earth's many winters, for those whims to etch the rock and for the rock itself to break and fall and reroute the river's path. Over and over. Now that's time.

He would be glad to die here, were it not for the inconvenience. It would never do, tour buses sure to show up soon. Why spoil it?

A moment more.

Beverly is the last woman he will have made love to, and he wishes it were Jane. Alas, all thoughts lead to sex. He laughs at himself, but ruefully. He does wish it were Jane, ardently so. He can't remember the last time they were joined, though probably there was anger in it, stiff hostility, his desire an unwelcome pest. No amount of anything else—mountain summits, women, money—has ever made up for losing her, and that's a thing he didn't expect of life. Not that there weren't other things to be found, or that you couldn't take the philosophical stance. But still. A loss remains a loss.

And yet. Here was morning, bird flight, breeze.

Then the day flattens out, the tour buses, as expected, shudder to a stop and disgorge their contents. The earth is hard beneath his bony rump, and twinges sing in his bent knees. A mysterious knot in his right shoulder comes alive as if it were some electric coil in him, switched on. He resists them all, these tempting discomforts and their conscientious advice that he should rise, they should go. Go now, go— you're aching, you'll get worse. Instead, he remarks the dryness of the air, how easily breathed it is, light and fragrant. A large black ant crawls near his leg, antenna wavering. Virgil holds out a small twig, maneuvering it so that it is always in the ant's path. "Express elevator," he says, when the ant finally climbs aboard, and Virgil raises the stick closer to his eye to examine the sturdy creature, its armature, its stick legs. The ant throws its head about wildly casting for bearings and all at once Virgil puts the stick back down. As a child he'd spent hours hovering over ant trails on summer days with a magnifying glass, radiating unbearable heat onto their backs. Occasionally, one would crackle and burst. Which was the point, of course, but in hindsight the barbarity of it weighs heavily on him. Sage, mesquite, sand, immanent flame—he smells these things. This is a good way to live. He ought to have done it more. He closes his eyes and feels profoundly tired. Caroline still sits at the edge of the chasm, and he would give anything he had to know her thoughts, whether they're focused on the outward spectacle of time's reward or the inward crucible of the last month, but even if she tells him—oh, I was thinking about my father, or oh, isn't this beautiful—it will not be access enough. The essence of love is that no matter how close, how trusting, how communicative, there is still the gap, as she'd said last night, which only some confederation of fantasy, sympathy, and speculation can bridge.

She stretches, turns toward him, and the sun explodes off the down on her cheekbone.

"This is so amazing," she says, throwing her arms up into the air and fluttering her hands as if trying to clutch the atmosphere. Her pleasure in this place suffuses him. The trip was right.

He rises, goes to her, kisses her deeply, to her surprise. "I love you very much. Please don't forget."

Then he jogs backward. When he's back far enough, he stops and looks. Enormous sky, red canyon walls. If he runs hard enough, can he reach the other side? He runs.

Three steps on, he collapses.

chapter 6

By noon it was hotter than hell, and of course that's when the buses really started pouring in. The solitude we'd enjoyed in the early morning was long gone, and while there was a certain interest in watching people walk to the edge, look over, and walk away, as if checking a storm drain, eventually the heat and the haste got to me. At the very least I needed a Coke, if not a Grand Canyon shot glass or refrigerator magnet.

My thoughts bent toward home, and home apparently did not mean New York. Virgil needed care and rest. I had amends to make and contemplations to contemplate. I wouldn't be going back to Donald, that was certain, and I wondered if New York were perhaps used up. That can happen with a place—you make a life there only to discover a few years on that the tree's tapped out and a new tree must be procured, sometimes a whole new forest. I was experimenting with open mindedness, feeling a bit self-congratulatory on achieving the vaunted *que sera, sera* sensibility. I imagined myself taking the proverbial step back, assessing my strengths, my skills, likes and dislikes by working through a self-help manual. Thirty Days to Destiny! It was an oddly comforting fantasy, that I could go through a rational process, on the far end of which I would enjoy firmer self-knowledge and emerge with a practical plan for how to do what I wanted. Which was, essentially, nothing. Could I get paid to think? Did I have to get paid? Another way to say it is I wanted merely to live. What might that entail?

Such was the tenor of my imagination when Virgil started hemorrhaging.

I heard him stir, and watched as he lurched toward me. A deep kiss, so troubling in its pleasures, some backward steps, and then Virgil sprinted toward the canyon. When he dropped, I was on my feet, running to his side.

He lay on his back, breathing heavily, staring at the sky. "The fool falls again," he said.

Another tour bus had pulled up, and as its passengers began their sojourn to the rocky edge, I called out. A young man darted over to me.

"What's up? Is he all right? I'm an EMT," he said. Kneeling, he began the probing by which humans discern medical reality. "Take it easy, Tiger," he said to Virgil, who pooh-poohed the man away with wincing swats.

"You need a doctor for this one," the man said. "I'm outta my league."

"Help me get him to the car," I said, and we each took an arm and staggered through the brush.

The man gave Virgil his unopened water bottle. "Good luck," he said, then he caught up with his group.

I started the car, hospital bound, and Virgil lifted his head.

"Just take me to our room." He said it calmly, though his voice was pinched.

Idiotic, I told him, absurd. I would be his sternest elementary-school teacher reincarnated, but he slumped back down and didn't say a word. And we were in motion, exiting the parking lot, the air conditioner blasting full tilt, but not yet cooling us so that we baked together for a hot moment. Then we pulled onto the highway. I accelerated. The car chilled to an autumnal sixty-eight degrees, and once again everything was just fine.

Either way, hospital or hotel, we needed this road.

A spur forked off to the right. A square blue sign, emblazoned with a healthful white H, indicated where we should go, also right. I continued straight.

So I made a choice, doing sixty-two in a fifty zone, to do what he asked. I could have driven to the hospital, checked him in, flipped through a hundred channels worth of daytime TV, awaiting a verdict, the legal mapped onto physical. But I didn't, and I wonder why. Was it enough, knowing what he wanted, to give it? In the car, the length and emptiness of the land filled in for talk.

*   *   *

"I think something's happening," he said, onward toward eleven at night.

I was in the bathroom, brushing my teeth, and came out quickly. He lay on his back, shuddering. The water in the glass on the table next to him had waves.

"Come here," he said, and he looked so calm and lucid, despite the sweat gathering on his brow, that I simply obeyed, and sat beside him on the bed. When I stroked his arm, resting outside the bedclothes, it was cool.

"I should have told you," he said, and then he told me.

"You should have told me," I said, outraged and instantly in tears. "I'm calling the hospital."

"Caroline, don't." I stood beside his bed and he looked up at me, his face etched with pain and pleading. "There's no point, and it isn't what I want."

"I don't care what you want." I reached for the phone.

"You can't save me." He motioned to me to sit, and waited until I did. "Bury me out there." He gestured toward the window. "You know, where we were, by the dinosaur tracks." Then he reached for my hand and held it in both of his, over his heart.

chapter 7

Rain on gray cobblestones. A brown dog and a black one sunning on a spring afternoon, daffodils waving near them. Virgil flies from image to image, each a delectation. It is definitely he that moves. The images aren't within him. He visits each, a panoramic flyover shot. Not a photo album of loved ones as he might have expected, but a cockroach emerging from the bathtub drain in brown crackly armor, the texture of a shearling coat, a curve in the road along Lake Shore. The beauty in the random moment is what endures, so easily and often overlooked. All the mountains, the willful climbing, the hammering in of pitons, the foolish vanity of thinking you could choose what was important. He has to laugh. The rest of it, the moment-to-moment mundane—that's what wins out by way of sheer volume. Human life consists of lifting a spoonful of cereal to the mouth day after day.

He would like to direct his gaze toward a lover's unbuttoned blouse. Or the supple swelling of Jane's calf muscle, images he has hoarded for years, beauty spots in the midst of drear. But he has no control. David's red trike stands sentinel in the walkway to the house in early summer twilight, a smell of grilling meat in the air.

He hadn't known he'd noticed.

Joy flutters through him. Caroline says something, maybe just his name, he can't make it out. Her voice sounds distraught, confused. She doesn't know that it's good. He would tell her but opening his mouth is a thick activity, words slowed beyond possible comprehension. What he has to say apparently cannot be said.

More shudders, hot and cold, an amusement-park ride. He feels laughter. A glove he'd never known he was wearing has been removed and the lightness of the real air against his real skin intoxicates as he floats up and sees a curl of wave breaking at Atlantic City, glitter and sparkle of sun on the skein of green blue ocean. His father in a panama hat on the porch that wrapped around the house. A water-skiing boat tethered to a dock in northern Michigan. The pressure of Shelly's breasts, the heat inside her. A sparrow in flight, twig in mouth, spring in motion.

Who knew?

chapter 8

Virgil shook violently from time to time, but he appeared almost to smile. I continued to hold his hand and fought back my tears. It was early in the morning, maybe two, three o'clock. The table lamp across the room was on, and I dearly wanted a cigarette, to hear inanities from the television, and felt ashamed for such cravings. Watch home shopping while your uncle dies. That would be a good memory to carry forward.

Would Virgil meet my father? Would they recognize each other? Would they talk about me? My God, I was tired. Only by stopping do we truly know how we've been on the go.

Virgil shuddered again and said something, "nothing happened," it sounded like. I squeezed his hands and conjured the best things I knew—bacon on Sunday morning, lemons, the sight of them, their smell and their tang. Fat snowflakes wheeling in an updraft.

"I won't forget," I said to him. "You really loved me and now I know what that feels like, and I won't not have it, so thank you. I won't forget the way you were with me as a kid, you helped me be stronger than I would have been without you. I'm sorry." I apologized for the tears that were flowing now, and for saying yes to this trip when if I hadn't we'd both be safe and now we were anything but safe.

His breathing rattled hoarse and regular, raising my hands up and down on his chest.

I stopped talking. There was nothing to say, really, that couldn't be better expressed through silence. So I drew my breath in and let it settle. His hands wrapped around mine felt papery and cold, the odd mix of bone and vessel. These hands had wisdom that would now be lost, trusting the tiniest dent in rock to hold him. I remembered how he looked high up in that tree, beautiful against the night sky, defiant of gravity, charmed. Just now, his breath hoarse, mine jumpy with the first lashes of grief, we were profoundly together.

My arm hurt, awkwardly bent across Virgil's chest for over an hour by this time. And the hurt spread up to my shoulder socket. The air held the smells of previous occupants—stale cologne, old cigarettes, must. I arranged myself behind him so that he leaned against my chest, then I wrapped my arms around him. He released into me.

I could always fuck strangers and call it adventure. I could always work fanatically at meaningless tasks and call it fulfillment. I could always breeze in and take over and get accolades for doing it just so, without ever investing myself. But these actions made me a stranger in this world, and to myself.

"Virgil, don't let me pull this again," I said. "Make me promise."

Virgil gasped—a short exhalation, a surprise—and he shuddered one more time, then stopped. I watched him, all manner of storm ready to break wild within in me. His chest didn't rise, and he slumped. I held on a long, long time.

"Virgil?" I asked the air. "Virgil," I told him, "I love you. And I promise. I'll be good."

Finally, I disentangled myself—he was getting heavy—and stretched him out on the bed, arms open at his sides. All sorts of fussing notions came into my head, lists spontaneously generated themselves, phone calls and action items, noise. Headlights from the parking lot fanned across the room and I stood still, frozen by their movement. When they ceased, I cried. I cried and cried and cried. I tore the bedspread from the second bed, threw it down and kicked it, but it didn't help.

Such moments call for poise. It was my mother's voice I heard, and it calmed me. I sat beside him a long time.

Rising, I turned on the air conditioner—best to keep him cool—and opened the curtains. Morning was coming on. What would he want? To be buried by the dinosaur tracks, he'd said. That seemed doable. I'd drive out there later today. I'd call Jane, we'd find David, I'd go home.

But for now, I lay myself beside him, put my hand over his, and closed my eyes, summoning a small gift, the fragrance of lilacs.

Acknowledgments

Thanks to Tom and Sheila for offering safe haven, good times, and boundless enthusiasm. My mother told me when to let go. Katherine Wood's steadfast warmth soothed many raw spots. Gilbert Newman for years has helped me hear. Willa Rabinovitch, Wendy Nelson, and Mitchell Kimbrough read generously and without gloves. Miroslav Wiesner offered invaluable design guidance. Thanks to Robert Stone for his kindness and that dinner at Sarge's. Fate brought me Philip Spitzer and Tina Pohlman, and I am grateful. Finally, a special leopard thanks to Mic, for his a priori belief and so much besides.

About the Author

Jean Shields worked as a teacher, cook, sorftware developer and magazine editor before turning to fiction. A Michigan native, she has lived in Fairbanks, New York City, and San Francisco, her current home. She holds an MA from the University of San Francisco. This is her first novel.